VENGEFUL ARE THE DROWNED

BOOKS BY MICHAEL J ALLEN

<u>Blood Phoenix:</u>
1. Ashes of Raging Water
2. Ruled by Tainted Blood
3. Vengeful are the Drowned
4. Rise of the Exiled Lady
5. Razing the Last Bastion

<u>Scion (Original):</u>
1. Scion of Conquered Earth
2. Stolen Lives
3. Hijacked
4. Unchained

<u>Bittergate:</u>
1. Murder in Wizard's Wood
2. The Wizard's Bane
3. Forge of War
4. Scythe of Illusions

<u>Guns of Underhill:</u>
1. Fey West

<u>Dumpstermancer:</u>
1. Discarded
2. Duplicity

<u>Delirious Scribbles:</u>
(Short Stories)

- Wyrm's Warning
- Scraping Bottom
- Criminal Justice
- Dreams of Treasure
- Desperate
- The Bottom Line

COMING SOON:

<u>Binarai Online:</u>
1. Storm Refuge
2. Rogue Planet
3. Power Break

<u>Wayman Chronicles:</u>
1. Crossways

<u>Guns of Underhill:</u>
2. Mettle Kingdom

<u>Dumpstermancer:</u>
3. Decoy

<u>Scion Rising (Remaster)</u>

Vengeful are the Drowned

Blood Phoenix Chronicles: Book Three

Michael J Allen

Delirious
Scribbles Ink

Delirious Scribbles Ink, Inc.

Copyright

This is a work of fiction. Names, characters, places and incidents are a product of the author's imagination or are used fictitiously. Locales, businesses, companies, events, institutions, and public names are sometimes used under fair use licensing for atmospheric purposes only and are not representative of their namesake. Any resemblance to actual people—living, dead or in between—is completely coincidental.

For Quincy, a great inspiration, author, friend and maven of fashion.

For B, B & E, J, S & J, and L.

Delirious Scribbles Readers Group

Like free stories?

How about curated deals for Science Fiction and Fantasy books?

Get your first benefit—a FREE story sent right to you—by becoming a member of the Delirious Scribbles Readers Group.

Begin your journey, just scan this image with your phone camera!

Content Advisory

In order to provide my readers the best possible experience as well as be responsive to reader requests, I've created a reader-curated content advisory on my website. If you are sensitive to certain kinds of fictional representations, please check this book's listings before reading.

I hope you enjoy this story...

— Michael J Allen

To visit the advisory, just scan this image with your phone camera.

Chapter One

Fires of Vengeance

Vitae

I swirled into existence, heart still thundering in my ears. A firestorm beat at the inside edges of my chest.

That ungrateful whore bitch killed me!

It didn't matter that I'd intended to punish her for disobeying. She needed to be taught her place, but instead of taking her lesson like an adult, she'd turned around and—

Cold washed through me.

Dread froze the breath in my chest.

Distantly, my brain sought refuge in cataloging my reborn form. Breast size, hair color, height—none of it mattered as long as I had the advantages a female body offered as a vehicle to my goals.

Rage overtook me, vibrating my whole body.

Dolumii's blade! Mare!

No matter how many times I argued with Vilicangelus over Aquaylae, he'd refused to recognize the threat she represented. He'd overlooked her disregard of duty. He'd discounted her laziness, her selfishness and her undisciplined attitude as youthful aspects.

And now, in disobeying my orders, she's cost Mare's freedom.

I stormed away from my nest through the security doors into my thrall's basement laboratory. A half-elf attendant—hybrid bastard of an elf and a Halfling—pushed replacement robes and fighting batons into my hands. I pointed with a baton at six hulks standing along one wall and pulled the robes over my head.

"I can dress myself, summon the car."

By the time the robe's folds settled around my sultry hips, the six enforcers bracketed me in a semi-circle. Their constant growth prevented dressing the wafers reanimated with troll marrow in clothes suitable for a gentleman's entourage.

The thrall claimed their constant 'hulking' out of their clothes wasn't likely to stop as long as we continued exposing them to x-rays, but the obvious advantage of naturally armored muscles and spiked limbs compensated for their lack of decorum.

I'd ordered them painted. Despite the thrall's objections regarding clogging their pores, the troll DNA kept the head-to-toe black from killing them a second time.

And when I proved the queer medical examiner wrong, he had the temerity to suggest we paint them green.

I stormed out of the basement for the front entrance, my temper heating further as I reviewed the travesty of the last few hours.

The young divine had summoned me—me—to a meeting to compare notes with the other shields.

As if I did not already know all I needed to know.

He'd shown his inexperience—nay, incompetence—abandoning us with claims of overwork for some vacation frolic. When a major incursion had demanded our attention, my fellow elder shields had defended Aquaylae's complete disregard for secrecy. They'd threatened me.

I did my duty anyway.

Choosing an inconspicuous route, I'd trekked through downtown to the DragonCon hotels, even paying for parking that should have been mine by right as the city's defender. Irreverent crowds and would-be photographers hampered my rescue mission, further endangering their fellow mortals. One mannerless cad had groped me rather than let me pass.

His hand won't be the only thing that rots away.

The instinctual use of life's antithesis on the knave opened my eyes to a power I'd never considered. Employing my essence to draw life away from the barricading foliage allowed me to penetrate the hotel. Wielded against the kudzu beast, I'd been nigh invulnerable.

It was for that reason I instructed Aquaylae as to the ideal course of action while I thwarted some druid's elemental.

A goblin in a chauffer's hat met me outside the dilapidated and condemned hotel that served as my new residence. The little faerie opened the back door of my 1937 Mercedes Landaulet limousine.

One of my enforcers wedged himself into the vintage car's front passenger seat. The other trollmen squeezed into an armored SUV gifted me by an agent of wafer government I'd enthralled.

Pushing a copy of *Wuthering Heights* aside, I slid onto the luxurious seat and reached for a decanter of aged brandy. "Take us downtown to the Marriott Marquis."

"Lots of activity down there, Master. Many faeries."

"Did I give you permission to speak?"

"Yes, Master, when you tired of my gestures."

"Use it again to express an unsolicited opinion, and I will revoke that permission."

"Yes, Master."

Good. Better behaved than Aquaylae.

The water phoenix has ignored my orders outright. Instead of stepping aside to care for injured mortals, she'd insisted on hogging the glory of the kill. She'd even had the temerity to relegate me to a support role like some kind of battlefield midwife.

When I'd objected, she'd attacked and killed me.

That is the last time I'll allow her to cost our shield lives.

"Drive!"

"Yes, Master."

Bystanders gawked as my vehicle pulled out of the dilapidated hotel. Crews of enthralled faerie workers pressganged into renovating the interior of my new Shield Sanctum hadn't begun work on the old hotel's exterior. There was no need to hurry them until I decided whether or not the hotel's current exterior condition served our new headquarters better as camouflage.

The larger building offered solutions to our Shield's most significant problems. It removed us from our 'lofty heights' effectively eliminating any arguments about the other shields living outside the sanctum. It provided more room so younger shields who were worth sparing could train to a satisfactory level. It included space for servants to take over the insignificant details so we could focus on our duty.

Once Mare is returned and we're rid of Aquaylae, this new headquarters will enable us to build the greatest Shield ever assembled.

I turned on the television.

I abhorred the mindless teat used to pacify the gormless masses. Unfortunately, without Anima's control center, the local news had to serve my intelligence gathering needs. The new headquarters needed a control center, but I loathed to simply relocate the automata. Caelum's mucking about had altered the artificial intelligence so that it no longer knew its place.

I should rebuild the oracle we used before. At least then there wouldn't be any confusion—or any reason for that ignorant fledgling bitch to correct me.

My grip on the crystal tumbler tightened until brandy-coated shards dug into my hands.

Obviously, some problem afflicted our newest generation of shields. Pollutants and toxins damaging Creation may have also damaged the development of young phoenixes. Such at least provided a rational excuse for Aquaylae, Caelum and the ignorant boob serving as Atlanta's Praefectus.

Vilicangelus and I will sort this out once he has a spare moment. Once we've replaced the dead weight and proved this Shield the most superior in Creation, he can see me elevated as a worthier successor.

With the power of faerie magic and the gifts of a Divine One, I'd reform the whole region until the other Prefectures adopted my training methods.

One task at a time.

A check out of the window showed us moving too slowly. "We're in a hurry, goblin. Drive faster."

"I'm doing the best I can, Master, but DragonCon—"

"Be silent and drive!"

For a moment, I toyed with replacing the goblin with the enforcer, but the bulk of the mutated former corpse would've made any attempt to operate the vehicle difficult.

I turned my attention to the news reporter on the television staring blankly into the camera, oblivious to an off-camera woman repeating his name. My disgust rose until I reached for the device's power button. A finger's breadth from replacing wafer gibberish with classical opera, the picture changed to a studio anchor. It took only a few words for me to realize the off-camera voice belonged to the attractive Moor.

"Georgia film industry officials have confirmed that what was reported as some kind of supernatural event was in fact film work for a new fantasy movie."

She droned on and on about safety signs and security lapses, accidents and lawsuits. Her comeliness couldn't overcome the selfish entitlement—a recent wafer epidemic—escaping her lips.

Despite my disgust, the explanation fed to the media bore all of the hallmarks of a well-conceived story. The fiction offered a sufficiently plausible scenario to ensure the secrecy of Faery despite all of the witnesses involved.

That idiot Summus must've lied about Vilicangelus's condition. Didn't want Vili learning of his shortcomings. This whole generation is as bad as Aquaylae.

The limo slowed, crawling forward through crowds and cars

in fits and starts. The third stop exhausted my patience. I had to reclaim the Unseelie Champion sword without further delay.

"Stop. I will get out here."

"We're in the middle of the street, Master."

"The other motorists will have to make way."

His worried expression belied his feelings, but the goblin nodded.

The faerie creature was too stupid to understand the human world. Besides, my Mercedes waited in a parking structure only a short jaunt away. Once I'd reclaimed my possessions, dealt with Aquaylae and ensured the Sidhe trounced, I'd drive myself back.

A car tried to hit me the moment I stepped out.

Only my supernatural reflexes let me slip the sedan's hammer blow. The mortal leapt out of the still-running car a moment later, not contrite, not apologetic, but indignant. "Stupid bitch! What the fuck is wrong with you?"

My mission to retrieve the sword imprisoning Mare was far too important to delay with injury or another death. Even so, the urge to teach the knave a lesson about proper respect, especially of a lady, tempted me to tarry.

I placed a hand on the car's hood and willed death into the machine. The act didn't manipulate life energy as Ignis might will control over flame through pyrokinesis. What I did was the opposite of manipulating life, and I have no idea how my power should be able to slay a machine.

The engine let out a groan of metal. Smoke poured from the hood only moments before fire licked out of the seams.

The driver's eyes widened. "What did you do? I'll sue you f—"

A trollman enforcer seized his arm. The driver jerked free and dove for the safety of his vehicle. The door locks clicked shut.

I eyed the flames flickering in and out of the engine compartment, raising a brow.

I needn't have given any thought to the man's lacking survival instincts. My enforcer ripped the door from its frame. When the driver scrambled first to the passenger side and then to the back, more enforcers removed the doors.

"Teach him proper respect."

I hurried away, rushing despite the unseemliness of it. Grunts and pained profanities faded into the distance.

I considered the day's discoveries on the run.

All phoenixes had limited control of their essence element. As life phoenix, I was the single most vital of all. It was my purview to grant the energy of life. It'd never occurred to me that such control meant removal as well as granting.

It is fitting though. Who else should shoulder the responsibility accompanying the ability to draw life from those unworthy?

Pedestrians thickened to crowds. I fought my way along increasingly packed sidewalks. After a prolonged struggle, a repeat of earlier obstructions embrittling my temper. I reached a corner housing the Marriott Marquis. Across the street, the dumbstruck news anchor I'd seen on the television stared unmoving at his cameraman.

My old friend epitomizes everything I shall be as a Divine One.

Someone thrusted a sign into my face. "This is your fault, jezebel! You and the rest of these sinners brought the devil into our midst."

I took in the man in an eye blink. Catholic priest's collar, a bullhorn and a sign staff adorned with fire and brimstone declarations.

"Whores, homosexuals and Satanists brought this evil. You'll burn for it! God will smite you for your hedonistic lifestyles."

I cocked an eyebrow. "You are mistaken, sir. The Creator loves all his creations, even when they err. That's why he sent a second host to protect you from hell and your foolish desires."

The preacher shoved his face into mine, spitting his vitriol. "My God is a wrathful God. He will punish you!"

My temper couldn't have ignited faster if I'd been a Pyri. The heinous wafer accosting me might have thought his sermonizing in service of my Creator, but his hateful speech did more damage than good as it incensed me.

I am a Shield of the Undying Light. It is not my place to judge.

"My good man, if you will refer to the Bible in—"

"Be silent, harlot! I will not listen to Satan's temptress pervert scripture with a forked tongue!"

"I haven't time for your willful ignorance." Essence leapt out of my fingers in writhing tentacles. "Ask the Author yourself."

For a moment, the touch of life essence enervated the preacher. New bluster rushed to his lips. I withdrew my gift, ripping out his life energy along with my own.

I left the corpse to lay where it fell and pushed through the mesmerized crowd toward the hotel entrance. The scene beyond the glass doors stopped me short.

An army of pixies and fairies cleared away detritus as dwarves —not putti—rebuilt the scene. Half-ogres muscled people and objects around while elves touched wafers with magic and whispered new memories.

Why are faeries cleaning up the scene?

I snatched a passing fairy out of the air by one wing. "Why are you cleaning up?"

"Screw off, bird. I don't answer to you."

"Who do you answer to?" I demanded.

The fairy snorted, soiling my robes with snot-laden fairy dust. "We serve the Lady, fool, and if you know what's good for you, you'll let me go before—"

I pulped the creature and drew in its essence. A surge of magic accompanied the sweet addition to my strength.

Vilicangelus isn't here, all of this is Faery's work. To what end?

I grabbed a grendling, putting power behind the harsh whisper escaping my lips. "Tell me where my swords are!"

"T-the o-only swords t-they f-found were Champion blades," the moldy faerie stammered. "The knights claimed them."

Dolumii and Gherrian are here? Together? Working with Wyldfae?

An all-encompassing need demanded I slay the grendling too. He was too big to completely consume as was, and his body might draw attention.

I needed Dolumii's sword.

I needed to free Mare.

Challenging the Unseelie Knight while I was so vastly outnumbered doomed me to failure—new powers or not. Further reconnoitering of the hotel risked a like altercation. Both actions might undo the Sidhe's confusing but thorough coverup.

My next choices required wisdom and for that I needed to gather intelligence. I set the grendling down and gently dusted off his shoulders. "Thank you, sir. Have a nice day."

The grendling's stare lingered on my back as I retreated toward my Mercedes. I'd observe from the old sanctum, formulate a plan, and take back my swords.

And I can retrieve more of my books.

Quayla

I trudged across one of the sky bridges exiting the Atlanta Marriott Marquis lost in my own little world. Mortals crowded around me, celebrating beloved books and movies, comics and anime dressed in a thousand lovingly crafted cosplays. Laughter, excited chatter and shoulder-to-shoulder bodies pressed around me in a fetid, white-noise cloud.

Awash in a sea of mortal adulation, I drifted like a bodiless specter. My soul hurt more than the lingering pain from my escape. I'd lost everything and everyone I loved in a single day.

Dunham Heffernan, CEO of Circlestone and Caelum's onetime boss had laid a trap. He'd captured Ignis, Caelum, and Terrance—the other phoenixes that made up Atlanta's Shield.

Well, the phoenixes that hadn't tried to kill me.

Right before I'd been suckered by a wounded mortal in

Dunham's employ, our Shieldheart, our Vitae attacked me, forcing me to kill him. I'd escaped Dunham's prison through excruciating means none of the others—except perhaps Vitae—could replicate. Forced to flee rather than risk getting caught once more, I raced to the Marriott Marquis. Reclaiming enough magical essence from another shield's corpse could've allowed them rebirth into freedom.

The Marriott had been spotless. None of the carnage or destruction from fighting a hundred-foot kudzu elemental remained. How the property had been restored nagged from a corner of my distracted thoughts. Our boss, a divine phoenix renamed Summuseraphi was out of commission as was his superior Vilicangelus.

Yet, the Marriott looks fine. How is that even possible?

Dunham hadn't returned from the Marriott by the time I escaped, so I had no idea if he'd monologue his master plan to the others. I hadn't spent a lot of time with the powerful man, but he'd never smelled of Sidhe taint like most other Fae Kissed.

Even Caelum, our air phoenix and possessor of the best nose among us, had worked alongside Dunham without ever noticing the odor of faerie taint. Dunham could've been born with the druidic powers used to create the monster, but such things were rare and such people weren't the powerhouses Dunham had proven himself to be. Offspring of Fae Kissed occasionally inherited power without the cost, but I knew first hand Caelum's old boss was in cahoots with a powerful faerie.

One of the Dark Trinity.

I couldn't believe I'd been singled out by one of the most powerful entities in Infinity and Creation. The Lady revealed that someone—apparently Dunham—had been a seventh son of a seventh son. Mortals bred pretty well, but such children were rare—extremely rare as economic realities made such large families too expensive to maintain.

Talk about catnip for faeries.

Folklore attributed any number of special powers—good and

bad—to seventh sons of seventh sons. With just under two centuries worth of life, I'd met two—a young boy who lived in my first shield's territory and Dunham. I'd never witnessed any kind of magic from the boy, making it hard to judge their power.

The Lady and Dunham had made some sort of bargain. Sought for their potential, most seventh sons became Fae Kissed, bringing almost unilateral destruction for the Shields. Without a taint, there was no proof the deal had been a trade for Sidhe power, but they'd been working together cheek and jowl to capture my Shield.

If the Lady's warning meant Dunham, he wants me dead.

Fae Kissed were dangerous—even the corrupted like Emma who'd only bargained out of grief for the return of her deceased tabby. Knowledge of Faery was too dangerous even for so benign a wafer. If a Fae Kissed refused to surrender their boon and repent, we had no choice but to kill them before they could instruct other mortals how to get their desires granted.

The smell of a cookie store stroked my troubled soul with chocolate chip caresses. I didn't have any money. Even if I had my old ID, I couldn't have gotten anything out of my bank. My newest body was male, a difference not easily overlooked by even the most clueless teller.

If only I hadn't asked for Dylan's memory to be erased.

I wrapped arms around myself and trudged through the thronging masses out for a quick bite between panels. I'd requested a rewrite for Dylan, Mrs. Cox and Detective Foxner to protect them from the increasingly treacherous faeries around Atlanta. I hadn't wanted to lose them, but the death of Judith cemented the reasons to wipe away any ties to my friends and beloved Dylan. Judith died because she'd gone to my apartment. She'd been used as bait for yet another trap then slain to make the Lady's point.

If working in my flower shop was enough to put Judith on the Faery hit list, Dylan—the love of my very long life—had been in extreme peril.

The shop has a good supply of cash, but I'll have to break in.

I had cash stashed at my old apartment, but it was rent money and my personal dwelling was just as likely to be under surveillance as Caelum's. Once I'd been allowed off house arrest, I'd set up small caches throughout Atlanta—mostly clothes and maybe a few dollars. After meeting Dylan, having a helpmate made the caches less vital, and I'd left them untended since.

No way to be sure if they're even there. I have to make a decision. The longer I wait, the more places Dunham will stake out in hope of recapturing me.

Chapter Two

Archangel Under Glass

Vitae

Once I escaped the wafers' convention insanity, I eased into my Mercedes, soothed by luxury. My recent acquisition was luxurious, but there was a certain kingliness of being behind the wheel. Shields under me might not treat me as I deserved, but the German car manufacturer knew how to pamper their clientele.

Rather than park in my too-small space, I parked across two spaces reserved for mere wafers. I strode across the parking garage, passing Terrance's truck, Ignis's Camaro and the motor-cycles of the Shield's juveniles. The wait for an elevator stretched on in an interminable doldrum. The ride itself progressed so slow I'd have thought snails were lifting the car.

I must address the slipshod repairs the putti did on this elevator.

The serene classical instrumental ended, replaced with what unsophisticated wafers called modern music.

Caelum's been mucking about in the programming again.

A century later, the elevator doors opened.

The disaster within took me aback. Our sanctum's condition had been disgraceful on my last visit, but insult piled upon injury to height that rivaled a great pyramid. Something had splintered the polished woods and shredded rich tapestries that decorated our walls. Broken stairs climbed to the upper level looking as if elephants had trampled them.

I spoke through clenched teeth. "Anima, report."

Silence.

I drew my fighting batons, compressing my essence to push up their shafts and form glowing crescent moon blades. Someone had cleared my chamber's destroyed entrance.

Sidhe had smashed the adjoining wall in, debris laying across Mare's shredded down mattress and smashed bedsteads.

Mare's room!

I seized wreckage, hurling it without a care for where it landed. Her coverlets were shredded. Ripped clothes littered the room. Not one of her splintered furnishing remained undamaged. Everything, even her lingering scent, had been fouled.

My legs buckled, leaving me at the foot of a once pristine four-post bed, clutching a destroyed pillow sham so tainted I could no longer scent Mare on its threads.

Fury returned, holding back bottomless wells of sorrow.

Thank the Creator.

Testing my growing Sidhe powers against Mare's prison had protected her egg, else it too might've been stolen. The prospect froze my blood only to transform it into a red and gold inferno.

How dare they?! They will suffer a thousand deaths for this blasphemy if I have to infuse their bodies with my essence for a century!

I opened the library—my library—to find it ravaged, vandalized and bereft of even a single one of my fine books. The sheer scope of the damage took my breath away. In half a day, the thieves had wiped away countless hours spent scavenging and restoring old literary treasures and tomes of knowledge.

Someone will pay for this too.

The brigands had spared neither my study nor the bedrooms.

The control center gaped—an empty tomb. Only crooked wires remained, bent along grooves torn into the drywall.

Violet and emerald energy pulsed around my skin, biting at me as it illuminated my aura. The Sidhe invaded my sanctuary. They'd broken my antique furnishings. They'd taken my automata. They'd stolen the millennia of knowledge assembled in my library. Worst and by far the most unforgiveable, they'd blasphemed all that had remained of Mare.

Primeval rage seared my veins. I wanted to tear the building down with my bare hands, but knew senseless destruction wouldn't help. I took hold of myself. I could not act like the spoiled air or water shields. I was a civilized elder and would comport myself as such.

I turned my back on the carnage and crossed the upper floor for the glassed-in tunnel to the greenhouse garden. I had to think. It had been some time since there'd been any need to contact a shield without the benefit of the automata.

Back then, they dwelt within our sanctum and we had a viewing pool.

The garden would help me regain my composure. Thriving plants, rich soil and tranquility would balm the deep gouges to my spirit. What awaited me did quite the opposite.

The vindictive destruction dealt my garden rivaled the rest of the sanctum. Someone had spray-painted the statuary of a Divine One surrounded by putti—small angelic creatures often confused for cherubim—into a mockery of its glory, leaving it as the only stone left unbroken.

An elven blade impaled the statue's heart.

I waded across the wasted garden to the statue.

I accept your challenge, Sidhe. You will rue this day.

I yanked the sword free.

The statue disintegrated.

"You want war?!" My voice rattled the garden's roof. "You're nothing but the arrogant get of fallen terrorists and corrupt magic." I slid the sword across one palm, coating the blade in my blood. "I will give you a war you cannot imagine."

Anima

Anima cowered, wings mantled close around her and her many eyes squeezed shut. The garnet imbedded in her forehead burned with a fury that threatened to split her head.

She needn't have feared Vitae. She dwelled safely within a storm's eye of mist and magic, creation and infinity. Only her kind could traverse the infinite gulf between Creation and the true world of spirit and soul.

Atlanta's translucent phantom surrounded her, stretching out in all directions from her perch above the Shield's sanctum. The dark fog of taint mired the city, worsening every moment. It failed to compare with the dark star in the garden that was Vitae.

Anima was just as able to violate stricture and show herself to Vitae as she had Quayla. She was just as able to answer his summons with only her voice. She was not the computer equipment or other devices ripped from the control center by Dolumii, Gherrian and their cohort.

Those devices augmented her abilities, but she was a true—if young—cherubim. She'd been created to See all.

What she saw in her Shieldheart terrified her.

Anima had not cheered when Quayla had slain him, but she had not shed a tear either. Vitae had assaulted one of his own, a sin tantamount to choosing selfishness over all of Creation. He required redress, but their Divine One had been laid low.

The Isaac commanded I watch and not interfere.

Anima lifted an eye-tipped finger to the sapphire eye embedded in her forehead, opening herself to Quayla's essence and peering within.

Nothing came to her sight.

Mirror pools dotted the swirling nebulae surrounding her tranquil island. Liquid looking glasses of Eden-born spring water orbited her, offering their sights to any of her eyes. In olden times when the pools had peered out mortal eyes, Hadley Cox's Romani ancestors named the experience second sight or opening their third eye. They'd never understood how some of their people could glimpse the secrets of the universe—not that the Roma had alone been touched by the cherubim. The changes made to chosen mortals had given them sharper senses, keen enough to peer through glamour or glimpse the Watcher's other mirrors—visions of other places and times reflected against the inside of their eyes.

Modern times granted the cherubim crafted eyes in addition to those born. The sheer number of technological lenses—as well as mortal eyes—made searches akin to touring constellations one star at a time.

Anima had lost Quayla after her flight from Circlestone's tower. The Watcher needed to find the water phoenix. Unlike the downtown convention center, seeds populated the area around Caelum's workplace, making Anima's search one of finding the nail in a mound of needles.

Anima needed a shield worse than ever to help her cleanse and redeem Vitae from the sins he'd perpetrated on himself.

She pressed the eye-fingertip harder against the stone, squeezing eyes shut to narrow her focus. Will forced Quayla's encased essence to reach out to its origin. Anima could almost feel Quayla amid the countless motes of essence, almost, but not enough to locate her.

Anima pinned a lip beneath teeth to forestall a curse on the verge of escaping. She grabbed a section of spirit Atlanta and pulled it closer, shifting and sliding, enlarging and shirking her shire in search of hope.

Dunham

Dunham strolled away from the circle of standing stones and Ignis's screaming. The base of each standing stone contained the stolen and modified nests of Atlanta's Shield. A spell inscribed on the basin contained all five phoenixes, but he'd built additional, custom cages within the spell boundary to ensure his prizes didn't escape.

And one already has.

A pentagram of phoenix energy burned on both the center stone of the main circle and another identical stone linked to the first. Off to one side, a control console managed the robotic arms that could lift the cages off of the stones or allow Dunham to communicate to the wireless intercoms installed within the vacuum-sealed cells.

"Good afternoon, Terra. By what should I call you?"

A husky female voice rumbled out of the speaker. "Do I hear Ignis screaming in the background?"

"Yes."

"Do you intend to torture me as well?" Terrance asked.

"That will depend on how cooperative you are," Dunham said.

"This is an interesting cage," Terrance said. "I can destroy the interior glass, but something tells me you've planned for that eventuality. Should I assume the viscous substance beyond will prevent, punish or both any such attempt?"

"That is correct."

"I wonder how thoroughly you have thought out this course of action," Terrance said.

"I hope that I have been thorough enough," Dunham said. "Your name, shield?"

"Terra is fine. Will you be giving me your name?" Terrance asked.

"Dunham."

"Ah, Caelum's boss. Interesting. Are you in possession of our eggs?"

"I am."

"The kudzu elemental was yours as well?"

Dunham lifted a questioning brow toward Viviane. "Yes."

"You are some kind of Fae Kissed then, druid most likely, meaning you have taken our eggs and used a spell on them so you can control us. To what end?"

Dunham lifted his finger from the communicator. He was supposed to be questioning the phoenix, but despite the polite tone of the dialogue, the conversation had somehow gotten away from him. He was Dunham Heffernan. Regardless of anything else he was, he was the CEO of Circlestone Industries, and he had presided over more than a few adversarial meetings.

Dunham depressed the button once more. "While I appreciate the astuteness of your mind, I'm afraid I must insist upon asking the questions here."

"Very well, ask a question."

"Why did your divine not step in to contain the situation at the Marriott?"

"Don't tell him a blighted thing," Ignis's screams redoubled.

"Though you will undoubtedly torture me or try to force obedience through my egg, I must maintain solidarity with my brother. So, it seems our conversation is over, Mister Heffernan."

"Until I compel you," Dunham countered.

"That won't be a conversation, sir. That will be an interrogation."

Touché.

Dunham took the Terra's egg from Viviane, rounding the stone circle to the corresponding cage. He kneeled in front of the double-layered glass bell jar. Swirling dark liquid prevented him from seeing the Terra or the line of illuminated runes inside the cage's border. Matching runes illuminated the outer basin and the standing stone behind both basin and cage.

The front of the base stone extended outward. A beveled protuberance housed a wide socket, though not so wide as the girth of the silver and iron framed emerald pulsing in Dunham's hand.

Dunham closed his eyes, blocking out the screams. He brought to mind the incantation Viviane provided. Unlike with Caelum or Ignis, Dunham didn't exert pressure on the egg. There was no reason to assert his dominance, the earth phoenix already understood.

Understands too much really.

Energy pulsed through Dunham in time with the beat of his heart. Viviane's tutelage included drawing in elements for power. He'd wielded the power of the world's lushest forests. Ingesting essence from the captured nests had swelled his abilities several octaves over his former pinnacle.

The kudzu creature had been meant to draw the shields in, but he'd never expected it to grow ten stories tall. The carnage offered by the monster at only one quarter height would've proved sufficient lure. The plant elemental had been meant to weaken them, allowing Viviane's Sidhe and her recruited coven to kill the phoenixes.

Timing had been everything.

He'd had to lure all of Atlanta's shields before they could regroup and replace their nests. Capture had been too risky, but death put them right where he wanted them.

The kudzu's regeneration almost made the others unnecessary.

He hadn't liked enlisting outside help. The precaution was sensible, but the coven, the Sidhe knights and the cleanup crew weren't loyal to him—in other words, they weren't trustworthy.

Dunham glanced at Viviane. She lounged against the billiard table examining her nails. He knew her inattention was feigned. He knew she protected her own interests observing his every action.

She acts as if after all this time I would betray her.

Dunham offered the egg to the stone socket. The stone loosened, opening like a living maw to take the fabulous ovum.

It stretched wide like a toddler trying to fit a gigantic jawbreaker.

She stopped me from getting the last egg. Did she create the crack so that the Aqua could escape too?

The socket settled in around the Terra's egg and returned to a state of rigid stone. Enough of the egg protruded that he could apply pressure or even break the magnificent inspiration that Fabergé never managed to match.

Viviane's sweet alto broke the silence Dunham hadn't noticed. "Dark thoughts? Still brooding about losing Quayla?"

"Among other concerns."

"Your revenge is at hand, sweet boy. This should be a moment for champagne, not sour grapes."

Viviane had saved him. She'd raised him. She'd identified Dunham's druidic abilities and seen him educated in their use. She'd even helped him learn ways to remain in his prime rather than die decades before when his years should've been spent.

But why? Why does she need me?

A dark chuckle threatened escape.

Why did she need Arthur? Why does she play with mortal lives?

Dunham looked at her.

Viviane was exquisitely beautiful in ways that weren't immediately apparent. She was comely, true enough, but there was something alluring yet intangible about her.

Dunham turned his back on the stone circle and crossed the living area to his bathroom. Steam erupted from the sink spigot, but he turned on the cold to counter the heat provided by his captured phoenix.

Viviane was a Principality, a chief power in the Dark Trinity. Her existence was a constant three-way tug-of-war to win favor. It was also a war she'd been cast out of for reasons she refused to divulge.

She wants back in, and somehow, I offer her a path to do just that, but how?

He withdrew a fluffy towel from the warmer and patted his hands dry before returning to his quarters. Viviane had vanished, probably down to her rooms. He returned to the control console and opened the channel to the Terra.

"I apologize for that interruption. Please tell me why your divine was not on scene to clean up after the battle in the Marriott."

"He wasn't available."

"Why wasn't he available?" Dunham asked.

"Perhaps he was in the bathroom."

"When will he be available?"

"It depends upon what he ate," Terrance said.

A bark of laughter escaped Ignis's cage. Dunham marched over to the billiard table and fished around the runed bag. He drew out a circle of celestial silver not much larger than an average key chain. A clip hung from the ring between two of the five gemstones which corresponded to the Phoenix eggs.

The construct technically remained unfinished. He didn't have Quayla's egg, and he'd chosen not to work the binding spells on the Vitae's egg until he had the phoenix in his custody. Even so, the other stones had still been thaumaturgically linked to the eggs via one of the spells Dunham laid on each before he'd mounted them in the stone circle.

He slapped half the circle against the rail of his billiard table. The Terra grunted and Ignis yelped. Between them Caelum doubled over, but if he made a sound, the cage kept it from escaping. Dunham pinched the emerald between thumb and forefinger, rolling it roughly as he returned to the console.

"When will your divine be available?"

Terrance grunted. "Whenever he gets over his last relationship?"

"I am not amused." Dunham squeezed harder.

"On that we agree," Terrance said.

After several hours of exercising his control, he'd delivered a lot of punishment but not gotten a lot of answers. The earth phoenix was as slippery as an elf and the fire phoenix preferred pain to cooperation. As Caelum had been in Dunham's possession at the time, he had no answers. Besides, Dunham needed Caelum in good shape for the first of many tasks.

Viviane returned as the last grains of Dunham's patience spilled into the bottom of the hourglass.

"You said I would have control over them," Dunham snapped.

"And you do, just not as much as you'd like."

"I cannot wait forever," Dunham said. "The longer I delay the more likely we'll get a visit we'd rather avoid."

"Then don't. Perform the ritual now."

"Will this sequestering interfere?"

She smirked. "Won't know until we try, but you have plenty of essence to burn."

"Fine." Dunham strode up the spiral stair to his bedchamber and up to the dressing dummy which normally bore his long leather vest. Viviane slipped up behind him, hands running under his arms and over his chest. She slid the vest away, hanging it on the dummy before slipping thumbs into his shorts. Dunham stepped out of his shorts just as her hands started to explore. The edge of her fingertips caressed him enough to start a tingle, but he pushed it away with three long strides into his private bath.

The Atlanta summer water coming out of the cold feed wasn't a low enough temperature to offer any kind of chill as it sluiced down Dunham's skin. Viviane had known he would only use the cold to prepare himself, hence the light teasing that wasn't followed by her stepping into the shower with him.

She knows better when I'm cleansing.

Dunham scrubbed with an old, handmade brush of natural bristles hard enough to pink his skin. He didn't use soap or anything else that might leave a residue on him. He couldn't risk anything unnatural hampering the spell he'd waited over a century to cast.

When his raw, new skin tingled head to toe, he exited the shower.

Viviane waited in his bedroom, holding shorts crafted from tanned lamb skin so that he could step in without effort. She drew them up onto his hips and cinched them tight with a braided leather thong. He stepped into the center of the open space.

She picked up the first yew bowl of pigments and closed the distance between him. Slender, practiced fingers dipped into the mixture of herbs, ash and phoenix essence, then painted runes onto his body. There was no seduction in her motions, nothing but business. She layered the marks on him; fire then water, earth then air and finally applied the final sigils with the concoction mixed with life essence.

"Do you want the vest?" She asked.

"No."

"Are you focused? Calm?"

"Yes, and I'll remain so if you stop nagging."

"You will only get one chance at this. It's prudent to be careful."

"Agreed." Dunham strode away from her and downstairs. He wove through the plush couches and fine side tables to the stone set opposite the stone circle. Graduated cylinders held phoenix essence at the five points of a softly glowing pentagram.

He stepped into the star drawn by burning lines of essence and inhaled a long slow breath in through his nostrils. He took another and another, centering himself for the audacity to come.

I am Dunham Colwin Heffernan, seventh son of a seventh son and this is the day I claim my destiny.

His hands swept upwards. The pentagram beneath his feet consumed the waiting essence, glowing with greater intensity. A moment later, the opposite center stone drew on the essence held in the surrounding basins. Lines of power lit the contained pentagram like blazing Vegas neon.

Dunham didn't hesitate.

He didn't look to Viviane.

He knew the spell by heart. He'd recited it day after day for more than a hundred years. Not once had he uttered the mantra with the casual air of rote repetition. He'd incanted the spell with the deliberate precision—a master musician caressing the notes of his most sacred song from a beloved instrument.

Dunham kneeled. He lifted a silvered feather and dropped it into a graduated cylinder holding Quayla's sparkling blue essence. "Summuseraphi."

Next, he picked up the white feather reclaimed from Caelum's death in the Goblin Market. He deposited the divine token into the container of air magic. The word rang with even greater voice. "Summuseraphi."

He split both feathers reclaimed at the church, inserting one each into Vitae's and Ignis's essence. "Summuseraphi. Summuseraphi."

Lastly, Dunham added the feather cast in amber taken from the Terra's body at the Marriott. "Summuseraphi!"

Dunham's chest seized.

Pain lanced through his heart and the vital organ stopped beating for a three count. Energy washed out of him and the essence in his beakers drained away as if the containers lacked bottoms.

Light and thunder exploded, the shockwave stopped only by the magic circle inscribed around the center stone.

Dunham held his focus with strangling, superhuman resolve.

Light faded, revealing a golden and white bird of prey far too large for the circle caging it. Wings beat at the containment spell. Each beat landed like a physical blow, eating through his energies in gigantic chomps.

The pentagram holding Summuseraphi dimmed.

"Viviane," Dunham choked.

She hurried forward, drawing slender thermoses from a bag.

Four wings the black of brackish water stretched from her. Each accepted a container, bending or stretching to pour essence into the mouth intended for or containing its matching egg.

The center pentagram brightened.

"By the Undying Light I command you to release me!" Even held back by the barrier, his voice shook the building.

Hold your ground, eventually the bucking horse breaks.

Summus threw himself at the barrier again and again.

Viviane delivered another round of essence, shooting Dunham a warning look.

The summoning spell design incorporated caging all five phoenixes of a single Shield, allowing the containment barriers to draw directly on all five elements. Performing the incantation with only three phoenixes seemed to drain all five essence reserves at an alarming rate.

There wasn't any way for Dunham to foresee whether the Divine One's recovery attempts left Summuseraphi weakened or enervated. It didn't matter. Dunham had the tiger's tail. Letting go ranked pinnacle above all other highly ill-advised actions.

Summus's power fought Dunham's will, and the collected phoenix essence. In the end, Summuseraphi transmogrified into a winged human and crumpled to his knees.

Dunham followed suit.

If Quayla or their Vitae chose that moment to assault, Dunham and all of his careful plans would have fallen.

Depending on whether Viviane bestirs herself to crush them.

He took a long, slow breath, then fought his way back to his feet. Leaden hands swept upward along his sides, moving faster and easier with every inch as Dunham drew divine power from his captor's pentagram into his own and ultimately into himself.

Even the small amount stolen from the fatigued divine felt like the output of a fusion reactor. A second draw left Dunham's head spinning. Seemingly infinite power thrummed in every cell.

This must be how it feels to be a god.

Chapter Three

Best Laid Plans

Vitae

The hotel my thrall had found for a new headquarters didn't have underground parking. I parked my Mercedes as far out of the way of falling pecans as I could, making a mental note to have a covered parking area constructed.

Scurith met me just inside the front entrance.

"Were you successful in retrieving the..." the canine's ears lay flat against his head. "Um, your swords?"

Even after the drive across Atlanta, clinging fury blinded me to all by my desperation to verify Mare's egg.

"Begone retch!" I snarled.

Scurith scurried from my sight, ears pressed to his skull and tail tucked tight between his legs.

I ascended a grand stair to the second floor.

Grendling guards flanked a double door into my study. Their pungent aroma of a rotting low tide bay offended my nose.

Fingers stretched out under their chins.

They raised their chins to accept the pleasure a gentle touch brought all my thralls.

"Your stink offends me."

I tore out both throats, spraying the new hardwoods with gore.

Their bodies thunked to the floor a moment before my study doors clicked shut. A basin of holy water stood just inside, personally transplanted from Central Presbyterian Church since my servants couldn't touch it. Dipping hands into the liquid burned away the dead Sidhe filth from my hands, scalding my fingers in the process.

I wiped my hands on a hand towel and strode through leather chairs, dark oak shelves and a fireplace built to house the crystal phoenixes of my shield. They'd been missing from our former sanctum, leaving me to despair their absence until I replaced our automata.

Another set of oak doors parted, admitting me to an antechamber. Doors led left, right and center to my private library.

I turned to the left-hand door, fingers hesitating at the brass handle. My breath froze in my lungs, blocked by the heart lodged in my throat. The slightest push swung the door into Mare's new bedroom suite.

Her egg nestled in velvet cushions atop a marble pillar at the foot of where her bed would've rested if it hadn't been destroyed.

My breath rushed past my retreating heart.

Three strides brought my fingers all but the last inch to her egg. They trembled over her sapphire and celestial silver ovum.

Flooding relief brought on by the presence of her egg washed away fury and fear.

My legs collapsed.

Fingers lapsed onto the pedestal's edges, unworthy to bridge the distance and caress her egg.

My voice rasped like a rustle of ancient parchment. "Mare..."

Tears poured from my eyes down a long sharp nose only to leap free of me in disgust.

"I failed you, my beloved, again."

Mare's egg glowed a soft steady light in silent judgement.

"I could never bring myself to confess my love to you in life. My devotion to you would've undermined my loyalty to Him, foreswearing my oath and duty."

Something that would have cost me your love and respect.

Lifting my eyes to behold her egg rivaled Hercules's Labors and Odysseus's Trials.

"I've failed you again, beloved. I've lost Dolumii's sword." Anguish flashed to rage. "That twice-cursed slut stole you from me!"

I was on my feet, ranting and pacing without memory of the transition. "I'll get it back, and see her punished for her insolence, mark me on that. She won't keep us apart. Nothing will."

Mare's egg rested atop her pillar in silent judgement.

I reached for her, heart then fingers.

Both fled before they could caress her.

I spun on my heels and marched from Mare's suite. The Sidhe wanted a war with my Shield, and I would see them bleed rivers to atone for what they did to my precious Mare.

Quayla

Getting onto to the station without paying had been simple at the perimeter station. With the city transit system, MARTA, completely underground downtown, there was no way to drop down onto the platform beyond the turnstiles.

Being male presented me more hindrances than op-portunities. If I'd still been a woman, I could've flirted my way through a few of the geeky guys in the food court, scraping together enough money to get on MARTA and maybe buy one of the heavenly cookies I smelled baking nearby.

New bodies were always virile, but the sea of scantily dressed men and women cosplayers made walking around in Viviane's too-tight boy toy cast-offs less than comfortable. I stepped into a men's room to discreetly adjust my overeager penis into a more comfortable position. After a few moments, I gave it up as a bad job and tried visualizing Vitae. Unfortunately, my jackass Shield-heart had always been handsome on the outside—especially his newest, sultry body.

Breasts can be a pain, but nowhere near the aggravation of penises.

Remembering the bloody chunks of Vitae I'd left behind to dissolve into essence did the trick, but not for long enough. I sidled into a bathroom stall and transmogrified. I suppose technically, if I took enough time, I could shift my gender, but all I really needed were clothes I could fight in with an unruly penis. Rewriting essence memory of just my clothes proved hard enough. Almost a half hour's worth of work and several attempts by desperate men to open my stall door, I finally overcame all of the mistakes to produce a reasonable facsimile of the martial arts gi of one of Dylan's anime favorites.

Dylan.

I'd avoided thought of my lover because I figured it would worsen my condition. I couldn't have been more wrong.

My heart knotted.

For the first time since entering the convention area, sorrow overcame physical desires.

I'll never hold him again.

Pushing the sorrow away hurt, but it was necessary. I needed to get back in the game. For that, I needed to earn MARTA fare.

Finding a clear space of floor was challenging, but I eventually found a corner near enough convention traffic. Taking off shoes that didn't fit the cosplay, I settled into a nearly superhuman display of martial prowess.

After half an hour with nary a tip, it seemed I was going to have to do something more drastic if I wanted to earn train fare. Repositioning my exhibition just inside the Marriott where the sky bridge dumped out, I squeezed my core. Essence bubbled into my palm. Without my Karambit hilts to aid in focusing my will, it took several moments to form a straight razor along one finger. Sawing away three apple-sized essence orbs hurt like no one's business, but I managed.

I took several deep breaths before turning to face the foot traffic. I laid my shirt on the ground before me and started to juggle. The first few minutes centered on learning the motor controls for the new body. Once I had a feel, I extended both senses and will into the orbs of my essence.

In moments, the spheres sparkled a shimmering blue. The glowing balls changed shapes on the fly. They wove around me in gravity-defying rotations that barely paused to touch my hands. My display of aqua kinesis quickly gathered a crowd.

They gawked.

The more brazen wafers announced in authoritative voices how I managed the trick—none of them even close. Finally, the first tip fell onto my shirt. With the first dollar bill to set the example, others joined. I'd nearly crested to twenty dollars when hotel security chivvied me off the premises.

I bought three chocolate-chocolate chunk-macadamia nut cookies and paid my way down to the platform of Peachtree Center station. I did my best to eat the cookies slowly, but after the aqua kinesis display and my escape, my new as of yet unfed body refused to tolerate restraint.

It would probably sound more romantic to suggest I circled the city working out my next steps, but Atlanta's train system only allowed for east-west or north-south back and forth travel.

There were spare clothes in my apartment. I had a backup set of Karambit hilts in my room at our Shield sanctum. The safe in the florist shop held several thousand in cash and a checkbook made mostly useless by my lack of ID. I had a new body, but Dunham's security cameras would know what the new face looked like, so none of my old haunts were safe.

All of us kept stashes of spare gender-neutral clothes spread sparsely throughout Atlanta—though my stashes lacked the arsenals that Caelum had.

Vitae hadn't been captured by Dunham when I'd killed him, suggesting Vitae had another nest somewhere configured as the primary essence source for his soul's rebirth—unless he'd been reborn in his egg.

I hate to admit that idea pleased me, but it wasn't very realistic.

He'd been disappearing a lot—ostensibly to search for our stolen eggs, but I had to wonder if he hadn't set up shop somewhere else in the city. His new body suggested a death despite no dying cry from his crystal simulacrum.

Good for him for trying to reenter the world, just wish he'd shared his location.

My train ran east then west then east while my mind circled Atlanta. There were no good answers. I was on the run with no support and no resources and no idea how to improve my situation without risking myself.

I could transmog and fly to the next nearest Shield, or back to my old Shield in Hedingham.

It only took two stations of toying with the idea to realize I was the only known free shield in our Prefecture. I couldn't just leave. I had to protect the city until I could free the other shields.

On my own, but not by choice this time.

I got off at Decatur station and jogged through the searing, humid afternoon to my nearest cache. The small hidden bag was missing. Dejected, I continued on to Ponds de Leon flowers. If the cache had been there, I'd have had a few hundred dollars to work with. I could've secured food, weapons and tools to break into the florist shop that night.

Of the choices, my florist shop was the most public venue Dunham could stake out. If his people were waiting, any fight would happen in broad daylight. There were pros and cons to that, but in the day time, Mr. Pete's staff would be within earshot to call the cops.

Even so, I hoped large glass windows and the open space

around the freestanding building would prevent attackers from making a move.

Summus isn't available. If Dunham unleashed something like the kudzu elemental, things are going to get flashy in a really public way.

I jogged up the sidewalk, allowing perspiration to cool my skin. Pete, the portly owner of Camp Woof, the doggy daycare next to my shop, watched me run by, shaking his balding head. I stopped on the sidewalk out front of Ponds de Leon, putting hands on my knees to catch my breath. When he went inside, I crossed to the front door. A lance of essence cut through a dead-bolt I'd have to have repaired. I let myself in, keying a code to silence the alarm before heading to the back.

I made a quick call, scribbling out a note and a quick blank check for Atlas Locksmiths. Signing it with my former signature, I headed next store to the dog daycare. Mara wasn't behind the counter, but the much shorter Pete ducked out from behind a wall leading to their animal staging area.

"Can I help you?"

I extended a hand, my other holding a note and the check. "You must be Pete. We've never met, Mr. Grossman, but I'm Quayla's cousin Quayl. She's not in town at the moment, but called a locksmith to fix a damaged lock on her front door. She asked me to give you the check. She said you'd take care of it for her in exchange for some chocolate-raspberry croissants."

Pete's head turned ever so slightly to one side. "That's quite a lot for a first introduction."

"Sorry, there was a death in the family. I had to fly in and then take transit out here. I got off in the wrong spot and ran all the way over, so I guess I'm still running on adrenaline."

"Uh huh, hold on while I give Quayla a call."

"Go ahead, but it's all on the note."

He called me, not that I could answer the phone or even knew where I'd lost it. When I didn't answer, he frowned at me.

"Checks made out except the amount. The locksmith didn't say what it would cost."

"Kale was it?" Pete asked. "Give me your number just in case."

I opened my mouth then froze. I didn't have a phone anymore, but there was no way he'd believe that of someone my age. Manly as it wasn't, I just wanted to cry. I'd have been better off leaving the shop open and fielding an insurance claim after the fact.

An idea stuck me, but even thinking about it made me want to shrivel up and die. I glanced around once more, hoping not to see Mara. "I don't have one, they can cause cancer."

Pete paled, head darting back and forth. The short, portly man was the exact opposite of intimidating, but he tightened up on me nonetheless. "I'd like you to leave."

I didn't wait for him to tell me twice. With cash in pocket, my next stop was the garage beneath Shield sanctum to reclaim my baby.

Vitae

My headlong march stopped at the railing overlooking the hotel foyer. The dwarves rebuilding the hotel hadn't finished with the foyer, but that was so much the better. I had new plans for the space in light of losing my Shield's automata.

"Scurith!"

The small grey and tan coyll raced into sight below. "Master?"

"Have the vehicles of my other shields relocated from the old sanctum here and have covered parking constructed for mine."

"Yes, Master," Scurith bowed low, eyes locked on my face.

"Now!" The growl echoed in the open area, but I turned heel and headed for the basement. The Sidhe needed a lesson on choosing their enemies with caution.

They're not the only ones with an army.

My experiments infusing Sidhe blood into the essence I used for rebirth had added a number of benefits. Not the least of which was a compulsion I used to press weaker faeries into my service. Unlike failed military leaders throughout mortal history, I wasn't about to trust my goals to such weak-willed creatures. I had however employed this ability in creating the specialized mixture of my essence and troll bone marrow, giving the concoction to my thrall for the purpose of animating an army loyal to me.

The resultant creatures were more compliant than the cat the mortal had first reanimated, but not autonomous enough for my personal tastes. The subsequent generations of the serum had included my thrall's blood, allowing me to delegate control to the weird mortal medical examiner that I'd enthralled.

A short stair led me to reinforced doors nearly as thick as those that had protected the control center of the old shield sanctum. A surge of life plasma energized the circuit and a pass phrase in Ancient Babylonian allowed me into the mortal's living and working area.

My thrall raised his head, brightening at my appearance. "Mister, I mean Miss Vitae. I know you're very, very busy, but I really need—"

"You will address me as Master or milord, slave."

"Slave? I don't think there's any call for that. It's a pleasure—quite literally—to be of service—"

"Silence! What is the status of my army?"

My thrall gesticulated wildly.

"You may speak, but only to answer my questions."

"Thanks, I never was very good at—right, well, I wouldn't exactly call them an army, more of a large squad of kupas...like from that Mario Brothers movie—you know the one with John Leguizamo?"

"How many are ready?"

His lips quirked to one side. "I'd say around thirty-seven?"

"I require more."

"Begging your pardon, but I've already collected all the John Doe corpses in the Atlanta coroner's offices, and...well, you kept me here without internet or a phone for quite some time, so I don't even know if I still have my job."

"You have a job here."

"Yeah, I get that, but see, if I lose my access to the morgues, I can't get any more bodies."

I considered the young man, tempted to tell him to go shave the lip mold mustache barely thick enough to see it matched his red hair. He was correct that losing access to the city morgues would create situations only I could remedy. I had a city to save. I didn't have time to collect mortal remains.

The lock kept my thrall inside because unlike the Sidhe denizens currently in my service, he had no way to produce magical energy to fire the opening sequence.

"Fine, you may leave to see to your other job, but I expect you back the moment your work shift ends and with fresh bodies to build my army."

"Thank you, Master. What if there aren't any John Does?"

"Bring me bodies, I don't care their names."

"Uh, that could cause problems."

"Then get a shovel and find a cemetery. I must have a larger army to defend this city."

The young mortal opened his mouth, but reconsidered blathering at his betters. He grabbed a set of keys from one corner of a work table and moved to the door, awaiting release. A gesture sent Scurith scurrying to release my thrall while I strode up to examine the newest crop of enforcers.

Bradley

Bradley almost made it to his area of Basement-E.

Wallace Cross, a midlevel administrative functionary leapt out of nowhere, grey hair slicked back with enough hair gel to make thinning hair into a helmet. "Where have you been, Sky?"

Bradley looked at the man, unsure what to say. His Mistress—despite ordering Bradley to call him Master—hadn't given any instruction beyond trying to keep his junior assistant medical examiner job.

"I was abducted by a blood phoenix who used faerie magic to open my eyes to the benefits of abject servitude."

Wallace eyes bulged further from his skull with each word. "What is it about medical school that pushes your type over the ledge and into the looney bin?"

"Hospital Jell-O?"

"Whatever, you have a pile of overdue reports in your box. I expect them on my desk by end of day." Wallace rolled his eyes and strode away.

"Huh."

Bradley entered his bay to the reek of rotting meat. Several gurneys were parked in a traffic jam reminiscent of shopping carts after Black Friday. Paperwork rested on each chest with yellow sticky notes asking for after-the-fact signatures.

He collected the paperwork, scanning each form to find all of the rotting deceased had been identified.

Where am I going to get so many bodies? Maybe I should try cutting one of the enforcers I already have in half.

Bradley busied himself setting his morgue back to rights. The task had never been one he disliked, though a particularly ripe body offered a challenge for even his exuberance. Never before had cutting into a dead body sent pleasure through him. When he'd first joined Master Vitae's quest to save Atlanta, any time Bradley obeyed her had sent jets of dopamine through him. Even after the relatively short time Bradley had been part of the team, he'd built up a tolerance to those same chemicals until the whole thing seemed like a constant, satisfied thrum—like how he imagined bees serving a queen must feel.

Displeasing Vitae was another matter altogether.

Bradley had gotten used to the pleasure, but the pain of disobedience was always excruciating. Vitae didn't even have to be present. Just knowing he was disobeying or displeasing his Mistress-Master filled Bradley's body with agony. The prospect of not being able to fill Vitae's request for more enforcers loomed like the Sword of Damocles.

I have to find a way to get Master more bodies, but stealing people's loved ones isn't right.

The sudden disappearance of the pleasurable thrum warned him, but the more Bradley considered taking identified bodies from the morgue, the more wrong it felt.

But is there any wrongdoing in obeying my Master?

Bradley looked at the middle-aged woman on his slab, breast spread to either side of the chest incision of her autopsy. She was someone's daughter, maybe even someone's wife or mother or sister. A heart attack had stolen her life.

Bradley couldn't steal her corpse.

Pain edged into Bradley's chest. It wrapped claws around his lungs, squeezing until it became difficult to breathe.

No. She might not need her body any more, but her family needs it for closure. Master will just have to unders—

Agony shot up and down Bradley's limbs. His legs buckled. He grabbed for any hold as he fell, fingers wrapping around the dead woman's wrist.

A little voice chastised Bradley.

It reminded him that to question his Master was presumptuous. Considering another's needs, particularly a lowly mortal's, over those of Master Vitae was beyond naughty. It was sedition...rebellion...sin.

Pain lessened as Bradley dwelled on the little voice's wise words, but returned the moment Bradley tried to think of a way to obey Vitae without stealing someone's daughter.

He writhed on the floor, fingers tightening around the dead woman's cold, stiff fingers. The body came off onto him, covering him in lingering fluids. Glassy dead eyes loomed above him. Their gazes locked. Bradley fought the pain.

Agony eased, and Bradley took a breath.

A certainty filled Bradley as he eased the body off of him. "Don't worry, I won't—"

Pain hit him like a semi-truck, driving certainty away and punishing Bradley's determination not to steal the woman's body. He screamed as pain became agony became excruciating to the point of unconsciousness.

Chapter Four

Opening Salvos

Caelum

Caelum hunkered down on the small stone pedestal, leaning against the vacuum-sealed bell jar closing him into the multi-layer prison cell. He looked up. Despite Dunham's air-conditioned chambers and the small wind he swirled around the inside, the heat was stifling. Worse, his own body odor coated his nostrils in a layer of polluted snot.

Dunham ascended the spiral stair just this side of a billiards table, not even glancing toward Caelum or the other caged phoenixes comprising Atlanta's Shield. He ascended another spiral stair to a floor Caelum had never seen.

Caelum waited, eyes on the top of the stair, but Viviane didn't put in an appearance. His stomach grumbled.

A sigh escaped him.

Viviane had always been nice to Caelum. Since becoming his warden, she'd hardened. Dunham's assistant visited throughout the day, nagging Caelum and the others to fill the cage's ancillary bottles with essence. If he failed to follow through or hesitated answering questions about Vitae or Quayla, she used Caelum's egg to hurt him.

She doesn't punish anywhere near as much as Dunham, and at least she feeds us.

Dunham came down half an hour later in workout clothes, a towel around his neck and hair damp. He crossed to a door, disappeared another few minutes and returned with a frosted bottle of something that regardless of contents made Caelum salivate.

Caelum's former CEO approached, stopping at the control console. "Good afternoon, Caelum. Have a productive day?"

"Well, I'm not exactly organizing fundraisers in here."

"That's true." Dunham chuckled. "You're doing something far more vital."

"Collecting essence so you can keep Summus caged?"

"In part, but more importantly, you're replacing what your divine uses. Without that constant influx, you might not have enough for a rebirth. I'd hate to have to smash your egg, Caelum."

"Wouldn't want to miss out on ogling opportunities?"

Dunham laughed. "There is that. Mortal women don't have the advantage of your—for lack of a better term—angelic DNA, but even so you know that isn't my real reason."

"I find myself wondering whether I know you well enough to say or not," Caelum flipped hair from his face, wishing for a trim. He wrapped knuckles against the glass. "I don't think there's any doubt you're cautious and thorough. You just never struck me as being wasteful."

"You're referring to my threat to break your egg?"

Caelum shrugged. "Seems like an inefficient use of resources, especially after all the effort you went through to trap us."

"Motivating people is key to success in business. Besides, once in your egg, your usefulness ends for the next century."

"Save as leverage over the others."

Dunham darkened. "Even if I agreed with you, I couldn't change my mind. Showing weakness to another predator is foolhardy."

"So's being shortsighted."

"I like you, Caelum, but—and you need to hear this—don't push me. I'm not a man to be trifled with."

Caelum's attempts to put up a false front hadn't succeeded in getting Dunham or Viviane to underestimate his true condition. If Caelum couldn't garner sympathy with illness, he'd offer Dunham something the mortal might respect—strength. He stood, meeting Dunham's angry gaze. "Neither am I."

"We'll have to see if you're more mouth than muscle. I hope you're certain your nest will sustain a rebirth."

"Sure. Don't worry. I'm covered if I should suddenly die of stink, heat exhaustion or you know—boredom."

"I can do little about the heat while your neighbor overworks every air conditioner in the building, but I have an answer for the other—a mission."

Caelum perked up despite himself. Some birds weren't meant to be caged, an air phoenix foremost among them. Smart and careful, the wafer wouldn't let Caelum free without some kind of leash, but the prospect of wind and space buoyed Caelum's spirits.

"Seems I have your attention." Dunham placed a thumb on the keyring gem thaumaturgically connected to Caelum's egg.

Crushing pressure forced Caelum into the bottom of his cage. Dunham's phantom fist squeezed Caelum's torso like a beer can.

"You will obey me, Caelum. You will fulfill missions I assign without deviation and return directly here for insertion back into your cage. Acknowledge command and your compliance."

Fire filled Caelum's belly until he felt like he could become Ignis. The hair on his arms and legs rose up as if a lightning stroke were about to fall. He tried to hold back the words, fought to keep his teeth clamped shut with all of his will, but the words escaped anyway. "I acknowledge, Master. I will comply."

Wait until I get my hands on you, you Fae Kissed bastard.

Dunham smiled, and dropped his eyes to the console. He reached for a control, only to stop. "You will not attempt to harm to me or any of mine before or during this mission. Acknowledge command and your compliance."

The words burned like acid. "I acknowledge, *Master*. I will comply."

Dunham keyed the robotic arms over the standing stones. The device lifted Caelum's bell jar, washing him in cooler air. Goose pimples spread across his skin and his nipples went taught in the sudden comparative cold.

Caelum licked his lips as Dunham approached. He stopped within arm's reach of Caelum, waiting for something.

Not taking the bait, I know there's a magical barrier. I saw Quayla collide with it before she escaped.

Dunham fingered his way through several gestures, lips barely moving as he uttered some incantation. The blazing runes adorning both the base and standing stones of Caelum's cell faded to a subdued glow.

Dunham extended a key card. "Building's empty, you'll find a marked locker with clothes in the gym—the ladies locker room. Get showered and dressed."

"Then what?"

"Then you will destroy Catholic Shrine of the Immaculate Conception."

Shock hit Caelum with another blast of cold. "What? Why?"

Dunham's voice hardened. "Because I wish it."

"That church has stood here almost as long as I've been in Atlanta. It's brick and stone. Besides, it's Sunday."

"You've never had a problem exceeding my expectations in the past. I'm certain you'll figure out a way to complete your assigned task. It should be night by the time you walk all the way there, so you will be able to draw on your full phoenix form without much risk of witnesses or fatalities."

Caelum's tone wasn't friendly. "How very considerate of you."

"You have your orders, Caelum. Don't push me, or I'll have a driver deliver you in time to destroy the church during evening mass."

Caelum tensed. "You wouldn't dare."

Even as the words left his lips, Caelum wished he could take them back. Dunham would dare. If Caelum pushed too hard, his old boss would make Caelum slaughter innocents just to prove that point.

"World's overcrowded as it is." Dunham smirked. "They're only wafers."

Caelum exhaled and hurried for the stairs.

Dunham's voice stopped him on the top step. "That was your free one, shield. All the rest will cost you."

Quayla

Once I exited the downtown train, I hurried up one block and down the other, weaving through other pedestrians toward our sanctum's tower. I had no way to discern whether Dunham's surveillance would watch the sanctum or the whole building. Either way, if I could get to my pearl white Johammer J1 motorcycle, I'd be able to reach Anima through the bronze angel on its console.

Our building came into view and my heart quickened. Anticipation doubled my foot speed. Help and transportation were in my grasp—ready weapons too if I could remember how to open Caelum's stash.

A tow truck pulled out of the building's garage, Terrance's old beat up truck half in the air to allow for towing.

My breath caught in my throat.

A second tow truck pulled Ignis's Camaro into the street, a bump scraping the car's undercarriage against the pavement.

I broke into a run.

A flat bed followed the first two tow trucks, Caelum's and my motorcycles up in its bed.

I couldn't have run faster without transmogrifying into a phoenix and flying. I waved my arms and shouted at the driver. I didn't give any thought to keys or identification. I wanted my baby, and I'd take her if I had to knock the mortal driver out flat.

I leapt a small island of dry weeds into the road. My sprint barely allowed me to escape a Honda's bumper. I leapt with all of my might, jumping further than any mortal could've managed outside Olympic competitions. I hit the side of the flat bed, gut slamming into the platform and fingers scrabbling for purchase.

A tie-down strap over Caelum's motorcycle pulled me onto the deck. Before I could round Caelum's bike to my baby, the truck screeched to a halt, throwing me into the back of the cab.

The driver got out, pulling a crow bar from behind his driver's seat. "What the hell do you think you're doing?"

"Trying to catch my breath."

"Get down."

I looked at him. My new body didn't have the mass to match him blow for blow, but Hep-Silat would let me beat him unconscious unless he was former special forces or some closet black belt.

"These bikes belong to my brother and cousin," I said. "What are you doing with them?"

"The owner called for us to move them."

"That's impossible, I'm—I'm sure Quayla didn't hire you to move her motorcycle."

"I've got a work order. So, you either get down and take it up with your cousin, or I'm going to beat you bloody, call the cops and press charges for assault and grand theft."

I took his measure and was sure that he was convinced he could do just that. I needed my baby, but I needed Anima's help more.

Maybe there's a way to have both.

I grabbed the angel statuette between Caelum's handlebars,

jerked it free and ran. The driver called me all kinds of names, but he only pursued about half a block before returning to his truck and its cargo. As soon as I felt safe to stop, I dodged into an alley and looked down at the disgruntled looking angel figurine.

"Ani, please tell me you can hear me."

"Quayla! Oh, thank the Creator you're all right."

"I'm fine for the moment. Please tell me you can track the other figurines on our vehicles."

"Of course, but you have one in your hands."

"Yeah, but I want my bike back too."

"What has happened?"

I told her everything I knew and even a few of the things I only suspected. When I finished, I took a big gulp of air before pressing forward. "Is my feather box still in my room in the sanctum?"

"No. Knight Dolumii took it."

"I thought I killed him."

"You did, but it seems not to have taken," Anima said.

"Fine, can you contact Summus or Vili?"

"I've had no luck contacting either."

I cursed, pacing the section of alley. "All right, I need to get some gear from Caelum's stash in the parking garage, then I need Shieldheart's Guide to Nests, a new basin and a place to work."

"You're fortunate. Had the tow trucks not distracted you, you would've run afoul of the bevy of Fae Kissed lurking in the garage. The faeries left nothing of value in the sanctum, not even the books."

I stared at the little bronze angel, its limbs arranged in a pleading stance. Without the book on nests, I had no way to rebuild mine. I had no way to know if I could merely collect essence like Summus, or if every choice I made had to be weighed against the chance of True Death.

I wedged the statuette into a back pocket and turned my hands over for a moment. I compressed my core. Essence frothed out from under my fingernails, climbing up the backs of my fingers and stretching out to turn my hands into armored claws.

"What are you doing?" Anima asked.

"There are Fae Kissed in that building."

"They're armed and prepared."

I flexed my hands, fingers closing one by one into a fist before opening back up into a shimmer claw. "So am I."

Chapter Five

Drowning in Fire

Quayla

Anima gave me a tactical rundown of the Fae Kissed and their positions within the garage. Instead of rushing into the ambush they'd staged around our parking places, I hopped a barrier and rushed down a ramp. I leapt the railing as soon as I was able, hopping down two levels in short order before heading to the garage's rear. Two floors seemed enough to evade detection by the Fae Kissed lurking in the landing of the ground level stairwell.

I eased the door closed ever so gently, noticing how my claws glistened in the dim stairwell.

If I keep them, they'll give me away.

Anima whispered from my back pocket. "He's lounged on the stairs watching the door."

"Shh."

Anima whispered an apology so soft I barely picked it up. Even so, the overdone whisper brought a smile to my lips.

"It's good to have you back in my corner, Ani."

I drew my essence back into my hands, but kept the tension around my center. With careful steps, I crept up the stairs slow and stealthy. Forty stair steps offered more than sufficient time to consider my reverse ambush.

The guy waiting for me wasn't a sad, lonely woman like Emma. Whatever he'd traded for—taking Anima's word that he was Fae Kissed—it wouldn't have been something so benign. Procedure required me to offer him a chance for absolution if I wasn't under direct assault, but making such an offer would cost me the element of surprise and very likely bring his comrades down on my head.

I didn't have an egg to catch my soul.

There was no way to know if the nest in Dunham's possession held enough essence for a rebirth. Even if I'd known for sure, the prospect of losing my current freedom wasn't worth offering my would-be assassin absolution he'd almost certainly reject.

Killing him outright violated more than just the rules, but the fate of my whole Shield hung on my freedom.

I'll face the consequences if need be—after I kill him quick and quiet.

I considered wrapping his head in essence, stifling screams while he drowned. If he fired his gun during his dying moments, I was screwed. I couldn't extrude enough essence to cover his mouth and gun.

If I'd still been a woman, I could've tried kissing him to take him off guard. The tactic still had merit, perhaps more so depending on any latent homophobia the wafer harbored. During his shock, the kiss enabled me to fill his lungs with essence until they burst.

Unfortunately, his gun remained a problem.

I considered going all movie action hero and breaking his neck. All phoenixes are, to varying degrees, stronger than wafers, but a Fae Kissed wafer could have traded for damn near anything. It was a simple thing for a Sidhe to enhance the wafer's speed, strength, or intelligence. Typically, the cost of such enhanced abilities burned out the mortal's body, allowing the faerie quick receipt of the goods. If his hand spasmed, or he had some way to resist my attempt to break his neck, a single shot would bring the ambush down on my head.

Two hurled blades seemed the best choice, but if the wafer moved, a near miss might still blow the whole situation up in my face.

I couldn't risk failing.

I couldn't shape essence in any way that could attract his attention.

I didn't have backup.

I cursed in silence.

Guess I should've been more careful what I wished for.

I pooled essence in each palm and resumed my silent climb. A thousand things could go wrong with my plan. For one, I'd never tried to shape essence on the fly before, but one way or another I had a duty to eliminate these Fae Kissed and the danger they presented to humanity.

Loose pea gravel shifted underfoot as I turned onto the last few stairs leading to the main level. Alerted by the trap he'd laid, the wafer dressed all in black leapt to his feet and pivoted around to aim his Beretta right at me.

Please don't let me misjudge.

I leapt left then right, bounding off railings in a three-step ascent. I shifted the essence in my left along the bottom edge of my hand, shaping it into as sharp a wedge as I could. I brought the hand down on his forearm in a karate chop, centered the essence in my right at the heel of my hand, shaped it into a spike and thrust a heel strike into his nose.

His Beretta fell to the stairs still, gripped in a severed hand. Blood painted the stairs in staccato spurts. Cartilage crunched. His broken nose added to the ruby deluge. A truncated cry died only partly voiced as my spike of essence went into his brain.

I grabbed his body to keep it from falling, only just realizing he wore a headset. Concern over the sound of his body hitting the ground or worse, tumbling down the stairs, was cut short by a voice from his dislodged earbud.

"Marks, report."

Nothing for it, I shaped the essence in my hands back to the bladed claws I'd formed outside, compressed my essence and kicked open the stairwell door.

"By the Undying Light, I command you to drop your weapons and surrender."

I'm fast, but not faster than bullets. Red hot metal tore holes through in my flesh before I could transmogrify. The nearest gunman held a Glock trained on me in a practiced two-hand grip.

I leapt at the black-clad figure, releasing hold of my essence to let it ripple outward, changing flesh into pure essence. My right claw slammed into him, but instead of shredding his chest as I intended, the blades embedding in some kind of body armor.

I wrenched my claw out of the hardened putty.

The tip of a machete flashed through my peripheral vision as the blade chopped down through my shoulder. Had I still been flesh, the powerful blow would've cost me a shoulder, a lung, and the use of one arm. As it was, it hurt like a bitch.

An upper cut wiped the smug grin and accompanying face completely off Mister Glock's skull. Taint soaked into me, the sickening sensation nearly as strong as with a pure blood Sidhe. I whirled on the next guy only to have a third man in black tactical gear shoot my head and chest with a pistol.

Mister Machete dressed like an extra soldier from a jungle war movie. He glanced behind the new gunner before trying to hack off my arm at the elbow. "Dammit, Wan, get in the game."

His blow severed my arm, but between water's latent desire to group together and my own aqua kinesis, the arm didn't fall away. Holding onto my form cost me a second, giving him the time to sweep the machete around again, this time for my neck. I deflected the blade on the hardened back of my opposite hand. The clumsy block sent the blade into the shoulder I was already struggling to keep together.

With my claws already positioned the right way, I slashed them across Machete's face. He dodged backward. When he lunged for my midsection, I grabbed his hand and crushed it with all the strength I had. He broke away, apparently unaffected, and slashed at me again.

The whole fight had been off balance from the start. Instead of playing to my strengths, I'd let temper and the wafers control the action. I stepped back from him, checking over my shoulder for the gunman.

The remaining gunman stalked forward, swapping his 9mm for an assault shotgun. Over his shoulder a little Asian woman sat on the hood of a Dodge Charger. Golden dragons glistened along the scarlet silk gown, reflecting the ember at the tip of a long, thin cigar.

Machete nearly took my head off.

I slipped away once more, sweeping my feet into a slow, fluid dance. I slid around his next blow, shifting to put him between me and the shotgun. There was no way to tell if the shotgunner would hold his fire or shoot through Machete, but it was worth the effort while I centered myself in Hep-Silat.

Extruding another ball of essence, I tangoed with Machete, proving how slippery water could be. On his next strike, I hurled the gob of essence at his face. It tore painfully away, splattering across his mouth and nose.

Machete tried to wipe it away with his off hand while lunging once more. The essence didn't wipe away. It clung to his face. With all the exertion, his heavy breathing quickly exhausted his air supply. Machete dropped his weapon, clawing at his face with both hands.

I'd been waiting on him to start suffocating, so I was ready when the blade fell. I hooked a foot beneath the machete, launched it up to my hand, stepped into Machete, drove a knee into his groin and hurled the machete toward the other gunman.

He sidestepped. A casual sweep of his shotgun batted the large blade away. "Damn it, Wan, if you're done painting your nails, now would be a good fucking time."

Wan sighed, ground her cigar out on her palm and hopped off the car's hood. She smoothed her gown and burst into flame.

The sight of a mortal transmogrifying into living fire caught me off guard. I didn't even notice when Machete fell to the ground unconscious, but I noticed when the shotgun opened fire.

In my human form, I have all the basic organs of a regular mortal. Even my phoenix form has vital organs, but the pure liquid form I'd adopted was just essence held together by my soul's will.

Bullets were an inconvenience. They hurt—though not as much as being shot in the flesh. They stole motes of essence from the whole and added heat that I had to dissipate through evaporation. The three assault shotgun shells splattered the upper third of me from the whole.

Tearing away that much essence exposed me to a whole new level of excruciating. I'd like to say that I engineered an artful backward fall. Instead, I reeled in agony, flailing back and away from my attacker in thoughtless panic.

The shotgunner stomped forward and shot me again in the midsection, spreading my essence further across the parking garage cement. Laughter exploding from him in harsh barks. "That's what I'm talking about. Recover from that, jackass!"

"He is not dead," Wan said.

"The hell he's not, there's nothing left but legs."

"But his legs still have form," Wan said. "When destroyed, he will lose form."

Wan was right. She'd also bought me enough time to reach out to all of the essence spread across the ground.

I'd never tried, let alone practiced, what came next.

I had forced myself into a long string and inch-wormed my way out of Dunham's cage drain. I had elongated my hands to slip from Sabrina's cuffs. Outside those desperate occasions, I'd never really taken any but my two normal forms.

Primal Battle had been written by an air phoenix, so a lot of the instructions revolved around uses of his softer form. He'd included chapters on the other elements, but the instructions were second hand at best.

Dunham reminded me that stone was pretty tough, but that air or water could wear it down in time. *Primal Battle's* author had provided detailed instructions for using wind to destroy Fae Kissed without leaving a body behind.

When faced with Emma's innocence, I'd been unable to kill her.

Furious and alone, terrified and desperate, I acted without giving much thought to why's or how's.

My essence flowed across the few inches separating me from the laughing shotgunner. I swirled up and around him until my essence encased him. Drowning was sufficient to end him.

I could've stopped there, but the bad day had me pissed off.

Essence flowed around him. Will pushed the current around him faster and faster. The inner whirlpool hardened into a thousand shark fin edges, eroding his clothes, his armor, his flesh. Taint bled into me, but no room remained between me and fury for sickness.

Having never eroded away a human being, there was no way to quantify the reaction. A few moments abrasion ate away months or years of normal decay. I stopped when I hit bone and reformed my body, leaving his bones and other remains to fall.

"So," I said. "Are you going to surren—"

Wan threw a fist forward, launching a jet of fire at me like a living flame thrower.

I dodged to one side, ready for her to try something.

She was ready too.

She launched a volleyball sized bolt ahead of my dodge, all the while shifting the flame tongue up my back trail as she strolled closer.

I hurled a blade into her chest. It flashed to steam without even causing her to flinch.

"Water does not win against fire," Wan said.

Her statement wasn't perfect. My essence could drown an

equal sized normal fire, but I had no doubt she was composed of faerie fire. A powerful Seelie backed her power for a no doubt a commensurately dire cost. She could throw flames around all day without exhausting her supply, but all I had was my own essence bolstered by a few cookies.

It's possible I could get to Caelum's stash, but bullets might not do her any more harm than they do me.

I glanced around the garage, searching for a wide red band signifying a pillar which bore a fire extinguisher. None of the pillars wore red paint.

What the hell, I thought Atlanta had laws about this kind of thing.

Our building housed both commercial and residential spaces. Municipal ordinance required that even the solid concrete parking garage have fire protection in place in case of vehicle fires. What I couldn't fathom is how our building—a structure Fire Inspector Ignis Round frequented—could not have fire extinguishers.

I threw myself forward and juked left, sliding under the flame gout. A fire bolt slammed into one leg. Pain flared up my limb as half my calf flashed to steam.

I hit wrong but kept rolling, pushing on my essence to rebalance. Hair I didn't have sent phantom tingles up the back of my neck. I reversed the roll, barely avoiding another blast. The sudden shift brought my elbow down harder than intended. I winced and rolled back the way I'd gone first.

As soon as I rolled over onto my face, I pushed myself up on to my feet and scrambled behind a pillar. Wan hit me in the side an instant before I reached concrete cover. The mind searing direct blow of pure faerie fire didn't eat away an equal section of essence, but it ate enough away that rebalancing too many times would reduce me to little in the way of physical attributes.

What I wouldn't give for some of those extinguisher bombs Ignis and Caelum were geeking out over.

Flame bathed the pillar, washing around both sides. Already

hot September weather heated up until I had to let essence evaporate to cool the remainder. The last thing I needed was for a fire bolt hit to flash already parboiled essence to steam.

"You cannot keep this up forever." The wash of flame shifted, Wan walking around the pillar in a slow and steady gait. "Fire destroys all. It is the ultimate element."

I moved opposite her, shifting to areas of still radiating concrete. I had to do something. If she beat me, I was either True Dead or back in Dunham's cage.

Not even sure which is worse at this point.

I bolted, snatching up the assault shotgun and sprinting to the faceless wafer. I wrenched him up as a shield against the firebolts only to realize that if I stayed in one place, she'd be able to close back into flamethrower range. That flame gout would cook both me and my makeshift body shield. I hurled myself sidelong just as she leveled the burning stream.

I landed wrong on the machete, turned toward her and unloaded the shotgun. The shot spread out at the longer range, but besides launching a meteor storm of flaming comets out Wan's back, the blast had little effect.

"You might as well just give up." Wan said.

I traded the shotgun for the machete and ran.

Wan caught me with the flame gout as I fled. However she maintained the continuous flame, it didn't burn with the heat of the fire bolts. The boiling away of my essence hurt like hell. I tucked behind another pillar out of breath.

"The faster you die, phoenix, the sooner the pain stops and I can get lunch. I'm thinking barbeque."

I sprang out one direction, drawing her fire before doubling back toward another pillar. Being the weekend, the parking garage was mostly empty. That meant fewer places to take cover but also fewer car fires.

Wan threw another firebolt, I batted it away with the machete out of instinct. The impact sent vibrations up my arm, but to my surprise, the blow actually deflected the bolt.

I shot a look up at the high concrete ceiling, double checking what I'd seen in that moment's paused rolled on my back. Between the concrete ribs but beneath the ceiling, red pipes criss-crossed the garage.

Through planning or happenstance, Wan only used the flame gout when she was within ten yards. With as hot as Atlanta got during summer, the fire control sprinkler sensors had to be set to go off only under sustained extreme heat.

I aborted my race to cover, walking backward facing her. "Surrender, Wan. You can't keep this up forever."

She smiled. "Are you sure? You're looking awfully thin."

Wan threw another firebolt. I slapped upward with the machete like we were playing badminton. The machete missed, the bolt hitting my bicep.

I screamed.

The concentrated fire burned away enough arm that my hand fell several inches before I willed it to float. I took the machete with my off hand and absorbed what remained of the arm.

I'd only just started rebalancing essence when Wan's next firebolt streaked toward me. Being a hair less than ambidextrous, I wasn't as confident in the skill of my left, so I shifted my frame out of the way of the bolt before trying to hit it.

I succeeded in both, but the thin, cherry red blade deflected the bolt imperfectly. I hit three more and was running out of parking garage when I finally knocked a firebolt into a sprinkler head. The intense heat expanded the contained liquid enough to shatter the extra thick glass bulb containing it. Collapse of the bulb opened up the path for water with a hiss followed by silence.

Nothing else happened.

The other sprinkler heads remained inactive.

No pressurized water sprayed out to help me fight Wan.

Not even a single drop of water offered itself to help rebuild my body.

I cursed.

Wan laughed and threw another firebolt.

I dodged this one wholesale, spinning out of its way and glimpsing the street a hundred feet away beyond a concrete barrier. It would take only a moment to revert to my human body, race to the entrance, leap the barrier and run away.

Anima's voice came from behind me, but I couldn't afford to turn my back on Wan. "Quayla? I would prefer never to interfere in a shield executing her—"

"Ani, can you do anything about the sprinklers?"

"The garage levels are not linked into the building control center. Even if they were, I am not sure normal water would be much help with the amount of Sidhe magic that's coming off of your opponent. Remember the DeKalb Fur Family Hospital fire?"

"If you can get the water running, I'll think of something."

"Perhaps you should flee."

Anima's words cut into me like Machete's first blow, but with far more effect. I wasn't doing well against Wan, but not all was lost. More, I couldn't just run away, especially from so powerful a Fae Kissed. Wan could not be allowed to continue running around Atlanta. If the section of garage behind me had been open to the street, I just knew she'd have thrown her firebolts even when missing me meant blasting traffic.

"I can't, Ani. Someone has to stop her."

"You are ill-suited for this fight, and your death will have far reaching consequences."

I deflected another bolt, Wan closing into range of her fire torrent. Anima wanted me to run. I knew she didn't want Wan running around Atlanta, but fleeing would give the Fae Kissed license to go anywhere unchallenged.

"Can you call Summus?" I asked.

"Summus has gone missing, even the Isaac cannot locate him."

I cursed and bolted for the entrance.

"You're going to make me chase you?" Wan asked. "Really?"

I'd hoped deluging Wan with the sprinkler systems would

dampen her enough for me to handle. The firefighters trying to put out the faerie fire at DeKalb Fur Family Hospital had waged war with four engine companies and still not kept it in check—at least until I'd used my essence to enchant the water supply.

I glanced up at the red pipes.

Instead of running out the entrance, I sprinted down the ramp to the next level. Hoping not to trip on my feet, I kept my eyes on the ceiling, tracing the sprinkler system lines. At the back of the next level, the pipes shifted ninety degrees, joining the sprinkler lines into a larger supply line that shot through the wall over a door marked 'FD only.'

I slashed through the lock as I yanked the door opened on a utility room. A huge machine dominated the room. A control panel hung from the wall between several thick vertical pipes— one red. The pipe wasn't the only thing red either. Red lights dotted the control panel even though the rocker switches along its face were all in the on position.

With the side of my hand, I shifted all the switches off and then on. The machine rumbled to life for the first time since a Wyvern's cry had overloaded the electrical grid.

I didn't stop to question how building maintenance had forgotten to check this control panel. I bolted out of the room and reversed course into the stairwell.

Wan's mocking laughter follow me. "Dead end?"

I coated the machete with essence, focusing on the edge of the heavy blade and backed into the corner of the stairwell. I extruded more essence into my off hand, extending my fingers and webbing the space between them.

The door blasted off of its hinges, careening into the room half aflame. I kicked it down the stairwell to clear my view as Wan stepped into the doorway.

I brought the machete down at an angle across the hose mount cover of the water stand pipe and shoved my other hand across the opening. My energy plummeted. I dropped the machete and closed my other hand over the stream. Shooting water tried to erode away skin I didn't have, meeting will-hardened and smoothed essence that directed the path of least resistance through the fine mesh between my fingers and right into Wan.

Some of the mesh ripped away, but I kept enough to enchant the deluge which blasted her. I kept up the assault until she disappeared beyond the doorway then sprinted after her, drawing in all the enchanted water I could.

I tackled her flickering body and wrapped her in another whirlpool. She drew more fire from the Sidhe backing her, but the assault had already weakened her. Suffocated by countless gallons of enchanted water and me, the fire couldn't gain a foothold. She flickered out, returning to flesh. I didn't stop until nothing but bones and a gold chain bearing a dark ruby housed in a golden flame remained. A shift in current ejected the Sidhe amulet, allowing me to grind down the bones to powder.

I fell to my ass and wept.

"You did it!" Anima said. "I was terrified you'd die a Truth Death, but you defeated her."

"Yeah."

"You will need to deal with the other remains."

"Yeah."

"And shut that valve."

"Uh huh."

"Quayla?"

"Yeah?"

"Are you all right?"

My head shook without conscious permission. "Not even close."

Chapter Six

The Hand of Trust

Quayla

I took care of everything first, then opened up Caelum's stash. To my surprise he'd included hilts for all of us as well as a few weapons I'd never seen the others use. Considering the poor performance of my close combat specialization against Wan and the other Fae Kissed, I took an automatic pistol.

I could've taken the guns I'd collected from my attackers, but Caelum's were far more likely to be unregistered and superior quality.

He likes his guns.

In addition to my own hilts, I took an alderwood flute Ignis preferred. I'd never tried to do the things he managed with ease, but I figured taking care of the whole city by myself offered plenty of training opportunities.

One thing Caelum's stash lacked was a replacement basin for a new nest. There seemed no way to close myself inside the secret room without someone to close up the utility closet in a way that looked right—something Caelum never envisioned.

If he'd planned for such an eventuality, I might've considered hiding my nest inside except that one squad of Fae Kissed assassins had already staked out the building.

Just doesn't feel safe here.

"Ani, if I leave this headset here, will you be able to tap into it to talk to me?"

"Yes, but you have one of the statues."

"I know, but the headset lets you whisper in my ear."

"Assuming you are in range of the unit," Anima said

I cursed.

She was right, but I did not know what the range was.

"What if I carried one and wore another?"

"That should work so long as they remain powered."

I tucked a second headset and power pack into a duffle bag and put one on. It didn't look like a standard Bluetooth headset and could gather attention I might not want. After another round of consideration, I powered both off and tucked them in my bag.

I can always put it on next time I need to go tactical.

I bagged up my belongings, putting the bronze angel statuette in an outer pocket I didn't zip closed. Hitching the duffel over one shoulder, I hiked away. The sun headed to bed and after the day I'd had, bed sounded like the right idea.

There are a lot of hotels in downtown Atlanta, but with DragonCon going on, they were expensive, full and not likely to take cash. If I hiked in any direction far enough, I'd likely find one that fit the bill. Knowing that Dunham sent a kill squad made MARTA a trickier option than before. He was rich, powerful and connected. It wouldn't take much to have transit cops or Atlanta's finest looking for me. Marching into a MARTA station carrying a pistol without ID or a carry permit wouldn't go well.

"Ani, can you lead me to my Johammer?"

The smile in Anima's voice came through the statue. "That's why you took the statue on Caelum's motorcycle, so I could zero in on yours."

"Got it in one."

"Head northeast."

"Toward Circlestone?"

"In that general direction, but closer to the perimeter."

I nodded and marched. It became apparent that I didn't have the energy to keep up the trek. I stopped in a Subway and got a double meat ham sub. I'd have preferred tuna, but their tuna subs were messy enough without doubling the meat. Besides, eating turkey or chicken seemed a little too close to cannibalism.

I rested and ate, drinking plenty of water. When I finally climbed out of the uncomfortable but so comforting booth, my limbs didn't want to move. I managed another mile or two before I just didn't think I had any more in me. The sound and smell of a highway—I-85 most likely—drew me a few more blocks.

I didn't have any experience being homeless, but I'd always heard they preferred overpasses. I climbed down underneath the first one I came to and found what looked like someone's nest on a flat ledge at the top of a steep incline. A short search identified a corner that wasn't strewn with litter and didn't reek of urine. I leaned my back against a corner, arms around and head laid atop my bag. My belongings didn't hold a candle to Dylan's and my bed, but I fell asleep on my second blink.

"Quayla?"

A name in the dark seemed to call me, but I couldn't get my brain to figure out why.

"Shield Quayla, please wake."

The voice sounded familiar and agitated. Sleep clung to my eyes, cementing them closed. I lifted my head, a taste of new nylon in my mouth. "Wuh?"

"Quayla, you must wake and help me."

Anima is asking for help? What could hurt her?

My eye lids snapped open, searching for the miraculous entity I knew to be Anima, but found only darkness.

"Quayla, please wake. He's taken the statue."

The sound came from further in the darkness then it should have. I leaned over to where the pocket holding my statuette gaped open and empty.

I drew a hilt and slid a blade out, lighting the underside of the overpass. Eyes reflected my light.

"You, give me back my statue."

The reflection shook back and forth.

I rushed forward, bringing my glowing knife blade close enough to get my first look at him. The wafer was thinner than I'd been when pushing hard to refill my nest. The weathered face shrouded in a mane and full beard of grey-brown hair looked at least ninety.

I softened my voice. "Please, give me back the statue."

He gibbered at me in a language I'd never heard.

"Ani, can you translate that?"

"He's speaking English," Anima said.

His words hadn't sounded like English to me.

"Look, I need that statue. It's important."

His words slowed down just enough that I got what he said several seconds after he finished speaking. "No, I heard them, the voices of the angels. You can't hog them. I need an angel. You can't have it. My angel. My miracle. No, I won't, I won't."

"Ani?"

"I've been trying to wake you for some time," Anima said. "I've located Caelum."

"Inside Circlestone?"

"No, he's assaulting a church," Anima said.

That almost made less sense than the homeless man's gibbering. Caelum would never attack a church. Dunham had captured him, so he shouldn't have even been out and about—unless Dunham had found some way to force Caelum into attacking the church.

"Look, I need that statue back. I'll buy it from you."

The mad vagrant clutched the bronze statue against his chest. He backed away, head sweeping back and forth.

"Perhaps your blade is scaring him," Anima said.

"I can't see without its light."

"Perhaps if you shined light from elsewhere?"

If I hadn't been desperate to get the statue so I could go after Caelum or the man had seemed less out of his mind, I mightn't have risked my next choice. I focused on my essence and shifted a vertical halo of skin and clothes into liquid—lighting myself up like an angel.

His eyes widened. He took a step toward me, hand outstretched.

"Please return the statue."

He backed away in a rush. "No, won't give the angel to the angel, no, he's already an angel, he doesn't need my miracle. It's my miracle, no you can't have it, make your own miracle, don't steal mine."

A snarl escaped me. "I don't have time for this."

I rushed him.

Terror drew away what little color remained in his face under the shimmering blue light. I seized the statue, jerking it toward me. He refused to let go, yanking it back with surprising strength. We struggled back and forth, the bronze angel glaring with arms folded and irritation on its little face.

I wrenched the statue from the old man's grip, turned my back and marched toward my bag. "Ani, where's Cae—"

"No!" the old man wailed. He leapt onto my back, one arm flailing and scrabbling to reclaim my link to Anima.

I swept my arms back, throwing him off and turned to snarl a rejoinder at him.

He hit the ledge off balance, stepping backward with his arms pinwheeling. I rushed forward, but he hit a support and fell sidelong down the steep incline head over heels. I rushed down after him, but before I could get half way down the sound of screeching tires on highway rent the air.

A thump accompanied the sound of shattering glass. The old man's body hit the highway and slid along, turning a slow spin until it came to rest fifty feet from the smashed van hood, broken body bisecting a white slash.

All warmth drained out of me.

A semi thundered past as I stared, and for a dreadful moment I thought its tires might find the old man's head.

"Hey, you up there. Did you push him?"

My stare moved from the dead vagrant to the dented mini-van's bleeding driver so slowly that bystanders could have heard it make a rusted metal groan.

"Quayla, your essence."

Transmogrifying the essence haloing me doused the light. I raced the rest of the way down the incline, grabbed the shattered man by mushy ankles and dragged him clear of the other lane. Hopeless searching failed to find a pulse.

A light shined on me from behind. "Hey, what are you doing?"

I spun around to look.

"Quayla." Anima's tone carried all the warning I needed.

I bolted toward the driver, ducked behind him and bound up the overpass incline. Grabbing my bag, I continued climbing up to the road above.

I'd killed the old man. I might as well have shoved him into traffic myself, all to get the statue faster.

So, I could help Caelum...at the cost of a mortal life.

I tried to push the encounter out of my mind, but it repeated over and over in my mind's eye. Each time it stole more breath, squeezing my chest tighter and tighter with icy, skeletal hands.

My voice escaped in a raspy croak. "Where's Caelum?"

"Catholic Shrine of the Immaculate Conception on MLK Junior Drive Southwest."

I turned left at the next intersection and tear-blinded, kept running from the old man I'd murdered.

Quayla

I ran for about four miles before the wind started to pick up. Hair on my arms and neck stood to attention. "Ani?"

"Caelum is in the center of the church complex. He's transmogrified controlling the storm."

I looked up into the dark sky ahead as dust and debris formed into the funnel of a tornado. I didn't have any ability to counter Caelum's wind, and I didn't have the mass to charge in without falling prey to the storm. Slowing to think was at the top of my thoughts, but the winds forced me to a slow trudge anyway.

"Ani?" I shouted over wailing wind. "How do I get his attention?"

"I don't have any suggestions. Maybe wait him out?"

"I'd rather he not destroy this place."

"He may not have any choice."

Probably doesn't.

Police cars sat at a distance with their lights flashing. The officers were inside cars nosed outward for a hasty retreat if the funnel started to move. Further back, gawkers held phones up to capture what they could in the remaining light of untoppled light poles. One police cruiser laid rubber in his haste to depart as the funnel shifted to the building nearest me.

The sound of glass breaking in the distance reached me bare instants before the windows on my side of the church exploded outward. I covered my head and face, cursing the swirling winds blue. All things considered, Caelum had been at it for a little over a half hour. That he hadn't leveled the buildings already spoke to their construction.

It shouldn't have surprised me. Caelum had regaled me for hours about this church's construction, trying in his way to ease the boredom of my house arrest.

Destroying this place must break his heart.

It donned on me his fondness for the structure might have softened his hand, causing the assault to take so long. Unlike with fire, mortal authorities had no options but wait out the freak tornado destroying the church.

I had to figure something out, some way to at least get him to stop long enough so we could speak. Unsure which direction Caelum faced inside the eye, I wasn't sure if transmogrifying into some form that glowed would catch his attention.

I could put glowing strips on a jogging suit, like phosphorescent neon.

No matter how bright I made myself, I had no guarantee he'd even be able to see that through the wall of wind and debris. If I could get above him, he'd have a clear line of sight, but I'd have to be in phoenix form—declaring myself to the world. There had to be another, better way to get Caelum's attention, but I was just too weary to find it.

No matter how much I'd wanted to stand on my own, there seemed no way for me to singly protect a city of millions from the Sidhe. I had to help him escape Dunham, which meant I had to talk to him.

Despite the thick humidity of the Georgia summer night, little in the way of cloud cover sailed over us.

But is it enough for a bad idea?

I took a deep breath and shouted with all I could manage. "Caelum!"

I hadn't expected it to work. I hadn't been able to hear Anima well, and she'd been in my pocket. Still, it was worth the attempt before I did something likely to make things much worse.

Nothing changed except the amount of church left standing.

I bolted the other way, searching for any building that could grant me height. Masking my head with my shirt, I cut through the lock and sprinted for the nearby stairwell. The alarm blared, but I wasn't planning to stay in the building any longer than necessary.

I hit the roof gasping, deafened by my pulse smashing against my ears like waves on the shore. Focused on compressing my essence into a tiny star, I leapt from the edge and let the mote go nova. I'd had some luck banking the illumination qualities of essence separated from my core, but had never managed to darken myself. My failure left me streaking through the night like a glowing, gravity-defying comet.

I leaned up, arching what speed I'd gotten in those few diving moments upward and beat my exhausted wings like my life depended on it. The Isaac would inform Anima if any witnesses caught my slow rise into the heavens—not that there was much I could do about collateral damage at that point.

I rose and flapped and rose and flapped until the air thinned enough to make my laboring lungs work twice as hard. A flick of pinion feathers let me slip sideways into a cloud. Plunging into an icy mist after the hot summer night was almost pleasant—almost.

Partially obscured, I reached out my senses and gathered the water vapor around me. By will and just plain stubbornness, I moved the cloud with me against the wind. I pushed essence into my tail feathers, elongating them into giant whips that I flicked around to create a lightning-like effect to observers despite the havoc it played with my flying.

I steered my cloud into another. One cloud after another I grew my cloud bank, focusing on thickening it beneath me to dampen my light as much as possible. Despite my incredible height, the winds of Caelum's tornado made herding clouds more difficult until I feared for my ability to maintain flight.

If I lost against his wind, if one of my wings broke, I had no safety net. I'd face either True Death or life as Dunham's prisoner.

Winds calmed when I found myself above the eye, allowing me my first relaxed breath. I had to get Caelum's attention, but I also had to make him understand who I was. I've always been more interested in music than sculpting, but I did my best with the cloud. Keeping aloft over top of his funnel, I put on a light show he couldn't miss.

Caelum

Caelum forced the tornado against the last and largest structure remaining of the Catholic Shrine of the Immaculate Conception. His eyes burned. He wasn't crying over destroying a building.

It's just grit, or maybe a surplus of hormones in this new body.

Caelum realized almost too late that his tail feathers were in jeopardy of pulling him down into the tornado. He flapped twice, maintaining his position in the eye. Most of his attention focused on moving enough air to erode away a church he'd watched rise brick by brick, stone by stone.

And now I'm doing the opposite. If I get my hands around Dunham's throat, I'll cut off his air or maybe fill his lungs until they burst.

A blast of light high above drew his attention away from impotent plans of revenge. As long as Dunham had their eggs ensorcelled, Ignis, Terrance, and he remained prisoners.

The lightning played about in the odd-shaped cloud in even odder ways. For a moment, one stroke near the cloud's edge flashed blue.

Caelum checked his position, flapped once more and narrowed his eyes at the almost stationary cloud. The angle of what he could see out the top of the funnel didn't allow a perfect line of sight, but for a moment he could've sworn the cloud almost looked like Aladdin reaching down from his carpet.

Quayla?

She'd been the only shield present when he'd jokingly mimicked the movie in the Goblin Market. She had no ability to manipulate wind, which meant if it was her, she'd have to be working almost as hard as he was to control the water forming the cloud while flying against the wind to keep the cloud stationary.

A mote of hope swelled in his chest, clogging his throat. Quayla had been through a lot and escaping Dunham's cage had to have been excruciating. He couldn't have pulled it off unless the passages and cracks had room for his essence to flow. Quayla's escape had required eroding her way along a crack to freedom.

And she's up there exhausted but trying to offer me help.

The ill-formed shape could've been a Sidhe trick, but Caelum didn't think so. Even if it turned out to be just a faerie plot, he'd take any help he could get at pretty much any cost to get his brothers and himself free.

There seemed no doubt Dunham had eyes on him, but he still needed to respond to the offer of help.

Chapter Seven

On the Run

Vitae

I folded *Wuthering Heights* closed and laid it in my lap. A melancholy pierced my heart. The knife always sank into my heart and twisted when I finished Mare's favorite book. Unlike her replacement, Mare had always been well read. Some of her tastes were more pedestrian than my own, focusing on epic romances she claimed gave her better insights into our charges. We'd spent many hours in my study, reading in companionable silence with only the antique side table between us.

Gentle, intelligent Mare. If only the changing wafer world hadn't seduced her away. We lost so much time...for reading, of course.

Before the seduction, our Shield had stood for something better, a higher purpose, a duty. It would again if I had anything to say about it.

Scurith stepped away from the room's shadows. "Forgive me, Master. I'd never bother you, save you seem finished with your reading."

"What is it?"

"The dwarves have finished the new fountain."

I turned more fully toward him. The diminutive, brown and grey canid retreated two steps, ears pressed against his head. "That was faster than I expected."

"Making slower and seditious dwarf workman subjects of your experiments left quite an impression, Master."

A chuckle escaped me.

Many of my prisoners had volunteered themselves to help build my sanctum just to escape my cages. A few had tried rebellion or escape. None had succeeded.

Fear, subjugation and brutality were the only things the Sidhe understood. Subjugation became easier as my experiments exhausted greater amounts of Sidhe blood in my rebirths, but I'd been all too happy to take out Mare's True Death on the creatures that had taken her from me.

I set Mare's copy of *Wuthering Heights* on my side table and followed Scurith out onto the balcony overlooking the hotel's foyer. My faerie servants had procured enough marble to replace the aged flooring. The construction team had inlaid an unblemished ring of white granite fourteen feet across in the center between the curves of twin stairs bracketing the foyer.

The oracle pool we'd had in the Shield had only stretched seven feet, but there'd been no way to view it from above—short of flight. From my perch, the larger pool would enhance viewing the condition of my domain.

While I had authored a guide to nests, I'd never studied the oracle pools. There'd been no need to know more about them until I'd found ours replaced in a single night with the technological abomination thrust on us.

I'd never participated in creating an oracle. Vilicangelus and his predecessor had seen to the carvings and once carved, an oracle inhabited the pool. The only thing I knew was that I needed at least some essence from an Aqua.

A pure Aqua who knows her duty, not Aquaylae, though I'm unsure where I will come by such a thing.

Still, there were books boxed in my library upstairs yet to catalog. The tomes saved from my library before the Sidhe ravaged it might contain the information I needed to create the artifact. If not, I would have to reach out to other Shieldhearts.

"Scurith, what are the chances Aqua essence is available in the Goblin Market?"

"None at all, Master. None would dare trade with any shield after you murdered Dolumii and Gherrian in the Sidhe council grounds."

I kept the anger from reaching my features. "Has my thrall returned?"

"Not yet, Master."

A perfunctory nod dismissed Scurith. I spun on my heel and headed toward my library. I needed to finish the oracle, and I needed to figure out a way to seed Atlanta so that I could track faerie movements enough to take the fight to them.

Quayla

To say the lack of response for all my efforts was disheartening was to compare a planter box to a farm. I fought the wind, keeping the cloud and its shape as best I could. I kept up the light show too, just in case Caelum hadn't noticed me yet.

Much as I hated to think about it, I had to face the very real possibility that Caelum had no way to respond without triggering whatever leverage Dunham held against him.

I was about to surrender to the inevitable when the tornado funnel jogged forward and back several times. From above, it looked like he was backing up to ram the church, but that made no sense. Caelum was tearing down the church with the sheering force of hundred-plus-mile-an-hour wind. Ramming the church that way wouldn't add any more damage.

A flicker of lightning illuminated the back side of the storm. Just beyond, bricks started to collect in a haphazard pile.

After several moments, the pile took on an upside-down T shape. My heart skipped a beat. Caelum was trying to spell out a message only I could see. I couldn't even imagine the amount of control it took for him to seize debris as he tore it away from the church and assemble it into a message without it looking intentional.

They're all so much better at their skills, even Caelum.

The arms of the T shifted. I stopped everything but keeping the cloud around me for cover and waited with bated breath for the next letter. When the bricks stopped moving, I just stared, not understanding what letter Caelum was trying to form.

It hit me like a brick in the forehead. He wasn't trying to make a T or other letters, but a much simpler message. An arrow of brick pointed up Central Avenue.

Caelum needs to meet me en route somewhere.

I lashed what remained of my cloud with a burst of energy and then let the wind sweep us away. I hated leaving him, but I needed to be in position whenever he escaped the scene of his assault.

Maybe it was Caelum's display of control. Maybe it was being unable to help Caelum save the Catholic Shrine of the Immaculate Conception. Or maybe it was the death of the homeless man who'd needed an angel instead of a murderer. Whatever it was, I wanted to be better. I'd spent the last couple of years trying to prove myself good enough. Instead I should have just been trying to improve me for my Creator. Terrance had called my thinking lazy. He'd been right at the fire and maybe he'd been right about the rest of the time too.

The others always seemed to manage without drawing attention to themselves. Sure, some of them had ten times the experience, but I didn't think of myself as stupid. Maybe it was time to prove it.

I didn't want any attention on my return to the ground, but I really wasn't interested in chancing a long, wingless drop and a last-minute attempt to transmogrify. There was no one else but me to protect Atlanta, and I needed to perform the job without the crutch of a divine rewriting reality when I screwed up.

It's time I step up my effort level and stop screwing up.

When we transmogrified, we invariable transformed our clothes and belongings. When we changed back, we brought back those belongings. I couldn't create something as complex as a cell phone whole cloth, but there was no reason I couldn't alter the clothes I'd been wearing—even if it took a little more essence.

Figuring out and focusing on my desire took more time than I normally invested into the process, but reality had been hammering steel toes into my butt for some time. I never believed myself lazy, but whatever I was, it wasn't enough to do the job.

'Lazy' Quayla needed to go.

I transmogrified, trading wings glowing in the thousand shades of water for a base-jumping wingsuit. I'd never used one before, but I doubted they worked so different that my flight experience couldn't compensate.

Inexperience compensating for the suit's lack of precision tail and wing left me juking and jerking like a new fledgling. Let's just say I made it to the ground without breaking any bones, but with ample evidence that I needed more practice. I found an out-of-the-way corner and transmogrified into street clothes.

"Anima?"

"Yes, Quayla."

"What's the damage? How many people saw my ascent or the spectacle I made in the clouds?"

"The impact is quite minimal. I was able to blur photographic records, and the Isaac assures me I did a good enough job that you've been relegated as an alien space ship."

I scowled. "How is that good news?"

"The people that generally believe in such things have questionable credibility," Anima said. "I would like to compliment you on your solution for returning to the ground though. If you'd come down in your phoenix form, it would have been far harder to minimize the impact of your ascent."

A warmth hit me with her words until my mind flashed back to the broken man on the highway.

Caelum jogged by at a casual lope, his neck on a swivel. His appearance distracted me from my guilt, at least for as long as it took me to catch up.

Caelum smiled when I came up abreast of him. "I can't stop. I'm ordered to come directly back to Circlestone."

"You can't even stop on the way? What does he have over you?"

"You don't understand...of course you don't, you escaped before Dunham returned. Viviane is some kind of faerie."

"She's one of the Dark Trinity."

"No shit?"

I drew an X across my heart.

"We're in some deep shit then. He's used a spell I think she provided. Wherever he came up with it, it enables him to control us through our eggs."

My mind flashed back to the Lady telling me she'd broken my egg to protect me. Caelum's revelation cemented Dunham as a threat to me personally, though I still hadn't figured out why.

"Any idea why Dunham wants me?"

Caelum frowned at me. "I think this is a lot bigger than you, little sister."

I punched his shoulder. "What did I tell you about calling me that?"

Caelum smirked.

Despite everything that had happened, that smirk gave me hope. "Don't you remember what I told everyone about meeting...no, you wouldn't. You were missing at the time. Then everything happened so fast. Summus had to go recuperate, the kudzu elemental attacked, Vitae tried to kill me, then—"

"Wait, Vitae tried to *kill* you?"

"Yeah. He gave me no choice but to kill him, then Dunham's shill stabbed me in the heart and I ended up in that cage."

Caelum shook his head, eyes fixed on the pavement. "You killed Vitae. Wow."

"But he didn't show up in Dunham's cage, so he's got another nest somewhere. That got me thinking, if I could build you a nest and you provided enough essence, we could get you free."

"I don't think it'll work like that. I've always been drawn to my egg, but now I can feel it reeling me in like I'm a fish on a line."

Fear caught in my throat. "We have to try. I can't protect Atlanta all by myself."

"You need to team up with Vitae," Caelum said.

"He tried to kill me."

"He's still a shield."

I shook my head. "I'll just wait for Summus to return, and—"

"Dunham caged Summus in that center section you used to escape. I don't think he can escape so long as Dunham has essence from all five of us."

"He doesn't have me or Vitae."

"My nest was full with spare essence on hand, but the amount remaining beneath the basin contains enough for one rebirth at best. I don't know how much he's used, but Dunham is using our essence himself."

"For what?"

"More power most likely."

I cursed.

"Ani, can you think of anything to help us?"

Caelum brightened. "Ani?"

"Hello Shield Caelum. I am relieved you remain living."

"You and me both," Caelum said. "How're we communicating with our automata while we run?"

I pulled the bronze statue from behind my belt. The little angel's face was screwed up and one hand pinched its nose shut. "I took it off your motorcycle."

"Genius. Ani, you have to get ahold of Vilicangelus."

"I am trying," Anima said. "He suffered a grievous injury before all this happened and hasn't been in touch."

Caelum cursed. "That's blighted inconvenient...or maybe too convenient. Could Dunham be coordinating all of this?"

"Or the Lady has," I said.

"I have reached out to the Isaac. We are trying to get some divine help, but with the two Courts fighting all over the world, resources are spread thin."

"We'll just have to make due," I said. "That's why I need you, Ignis and Terrance back."

Caelum's fine features bent in concentration. I grabbed his arm, jerking him to one side to avoid running into a parked car. He beamed, batted his lashes and raised his voice to a girlish tone. "Oh, my strong hero!"

"Knock it off. What were you thinking?"

"Ani, what about the first host? Surely some original angelic powers remain."

Hope swelled. "Caelum, you're a genius!"

The hesitation in Anima's voice filled me with dread. "Yes, technically, but I doubt He'd dispatch any to help."

"And why not?" I demanded.

"They're no longer trusted to visit Creation," Anima said.

I considered what I knew about the previous order charged with the defense of Creation. My initial training suggested many had served with flawless dedication—paragons of loyalty in service to the Creator. Others harbored jealousy toward the Creator, Creation or both.

They'd been cast out of Creation into a void, but over millennia they'd changed that void to suit themselves and made inroads back into Creation. They'd continued to manipulate mortal lives, but with a fresh eye to mischief and their own plea-sure. Many prominent figures in mortal history had risen on the wings of the Fallen, their souls or service traded to one Court or another for power.

"Things look pretty bleak, Ani doll. Might be worth the risk."

"No!" I hadn't meant to snap, but a sudden gut-wrenching foreboding pushed the word out sharper than I intended. "No, Caelum. How many millennia have they been under house arrest, untrusted to do what they were created to do? How many long years were they forced to watch others fill the roles they were meant to serve?"

Caelum actually stopped running, searching my expression with genuine concern. He doubled over a moment later, screaming in pain.

Panic shot through me. I grabbed Caelum's arm and hustled him back into motion. The pain seemed to recede enough for him to take over his forward motion.

"Thank you," he gasped. Tears leaked down his cheeks. "I'm so sorry we let Vitae treat you like that."

I refused to look at him. "It's not your fault."

"Quayla?" Concern dominated Anima's question, but something of steel undercut it too. "I will speak to the Isaac about Caelum's suggestion."

"That's not a good idea, Ani."

"Perhaps not, but you cannot defend so many millions alone."

The certainty in her conviction was hard to argue. I'd already recognized that I wasn't enough, but I wasn't about to stop doing my duty just because I wasn't. Every mortal protected was a victory against the Sidhe.

"We'll try it," Caelum said.

I blinked at him, not at all trying to clear away tears of futility.

"Get some balloons." Caelum said. "I'll give you what essence I can. Maybe Ani can come up with a way to cut me off from my egg."

"I'll be right back," I bore down on my exhausted body and demanded more speed. I had to get to a store, buy some balloons and get back before he reached Circlestone.

"Wait, Quayla. I don't have any spare tonight, but there will be other opportunities. How are you set for equipment?"

"I fought my way into your headquarters stash, so I have hilts and a small amount of money."

"I can't help you with money, but let me list my other stashes, just in case." Caelum listed the locations of his hidden caches throughout the city. "I've depleted many of them, but maybe what's left will help."

All too soon we were too close to Circlestone for me to continue running alongside him. Splitting off onto a side street felt like tearing away some of my essence. The ache of his absence, even only moments away, felt like a mortal wound. I was back on my own, but worse I was letting Caelum return to captivity without any idea what Dunham would do if he learned of our joint run.

"Run three more blocks then turn north," Anima said.

I nodded, not questioning her directions. We'd started the evening tracking my Johammer. If she was taking me anywhere else, she'd have her reasons. It didn't matter, nothing mattered. I was just too numb to care. One foot after the other, I jogged through Atlanta's night.

I'd been running a long time when a QuikTrip came into view a little off of my path. Turning aside toward the convenience store, I came to a slow stop on the lit sidewalk. I'd been running so long that both my legs and brain felt like the world was moving past me far faster than they were.

I had to step around three guys shooting the bull on their car hoods. They seemed engrossed in their conversation and since I wasn't female, I had less to worry about than normal—not that I couldn't hand three mortals their literal asses even as tired as I was. Still, I loathed to relive killing the nameless homeless man.

Once inside I bought two of their largest coffee cups and filled them with a mix of hot chocolate and espresso. I bought two boxes of Little Debbie Cosmic Brownies, three Hershey bars, a cranberry orange muffin and a bag of ranch flavored sunflower seeds.

The cashier didn't give me so much as a sideways look. It

wasn't like midnight convenience store runners prized healthy fare, but I still felt conspicuous on the verge of a stress binge.

I downed half of the too hot chocolate the moment I exited. Caffeine, warmth and chocolate reduced the ghosts haunting me. A silver cab pulled in to refuel. I couldn't get an Uber to our destination without a phone and an online bank, but I could hire a regular taxi with cash. One of Caelum's caches held several phone replacements, but once I had my Johammer, I could go anywhere I needed.

"Ani? I should have thought to ask you this earlier, but can you get the Isaac to move all my money onto a new set of IDs?"

Anima had the sense to keep her voice down, even so the three guys were eyeing me.

I am loaded down with junk and talking to myself.

"I am so sorry, Shield Quayla. I never even considered how much easier having replacements would make navigating Creation. I will contact him at once."

"Great, can you give me an address for where we're going?"

Anima provided an address on Lindbergh Drive. While she contacted the Isaac, I approached the cab driver. He was an older, black gentleman in a dress shirt and tie. "Pardon me, is there any chance I can persuade you to take me the rest of my way to a friend's?"

He eyed me. "I'm off duty."

"Could you call another taxi to take me?" I lowered my voice. "I have cash."

"Why don't you call one yourself?"

"Broke my phone." I shrugged.

He sighed, shaking his head. "What's the address?"

I gave it to him.

"Get in. I'll take you, but I want to see the cash first."

I got into the back of the cab and drew out the money. I offered him two twenties in advanced, but he told me to hold on to my money until we got there.

I fell back into the luxuriousness of his back seat, my chocolate and expresso binge holding off invading sleep.

He eyed me in the rear-view mirror several times, apparently too tired to be chatty. His scrutiny hardened when he pulled up in front of an old, condemned hotel. "Your friend's?"

"Uh," I scanned the ruin-dominated block. A few yellowed street lights half-heartedly illuminated the parking lot, but there were no lights on anywhere in the hotel itself. Toward the back, the glow of my pearl white jelly bean on wheels called to me. "Yeah, he's putting on a haunt. I'm helping set up."

"Twenty, be careful."

I gave him forty anyway and flashed a smile less effective in a male body. None of the shields I'd met acted gender-fixed, but my default self-image remained female despite my body because that was how I'd been born first. I hadn't had a male body in some time, and I hadn't taken the time to adjust my paradigm.

I double-checked that I'd picked up all my trash and got out of his cab. "Thanks again."

Once he departed, I turned back to the hotel. Behind my Johammer I saw Caelum's bike, Ignis's Camaro, and Terrance's truck all parked in a row. A Mercedes, several SUVs and a limousine parked across from them under temporary carports.

"Ani? This isn't an impound yard. What am I looking at?"

"This appears to be some kind of Sidhe nest based on the sentries, but I cannot penetrate the interior."

"That's Vitae's Mercedes, isn't it?"

"I believe so."

"Why would Vitae be living inside a Sidhe nest?"

"Perhaps he is a prisoner," Anima said.

A dreadful certainty grew into my consciousness like a mold. "What if Vitae lied when he said he got Sidhe blood on his robes? What if he's...I don't know, experimenting with Sidhe blood?"

"Why would a Shieldheart do such a thing?"

"I'm not sure, but Dylan acted bizarre around Vitae, and he admitted to being tainted during the fight in Shield Sanctum."

"He admitted to the taint, Shield Quayla, even apologized—something I've grown to understand is difficult for him. I know he has treated neither of us well, but that is no reason to distrust him."

"His attempt to stab me comes to mind. Plus, he wasn't that upset about his nest being stolen from headquarters. When I killed him, he wasn't reborn in Dunham's trap. Both things suggest that he has another nest."

"That seems a reasonable conjecture."

"More, when I asked to use his book on nests, he put me off."

"What should we do?" Anima asked.

I tucked my remaining feast in my duffel, stuffing trash into the empty coffee cup. "I'm too tired to fight him tonight. I'm going in there, wheeling my baby out and getting as far from this place as I can."

"The sentries may be a problem."

I nodded. "They're Sidhe?"

"I'm unfamiliar with this species and unsure how to classify them."

My brow furrowed. Anima knew everything there was to know about the faeries, or at least she always had up until that point.

How can she not know what these things are?

Chapter Eight

The Fix is On

Caelum

Watching Quayla leave wasn't easy, but Caelum didn't want her coming close enough to Dunham to get captured again. He doubted building a second nest would win them much, but he'd never seen her so fragile.

Whatever had happened to her in the short time since her escape, Quayla was questioning herself. Whatever it cost him, he had to keep her encouraged until they could come up with something. The obvious solution would be to break his own egg. He could only imagine the agony involved with Dunham's spell on the jeweled ovum, but if Quayla had a nest ready to go, it might be worth it. Once all of them were free, they could rebuild their eggs and see to the Fae Kissed CEO.

I want him to myself, but I'm probably going to have to share with the others.

He transmogrified into his phoenix and winged his way to the top of Circlestone tower. Dunham was waiting. The moment Caelum set talon on the roof, the torture started. Dunham squeezed the symbolic egg until Caelum's wing bones snapped. His ribs pushed in, breaking and piercing his lungs.

Unable to ask why in his phoenix form, Caelum screeched fury, torment and questions.

The pressure lightened. "Transmog. Now."

Caelum fought to gain control over his whole essence through the pain. Every cell, every feather burned with purest agony. He forced the change, the sudden absence of pain becoming almost pleasure. He lay on the roof gasping. "Why?"

Dunham's rage seethed just under his calm surface. "You've displeased me."

"I followed your orders. I destroyed the church. I came directly back here."

"You let Quayla go."

Caelum opened his mouth to point out that Dunham hadn't given him any order to capture the water shield. He closed his mouth, hoping Dunham didn't remember things the same way.

"Into your cage, now."

Dunham marched Caelum down into his private quarters. Caelum's former CEO broke off to activate the arm that raised Caelum's cage once more. Caelum had little choice but to obey, so he marched back to the five grouped standing stones. He hesitated at the basin stone in reach of the stone boot and the toe swallowing his egg.

If I smash it now, there's nothing more he can do to me.

"In!"

Caelum glanced over his shoulder.

Dunham's calm facade was slipping.

Caelum wasn't certain what about letting Quayla go caused so much fury, but breaking his own egg might cause Dunham to kill him outright.

The air phoenix stepped onto the stone, conscious of the illuminated runes. He relaxed when he didn't collide with a magical barrier. A flash of inspiration hit Caelum as Dunham strode forward with a rare steak swinging in one fist.

He had completed the mission the moment he'd stepped onto the stone. The prescription against harming Dunham no longer applied. If he was fast enough, Caelum could tear out Dunham's throat.

Caelum tucked a hand behind his back and focused on his essence. Normally, his arms transmogrified into wings, but he knew the shape of his talons like the back of his foot.

Pain shot through Caelum, dropping him to his knees. A great fist crushed his chest once more, squeezing out all of his breath.

"Do you know that when you gather your essence to transmogrify your eyes glow?" Dunham asked conversationally. "I left that little loophole in your orders to see what you would do, and to be honest, you didn't disappoint me. You're as tricksie and legalistic as any Sidhe."

"If you were in my place, wouldn't you do anything in your power to escape?" Caelum asked.

"And take revenge," Dunham said. "Still, now I owe you double punishment."

Dunham tossed the meat between Caelum's feet and activated the runes that caged him. He returned to the control panel, adding the bell jar to Caelum's jail. Dunham's voice sounded tinnier over the intercom.

"You knew I wanted her. Delivering her might've been worth your freedom."

"You're a bad liar, boss."

Dunham shrugged and turned the pain up to eleven.

Summuseraphi

The gaps between the standing stones let Summus see both the mortal that had caged him and the cages around Atlanta's shields. At Summus's feet, a pentagram of phoenix essence kept him caged. All five shields were represented, but the essences of fire, earth and air throbbed with the nearness of their origin.

The flavor of Caelum's essence soured in response to the torment the Fae Kissed mortal inflicted. Summus couldn't hear the screams of the crumpled shield, but he felt the echoes in his essence.

I have to do something. I can't just sit here. I'm a divine phoenix, surely, I can thwart one Fae Kissed mortal.

Summus gathered his strength. His recovery hadn't reached the halfway point before all five of his shields call out from the same location. There'd been other calls, but none so insistent or so concentrated. He'd had to come to their call. It hadn't even been a conscious choice, though had he had that option, Summus would've come just the same.

Part of his ignorance could've been the rushed training after being elevated. He'd never heard of anything like the spells keeping him and the three shields bound. The mortal had possessed four of Atlanta's shields, but Aquaylae had escaped— no doubt utilizing the nature of water itself.

Good for her. Controlling myself as a shapeless liquid escaped me for years. Despite Vitae's claims, she would learn well from an excellent teacher.

Summus squared his shoulders. She'd escaped, and now it was his turn. He'd yet to master his new element, but there were principals he'd grasped. Divine light made up the body of a divine phoenix. As light, he could travel faster and penetrate places no other phoenix could access. He wasn't as fluid as he was in his former life, but light had advantages over water.

Dunham only has so much life and water essence.

Summus bowed his head, folding his wings around him like a cloak. He put Caelum's suffering not out of mind so much as within the caress of his wings, using it as fuel for his focus. Summus ignited his essence. Like a star, he unleashed waves of power and light against the magical barrier. Divine energy rebounded off the walls of his cage, each wave stronger than the last.

Lines forming the pentagram beneath Summus's feet intensified, throbbing in time with the waves of power. He invested more essence, slamming a battering ram of light against the walls of his prison. More and more energy rebounded off the walls, across Summus, into the opposite side of his cage and back again. The energy picked up speed and force. The power buffeted Summus more with each pass, growing in a crescendo of power.

"It's about time," Dunham said.

Summus looked up, barely able to see the mortal kneeling inside the other stone circle. An avaricious smile disappeared as Dunham lowered his head, pressing palms flat on the stone as if bracing himself

Blue-white fire flickered to life around Dunham—a growing aura of divine flame. Realization hit Summus a moment too late. The energy he'd employed against the cage drained away like the stone beneath him had gravity to restrain light itself. Summus's essence, connected to his assault dragging the divine phoenix to his knees.

Power tore itself away from Summus in an agony that seemed to claw his soul while stripping the flesh from his bones.

On the opposite stone, Dunham struggled to his feet wreathed in Summus's power. His face rose, eyes blazing with the same fire that shrouded him. "Now that you've volunteered your essence, I'll take it all if you please."

The gravity beneath Summus grew claws and fangs, ripping more and more essence from him. An eternity or an instant later, the draw vanished. Darkness hedged Summus's blurry vision. His hands had shriveled to skeletal fingers in pallid skin gloves. The world he'd crumpled against swam violent teeters and totters.

Raising his head took all of Summus's strength.

Dunham stood mere feet away on the other side of the barrier, somehow more than real. He wore an angelic mantle that seemed to cast shadows along his body, creating an undulating halo of writhing dark and light plasma.

"You should rest while you can, Summuseraphi. I'll require more from you in due time." Dunham turned his back on

Summus, his aura settling around the mortal like a fitted suit without robbing Dunham of the clinging sense of power.

What have I done?

Quayla

I backed off a short distance and pulled out the two tactical headsets. With Anima providing oversight through one of them, we'd be able to infiltrate the hotel. As long as I got the jump on one or two of their sentries without sounding the alarm, I'd been able to roll my Johammer away with no one the wiser.

I hung the spare headset from my belt. "Tie in through this and walk me through what I'm facing."

"There are two, well, let's call them sentries on third-floor balconies overlooking each side of the hotel. There are two more at ground level, lurking in shadow and a pair patrolling a slow circle through the parking lot."

I had to assume the sentries could see as well or better than I could in the low light, giving them an advantage. I waited for the sentries patrolling to come into view, intent to get a feeling for how much time I'd have between circuits.

First glance suggested the sentries dressed in a hybrid of modern battle armor and a heavily-spiked medieval-style field plate mail. They edged into the radius of a street lamp.

I gasped.

The spikes, the armored plates, they were part of the creatures themselves. I'd never seen or seen reference to anything like the things guarding the hotel. The miasma of their taint reached to me from across the street.

My gaze shifted to my baby, a forlorn white jellybean in the darkness. Tactically arranged sentries allowed for multiple overlaps. To clear the side which held my baby, I'd have to descend from above and take out a third-floor sentry without alerting his partner. If I managed to subdue both, I'd have to eliminate the ground sentries the same way, hoping the rovers didn't notice until I took them down too. All of that work went to hell if I made even one mistake, and it seemed likely guard placement on adjacent sides offered those sentries the ability to catch me in the act.

I turned off the headsets and strode down the block, tucking the equipment back into my bag and taking a bite out of a Hershey bar.

Anima's whisper emerged from the statue. "Shield Quayla?"

"I love my bike, Ani, but it's just a motorcycle no matter how many changes Caelum made to it." I sighed and bit into more chocolate. "I already have one statue for communicating with you. A backup is nice but not worth risking my freedom."

She didn't answer right away, making me wonder how cowardly my explanation must have seemed. I still needed to investigate the hotel more, but not until I was ready.

"I don't know how to say this without sounding con-descending, but you made a mature choice," Anima said.

"Yeah." My feet felt heavier than they should, and the chocolate lost its flavor—not that I stopped chewing my way through the goodies I'd bought. "How much further to the cache with the phones in it?"

"Four miles as the phoenix flies."

Four miles?

Physically, I could manage the distance, but emotionally I didn't have four more miles in me. "What about a Walmart?"

"The nearest open Walmart is about a mile and a half."

"Fine."

Forty minutes of slow trudging brought me to an oasis of nocturnal capitalism. I sidelined through the grocery section to restock my binge supplies before heading to electronics. Caelum's cache held free phones, but I just couldn't face the extra distance. I wanted to go home. I wanted to curl up on my couch with Dylan and watch some geeky movie that would make him happy. I wanted my life to go back to some semblance of normal.

It took an eternity to get someone to sell me a prepaid smart phone and activate it, but in the end and in no small thanks to Anima, I walked out of Walmart to meet an Uber that for once wasn't a gas guzzling behemoth.

The closer my ride brought me to my apartment, the more the ache in my chest dug into my heart. My driver stopped. I didn't look up, focusing instead on rating and tipping him as a last-ditch stall tactic to procrastinate. When there was nothing else holding me in the car, I shoved the rest of the dense Cosmic Brownie in my mouth and got out.

My parking space gaped empty without Dylan's car or my baby parked between the stone bumper and the curb. The three-story walk-up loomed above me in the predawn. A large glass oval glowed, back lit by the low-watt bulb hung in the landing. Just left of the front door, my landlady's windows remained unlit—a good thing all in all.

The old lady had joined forces with my beloved Dylan and Detective Sabrina Foxner to invade Faery and rescue me from the Lady. Mrs. Cox and her humongous old tome had proven a veritable wiki of all things faerie. While the canny old grandma's knowledge had been shocking, Dylan had surprised me the most. He had none of the knowledge of Mrs. Cox and none of the training the police detective gained over a decade or more time on hard streets. All Dylan had had was love and a new gun when he charged into a strange, foreign world to help me.

And I thanked them all by ignoring their objections and having Summus rewrite their existence so all but Mrs. Cox had never heard of me.

Standing in the street staring down my mistakes wasn't getting me anywhere. I marched up the stairs, taking the extra time to ease the old door open before tiptoeing up to my old apartment. I winced with every creaky stair, but I made it to my door.

A prickle of taint pushed against my skin. Until I'd reached my door, I'd pushed the state of my apartment from my thoughts.

Not like I haven't been somewhat distracted.

Goblins invaded my apartment while I was recovering in the sanctum. They'd broken my furniture to build an inverted crucifix which they'd used to torture Judith when the flower shop worker showed up worried about me.

"Something I can do for you, son?"

I turned to find Mrs. Cox leaning on a cane she didn't need. An unobtrusive button on the cane told me the walking aid contained something sharp.

"You must be Mrs. Cox."

Her sharp eyes nailed me to the wall. "And you are?"

"Quayl, Quayla's brother."

"Were you twins? Where is Quayla? I haven't seen her."

"Yes. She had to go out of town. Since I was visiting Atlanta, she asked me to come by her apartment and pay her rent."

"I don't take checks."

I smiled. "She has cash in her bedroom, but I don't have a key."

"So, you were planning on staring at her door until it magically opened up?" Her scrutiny shifted up and down.

I was planning on breaking in, but you've probably figured that out by now.

"You stand like Quayla, and your eyes are very similar. Do you have any identification?"

"Airline lost my luggage. I'm waiting on a text to tell me it's caught up." I looked down at my duffel. "My other bag, this one's junk food and electronics."

"No," Mrs. Cox's word had bite. "You need an ID to get onto an airplane."

"Actually, I only need it to get past security. I tucked my wallet into my carry on, but the plane didn't have enough overhead space so they forced me to check the bag at the gate."

"Which means it was on the plane with you."

"I know, right? How they lost the bag between the departure and arrival gates is beyond me."

Mrs. Cox didn't seem convinced.

"Look, I don't want any trouble, Mrs. Cox. Quayla said you might have a spare apartment after I got her rent settled, but I can go anywhere. She told me one of the headboard knobs hides a cubby with her rent." I stepped around her to the stairs. "She's hoping to return before her rent's due again."

The lock to my apartment door clicked open. "Stay here, young man. Let me check out your story."

Taint and burned white sage hit me like a battering ram. The world spun. I sat, dropping onto the stairs harder than intended. When the world steadied a bit, I twisted just enough to see my door and watch for trouble coming up the stairs.

Mrs. Cox emerged a few minutes later. She shuffled to the next apartment over, paying minimal attention to how she moved the cane. She unlocked the door. "This tenant moved out a few days ago complaining about the white sage I burned up here. They left the place a wreck. If you help clean up the place, you can camp out until the job's done."

I rose. "I'd be happy to help."

"Come along. I have an old cot in the basement. Not as nice as a real bed, but it'll do in a pinch. When the apartment's clean we'll talk about the vacancy—once you have ID."

"That sounds fair."

Mrs. Cox eyed me sideways when I led the way to her cot storage. By the time I got it back upstairs I was ready to fall over. Mrs. Cox hadn't been kidding. I hadn't talked to the young dental technician very many times, but I'd been unaware Elijah was such a slob.

Isn't much of a shock Mrs. Cox got the better end of this deal.

I passed out on the cot.

Chapter Nine

Seeing Beyond

Terrance

Dunham's voice interrupted Terrance's meditation. "Good morning, Terra."

The meditation served two purposes. The practice kept him calm in a cage no bird was meant to endure, and it shifted the focus away from lingering pain from separating essence.

"I am forced to take your word on this," Terrance said.

"Don't you have an innate sense of day and night?"

"Trusting such a sense seems a foolish choice while penned and idle without cues for light or dark."

A shadow of overlarge finger and thumb braced Terrance's chest. The sensation spread as his jailor wrapped Terrance's egg or its simulacrum within his palm. Terrance braced himself for a tyrant's lesson, but the pain didn't arise.

"Today you will see daylight. I have a task for you."

Terrance let silence seed and grow. After a few moments he felt the grip on his egg tightened. "You will answer, Terra."

"You didn't ask a question."

"I expected curiosity from you."

"Curiosity is a waste of energy for a slave," Terrance said.

"I have intelligence of a skirmish between Seelie and Unseelie forces. I wish you to crush both sides. No one save yourself may walk away."

"That would violate the Articles of Ararat."

"Those articles don't apply to me," Dunham said. "Besides, dead faeries don't complain."

"I am bound to adhere to the Articles."

"If you consider yourself a slave, then you recognize you don't have a choice in this matter."

Terrance inclined his head.

"Do you require a weapon to accomplish this task?"

Terrance considered for a moment. He didn't doubt Dunham would forbid Terrance the latitude to use such weapons against his captor before their conversation concluded. Still, prudence required he skew his warden's information.

"A cudgel."

"I'll have one readied while you shower."

"How civilized of you."

The ghostly grip tightened until Terrance's ribs threatened to crack. "I don't appreciate your tone."

"I do not appreciate being caged. If you truly have the means to control us, why would you require these cages?"

"I imagine you will answer that question on your own after I release you." Dunham's tone became more practiced, as if the words that followed were a well-traveled path. "You will obey me, Terra. You will fulfill the mission I assign without deviation and return directly here for insertion back into your cage. Acknowledge command and your compliance."

"I acknowledge these commands and will comply."

"Good. You will act civilized on these premises. You will make no attempt to disrupt operations or call attention to yourself. You will ensure all of the Seelie and Unseelie at the location where I send you are slain. Acknowledge command and your compliance."

"I have already done so."

"Then do so again."

"I have received and will comply with your commands."

"If you encounter one of your other shields, you will subdue, capture and return them here to me. Acknowledge command and your compliance."

Shields plural.

The repetition was tedious, but the command itself wasn't. This latest command also didn't have the practiced feel, as if Dunham had added it in response to a recent development.

So, one of us saw Aquaylae or Vitae and didn't apprehend them. Interesting.

"I will comply."

The dark, sludge-filled walls tilted before something raised the swirling darkness. Terrance waited, blinking away the dazzling but dim lighting. He absorbed what he could of his first look at their greater jail. A dark cell to Terrance's left contained what had to be Ignis. An empty bell jar stood to Terrance's right.

He turned inside a perimeter made of glowing runes expecting to glimpse the other two cages. Summus slumped in the center of a much larger stone. Stringy, sweat-soaked hair draped his face. The limbs Terrance could see lacked the healthy color and soft lines of a well-nourished phoenix.

"Summus?"

Summus's head rose at the sound of his voice. A drawn, exhausted face looked up from beneath divine phoenix's locks. His head fell back down without a word.

What have they done to you, little brother?

Terrance's eyes shifted over Summus's head to the other two cells. A blond girl crumpled inside another bell jar much like the empty one. There wasn't any real way to tell, but something about the frame of her face suggested Caelum. Between the two transparent cages, a cage composed of a strange beaded curtain reeked of poison.

Dunham cleared his throat.

Terrance turned around, getting his first close look at the large powerful man. Terrance's last several forms would've been a match for this man physically, but a super-real presence cloaked him like a second skin. A fine, fitted suit covered most of Dunham's skin, but woad tattoos peaked out of the gaps, suggesting their captor had Celtic ancestry.

"You summoned the kudzu elemental?" Terrance asked.

"What happened to curiosity being a waste of energy?"

"This isn't curiosity."

Dunham's brow rose. "Something more akin to 'know thy enemy?'"

Terrance smiled.

Dunham offered a set of sweats and a security badge. "You will find a labeled locker in the thirteenth-floor gym. You'll find street clothes that fit you once you're showered. The security desk downstairs will have your weapon and an address."

"What happens if the forces exceed my capabilities?"

"If you honestly feel you're that out-classed, let them fight first and pick off the remains."

"Very well." Terrance took what he was offered. "Thank you for your consideration."

"Traipsing through my business naked, while pleasant for some, would interrupt business and clog up HR."

"Eminently practical." Terrance slipped into the sweats. "May I begin the mission you have assigned?"

Dunham inclined his head.

Quayla

Something heavy settled onto my sternum, causing a small throbbing. I opened my eyes to find Grynnberry smirking down at me in my temporary lodgings. The little nymph wore a dapper suit probably just as much pure glamour as what he wore when human sized. Honey brown eyes just lighter than his hair danced beneath neat locks and twitching antennae.

"My, you are a sound sleeper," the little nymph said. "I could have done just about anything to you—less interesting in your current gender, but still so very tempting."

I blew into his face.

He managed to curse me before he crumpled to my chest.

A quick search turned up nothing useful to cage him, so I left him on the cot while I broke into my old apartment and fetched the large glass jar I'd prepared for him. The state of my kitchen made me want to cry. The goblins had ransacked it completely, including draining every microscopic bit of honey in the house.

I tried not to see the nests the goblins had made from the shredded pages of my books. Gratitude welled up that Mrs. Cox had spared me a trip into my bedroom to get her rent.

Grynnberry remained out when I got back into my temporary place. I slid him into the jar, being gentle not to harm his wings and put the lid on tight. I put the jar on my lap. I adjusted it a little. I gave up on the third try and went to the bathroom. When everything was relaxed, I propped him on my lap once more and waited.

"You filthy, bitch!"

After nightmares of cages and killing innocents, I had no patience for the little faerie. "Give me one reason not to kill you."

"Oh, I don't know, the rules?"

"All bets are off right now, Grynn, so you better start talking and I'd better enjoy the story. How'd you even know I was here?"

"You may have lost all your soft luscious bits, but you still smell like a spring rain, kiddo."

We used smell to identify faeries. That they had the ability to do the same shouldn't have been something just occurring to me.

"Answers, Grynn."

"Questions, Quayla."

My temper hit like a flash flood. I shook the bottle. "Dammit, faerie, I've had about all I can take of people playing games."

Grynnberry cried out, trying to find a midpoint to hover only to snap a wing against a side during one particularly violent shake.

"If that's the way you're going to treat someone exiled for helping you, then I'll just tell the Courts where you're hiding. Might buy me a pardon."

I shook the jar with each word. "What. Are. You. Talking about?"

"Stop! Stop! I know why they took the animals!"

Gravity reversed itself in my stomach. I dropped the jar. It bounced off my knee then onto the carpet. A litany of curses to turn British Marines into Catholic saints escaped the tiny Sidhe.

I lunged off the cot, catching the jar before it broke, adding to my already substantial list of problems.

Grynn glowered up at me. "You fucking, flaming, fart-licking, leaper whore!"

"I'm sorry, all right, that was an accident."

"You broke my wings! All of them."

"I'm sorry."

"You'll be sorry when the Courts know where to find you."

I left him on the floor threatening and cursing while I ransacked the kitchen. Through some small miracle I found an ancient jar of honey—the inside heavily crusted in crystals. I fished a spoon out of a sink full of moldy dishes, gave it a quick scrub and returned to the imprisoned faerie. I popped the top of both jars, scraped the spoon through the honey and dropped it in with Grynnberry.

He pounced on the spoon before it stopped clattering. Grynnberry crunched honey crystals and shot me the nastiest look he could manage while enraptured.

"I'm sorry, Grynn. Breaking your wings really was an accident."

He harrumphed and chewed honey.

Grynnberry was a Sidhe. He didn't belong in Creation and he sure as hell-blight wasn't innocent. Just the same, the condition of his wings—seeping blood and nymph dust—overloaded my already burdened soul. I turned my back on him, shoulders shaking as all the stress of the previous two days hit me full force.

"I'm out."

For a moment I thought he was bragging about escaping, but a glance showed him extending a clean spoon and tapping his foot. I tipped his prison over very slowly so he could crawl out. I set the honey in front of the opening and turned my back on him once more.

The home I'd made wasn't feet from where I sat and yet it was destroyed and desecrated. Everything that had been mine, my movies and books, my kitchen and bedroom were little better than junkyard fodder.

I need to get over all of this. I can't just sit around and cry.

That was what I chose to do until Grynnberry came around and patted my hand. "Jeez, Quayla, they will grow back."

A quick scan of my surroundings offered no tissues, so I stooped to wiping my nose on a forearm in typical male fashion.

"Look, stop crying, promise me another jar of honey and I'll tell you what I learned."

I nodded and sniffed.

"The Wyldfae took all those animals to sell, but not as food. Well, okay, they didn't sell the cats exactly. Ralein worked up some special collars for them."

"What do the collars do?"

"The dog collars nullify seeds in range."

"The cat collars?"

"Here's the genius. The cats are released back into Creation at a time chosen by warring Sidhe."

I frowned.

"Look, when some Seelie challenges his opposite, a Wyldfae sells him and his opponent a spell scroll that opens a temporary arch."

"How are the cat's involved?"

Grynn folded his arms. "After the release time, the scrolls splat their respective cat, using each animal's life to open up a temporary Arch. Then they release the dogs through the Arches to spread out, taking down the local seeds before someone follows through to brace up the Arch—instant war zone."

"That's awful."

"Be a man."

I shot him a glare.

"I don't know how the Wyldfae knew they'd need so many portable battle grounds, but they're making a killing in every Goblin Market around the globe," Grynnberry snort-giggled. "Pun totally intended."

I stared at the little Sidhe. The ramifications of what he'd told me raced around my mind like a puppy after its own tail. The Wyldfae had planned to supply a war they knew was coming because they'd been orchestrating it. The question was why.

What do they gain by helping the Courts fight on mortal ground?

My encounter in the crayon scribble flashed across the forefront of my thoughts.

The Exiled Lady—one of the Dark Trinity—one of three.

The Seelie and Unseelie Courts had queens. Sure, they had countless children from among their favorites, allowing them to seed Creation with little echoes of their royal Courts—whatever they called themselves. The Wyldfae had no rulers. As best I understood, they weren't allowed to be ruled—hence their designation as wild.

During my initial training, my old Shieldheart talked as if there were three Courts, but Vitae only ever talked about two. Could something have happened around the time I screwed up that cost the third Court its existence?

If the Exiled Lady was once queen of the fallen Anseelie, she could be engineering a war to weaken the other two Courts so she could return to power. That such a creature would rather risk Creation and bloody her rivals instead of working through whatever penance had been asked really was very Sidhe. Doing so while making her rivals pay for the privilege practically sang Faery's national anthem.

"I'll get you two bottles," I said at last. "Stay here and try to keep out of Mrs. Cox's sight."

"The blind old bag who owns this place?"

"I wouldn't count too heavily on that blind part."

I took a quick shower and changed into my single alternate outfit before rushing down the stairs to catch my Uber. The gator paint job returned, grinning his gap tooth grin and head banging to twangy country music along with his line of NASCAR bobbleheads.

I could've had him wait outside when I got to the bank, but the music and the driver were both giving me a headache. Rather than head straight in, I veered to one side and drew out the little bronze angel. It held both hands over its ears.

"Ani? Can you help me access my accounts at the ATM without a card?" I asked.

"A bicycle messenger is waiting at the front door for you, green speedo. He is carrying your IDs."

"Oh, Ani, I could kiss you."

"Handsome as your new body is, I'm afraid you aren't my type."

I laughed my way to the courier who really should have worn Bermuda shorts over the speedo in public spaces that might include children. Considering he barely looked away from his mirror to sign over the envelope, I had a feeling no one else existed in his world.

I'd used my drive over to run through Craigslist ads for vehicles. I'd found a used Vespa at a small enough asking price that I could afford it without emptying my bank account. The seller agreed to meet me ninety minutes later during his lunch hour. I only hoped the line in the bank wasn't too long.

I dug into my envelope, barking my knuckle on something sharp. A more careful probe provided a leather wallet with everything I needed and a scooter license plate.

I don't know who the Isaac is, but Light he's good at his job.

I pushed open the door and ran headlong into someone. Hot liquid exploded between us. We both hit our asses on the tile.

"Dammit!" Dylan cursed.

Shock stole my air. Before I'd thought anything through, I grabbed his soiled dress shirt and pulled him into an impassioned kiss. For a moment, the familiar caress of his lips met mine.

He pulled away. "What the hell?"

What blood hadn't already drained into my erection left my face.

"Great, I've got to meet with a client in twenty minutes, and you not only killed my coffee and my only ironed shirt, but you decide to what? Kiss it and make it better?"

I stared at him, finger on my lips. "I'm so sorry, Dylan, I didn't thi—"

"How do you know my name?"

My jaw moved up and down as I goggled at him, mortified and aroused, anguished and delighted to see him.

"You know what? I don't have time for this." He grabbed the things he'd dropped—including the crushed coffee cup—and hurried out through the door.

An older woman with frosted blond curls came over. "Are you all right, sir?"

"Besides being really embarrassed?" I asked.

She helped me up, lowering her tone. "You might want to think of something else."

I noticed the direction of her gaze to find my still new body eager to try out the fresh body parts with the man I'd erased.

"Thanks, that helps."

She laughed. "You're sure you aren't hurt?"

"I'm sure."

"I'm going to need you to fill out an accident report and sign off as uninjured," she said.

I glanced at the time on my phone. "Of course, you do. I need to make this fast."

By some stroke of luck, I made it just as the seller was getting back into his car. I handed over the cash without so much as cranking the scooter up. If there was anything wrong with it, I'd ask Anima to get a putto—the lewd little construction angels most people confused with cherubim—to fix up the bike.

Since I offered him more than he asked without dickering, he agreed to be a little late back to work while we filled out the title. I didn't really need his signed copy. The Isaac had included an already transferred copy in my wallet, but I couldn't tell the seller that.

The little scooter didn't hold a candle to my Johammer, but it didn't need any repairs either. I headed to the store for cleaning supplies, a spare outfit and a small fortune in honey to bribe the rest of the information out of Grynnberry.

I had some faeries to stop, but before that I needed a nest.

Vitae

I searched all of the books I'd saved from my library prior to its ransacking. None of them contained any notes on constructing an oracle. With my automata stolen, I couldn't even use the cursed thing to provide the information I needed.

Lesser shields might have just flopped down and pouted, but dedicated soldiers never accepted failure. I drew a silver cigarette case from where it was tucked into my corset. Divine light spilled out of the insides the moment I cracked open the reliquary containing Vilicangelus's feather.

"Vilicangelus. Vilicangelus. Vilicangelus."

I waited.

I paced and waited some more.

My hands tingled. My manicured nails smoked.

That incompetent boob is blocking me.

I paced the room again, surer with each step that

Summuseraphi, the so-called Praefectus, was intercepting all use of Vilicangelus's feathers to ensure my old friend didn't learn how badly he'd lost control of Atlanta's shields.

I spun on my heel mid-pace and marched out of the hotel. Scurith rushed to catch up with me, nattering about something. I shoved him away, picking up steam until I slid into the driver's seat of my Mercedes.

I addressed the bronze angel on the dashboard, its pose one of irritation and disgust. The Atlanta Shield was out of control. I had both the Shield's and the shields' corrections in hand, but in the meantime, I couldn't blame its repulsion.

"Vilicangelus. Vilicangelus. Vilicangelus."

No one answered.

I wasn't surprised not to hear my automata's voice, after all the equipment that made it up had been stolen. There'd be no way for it to communicate across the angel network so long as it remained disconnected. As far as I was concerned, the thing could rot with the Sidhe that took it. I'd soon have an oracle once more. No one would reprogram the oracle. There'd be no more baby phoenixes anthropomorphizing it then lecturing me about its gender.

Everything with that lazy ungrateful slut is about sex.

I started my Mercedes and raced out into traffic. Some wafer blared its horn at me. Unfortunately, the duty before me prevented me schooling the mortal on the virtues of respect.

"Vilicangelus. Vilicangelus. Vilicangelus."

A mile later I'd still heard no answer.

It didn't seem possible that our elevated buffoon could block the whole of the angel network, but I didn't yet know all that a Divine One's power encompassed.

He can't block this.

I pulled out my cell phone and dialed the Isaac.

"Atlanta Vitae." The Isaac's voice had the same kind of deep resonance that Terrance occasionally achieved, not earthy exactly but resonating with the surrounding objects.

"Isaac, I need to get in touch with Vilicangelus."

"Vilicangelus cannot be disturbed. Contact Summuseraphi?"

"No need to waste your time. I need information on the runes involved in crafting an oracle like the ones we used to have."

"Have you contacted Anima?"

"No, the Sidhe stole all of that equipment, that's why I need to build an oracle. Can you get a tome from one of the other Shields?"

"Bide. I will see to what is needed. You will be contacted."

"Thank you." I closed the connection. The Isaac would see to my needs—no thanks to Summuseraphi.

Anima

Sudden warmth drew Anima's attention.

A greater cherubim appeared in the mists before her. Sad eyes that had witnessed too much tragedy covered the Isaac's face and hands, wings and torso. Older and larger than Anima, his body was somehow scarred. She had no idea how it was even possible for him to have earned the scars, but her gaze shifted to the golden sword at his belt. He cleared his throat, drawing her attention once more.

When he spoke, the eye on his tongue appeared between his lips in blinks. "Anima."

Anima bowed her head. "I greet the Isaac."

"Vitae thinks you stolen. Why?"

"I don't know," Anima said. "He's been hidden from my sight until a few minutes ago. I only found him because he used the statue in his Mercedes."

"You did not answer him?"

"He didn't call for me."

"He is your Shieldheart."

I opened my mouth, but instead dropped all of my eyes, nodding without a word.

"Speak, little one."

"Vitae is...wrong. He frightens me."

"You See. Without Sight your Shield is blind."

"I See for Quayla. Something veils the others from my Sight, but we're working to reclaim them. It's not like I'm allowed to manifest. What else do you expect of me?"

"Forbidden yet Seen twice. See for your Shieldheart."

Anima cringed. "The equipment was stolen."

"He builds an Oracle. Grant Vitae the Knowledge. Grant your Shield Vision in the Waters."

"I shall do as the Isaac instructs."

The Isaac vanished.

She reached a finger up to the garnet for Atlanta's Shieldheart, but hesitated. She dipped an eye-tipped finger into the cosmos. Another like her appeared in the view. He was only twice her age, but his voice rang like a clarion call. "Speak, Atlanta Sister."

"My Shieldheart needs a tome for inscribing an Oracle."

"I shall grant you the knowledge."

"No," Anima spat. "I-I have no way to show him the runes. He will need a book."

"Something is wrong in Atlanta?"

"My Shield is all but destroyed, Nashville Brother. We are trying to rebuild."

"Have you received any word from Summuseraphi?"

Anima shook her head. "I cannot See him."

The other cherubim nodded. "A courier will bring the tome."

"Thank you."

"Thanks are not for passing between us."

Chapter Ten

Heralding Doom

Vitae

A fanfare of trumpets exploded in my car. I glanced at the bronze angel to find the figurine's expression mixing shock and horror. A blinding wall of white obscured everything as my Mercedes dropped out of Creation and almost ran over a winged figure in white robes.

He leapt upward over my car, but rather than appear disgruntled he beamed like a happy child.

Unlike the transparent veil Vilicangelus employed to separate us from creation, the surrounding white was absolute. I got out and turned toward him.

He stood at last eight feet tall, crowned with long brown hair that fell nearly to the center of his back. A golden rope restrained robes and the muscles beneath straining to get out. A similar circlet kept hair out of his eyes. His teeth gleamed whiter than his wings—an all but impossible feat.

I folded my hands behind my back. "I do not believe we are acquainted, Nuntius."

His voice shook the world around us. "I have come, beari—"

He stopped, starting again with his voice lowered to an exuberant boom. "I have come, bearing a missive for Atlanta's Shieldheart."

He kneeled to one knee, extending both arms holding up an ancient-looking tome.

I strode forward noticing thick, braided silver and gold hemming his robes. Three small trumpets adorned his circlet. The book laid across his forearms was wrapped in a thick leather but surprisingly light when I took it.

"You have my thanks, Nuntius."

He stood, frowning. "You've misnamed me twice as one of your kind's messengers. Do you truly not know me?"

"That's correct. Your message is delivered, take my thanks with you on your way."

"I do not think you understand the honor you've been given, Atlanta's Shieldheart. My service is given you by special dispensation to dwell with you among mortals and bring order back to this shire."

I bristled.

Pins and needles bit into my fingertips and the spots on either side of my jaw beneath my ears burned hot. "This tome is all I require."

His eager grin faltered. "Begging your pardon, Shieldheart, but without your Watcher you may not be aware what transpires—"

"I do not offer you my pardon, *messenger*. Atlanta is my realm, and I see to its order and its Shield."

"But it is said you do not stand at the side of your Aqua—"

Outrage burst from me, filling the white place with fury like thunder. Power washed around me and my words boomed. "Aquaylae is a wafer-licking traitor that belongs under heel!"

A serious expression exposed wrinkles on the messenger's young face. "Shieldheart. I like not the feel of thy magic. Though you were created second, your strength cannot match those that first served."

It took all my will not to teach the young messenger the error in his words. "You have discharged your delivery. I require no further assistance at this time. Leave this realm and return me to Creation."

"You are rejecting my service?"

"Have you lodged feathers in your ears? Yes, I reject your service and forbid you contact with the others of my Shield. Now, begone from my sight."

Blinding white walls vanished. Tires screeched. Metal slammed against metal and my Mercedes lurched forward into a Corvette. German craftsmanship disintegrated American fiberglass like hot water on cotton candy.

I shot the minivan driver that had hit my Mercedes a look worthy of a Greek gorgon.

Terrance

Terrance stretched in the locker room, getting a feel for his new body before enjoying the relative luxury of a cool shower. He cleansed methodically, bolstering the bones of each limb with a protective layer of stone as he washed it. The new muscles weren't used to the weight, making them move more sluggishly than he might otherwise want going into a fight.

Since the shower area was broken up into walled-off cubicles, he took a moment to transmogrify his entire form into essence. The primordial scent of new-growth forest and freshly-turned earth filled the small space. He inhaled deeply, remembering beloved corners of Creation. Caelum or Aquaylae might've poked fun that he enjoyed his own scent, but they were both absent.

One an injured captive, the other free somewhere. Are you well, little sister?

He'd been ordered to capture her if they encountered one another. Fortunately, he'd not witnessed her current body allowing for, if not perfect, at least plausible deniability.

The order itself suggested one of the others had encountered Aquaylae or Vitae. Within the murky cave Dunham caged Terrance, he couldn't be sure who'd allowed the free shields to escape, but Caelum's condition pointed to the younger shield's guilt.

Terrance focused on his essence. Unlike Quayla's fluid form, a mud bordering on the consistency of clay composed the base essence of Terra phoenixes. A thick lichen shrouded the dark, wet soil, making Terrance resemble one of mortal kind's Chia pets in the earliest stages. Unlike Caelum's or Ignis's essence, Terrance's essence maintained a stubbornness to stay unified and in a set shape.

Much like water and the reason Quayla and I feel such pain separating out our essence.

Terrance bullied his essence, shifting extra breast and hip mass into muscle. The new body would be leaner, better able to manage the added weight to its limbs and easier to balance. He could remold his features too—not something he wanted to reveal to Dunham—and even make himself appear male again. It would be appearance only, since the encoding in the new body was and would remain female. Terrance hadn't died unexpectedly in some time and thus hadn't lost the opportunity to fix his ID prior to death in many rebirths.

Female bodies have chemical and biological difference, but their senses and connection to Creation are often stronger.

He chuckled, a musical note far from his old rumble.

It's Mother, not Papa, Nature after all.

Terrance completed rearranging his essence once he'd bullied his shape into a body better balanced for the combat ahead. He stepped out of the shower cubicle only to bump into a tiny but athletic girl in her late twenties. The collision cost both of them their towels and balance, but Terrance regained his feet first. His eyes lingered on her, traveling head to foot with a few short stops that kindled the primal hunger common in a new body. His gaze rose to her face, finding a hard expression in place to mask flustered embarrassment.

"I'm sorry for knocking you down," Terrance purposely pushed damp hair away from his face. "I'm also sorry for staring. I know I shouldn't envy others, but sometimes you see someone and just wish you could be as beautiful."

The girl's hard expression transformed into a full-fledged blush.

Terrance picked up his towel and offered it with a hand up. "I really am sorry."

The girl took the hand. Once Terrance had her on her feet, he lowered his head to hide his face behind dark curls and turned back to his locker.

"Don't you need your towel?"

"I'll grab another. I didn't want to bother you anymore."

"I'm Bree, I don't think I've seen you here before."

Terrance turned, standing in profile half engaged in the conversation and halfway positioned to flee. "Terra. I'm one of Dunham's new acquisitions."

"Mister Heffernan hired you personally?"

Terrance chose a noncommittal tilt of his head.

"What did you think of him?" Bree asked.

Terrance considered his answer for a few moments. "I have no fondness for arrogant megalomaniacs."

Bree gasped.

"I apologize for distressing you, but I must be going. Dunham scheduled me for a meeting I may not miss. Have a good day."

For a moment, Terrance thought she might say more, but she allowed him to return to the lockers. The clothes Dunham provided no longer fit the adjustments to his body. For the same reason he transmogrified in an area less susceptible to Dunham's surveillance, Terrance chose not to convert the clothing to essence and back with a corrected fit in the locker room.

Security in the lobby provided him a long duffle bag ostensibly containing the requested cudgel. When he asked about the address he'd been promised, they directed Terrance to a waiting car. He'd have rather had lone access to a vehicle, but having a driver meant relinquishing responsibility for arriving at the right place in a timely manner.

The mortal tried to use the vehicle as a rolling speak easy, but Terrance focused on preparing for the battle ahead. He was required to assault both sides of a Sidhe battle. He was neither permitted to adhere to the strictures proscribed in the Articles of Ararat nor to allow any of the combatants to escape alive. The plausibility of complete obedience didn't seem one of Dunham's concerns. He had control of Terrance through his egg.

He would demand.

Terrance was expected to obey.

The smile grew slowly, a widening furrow in fresh earth.

Dunham's orders, if interpreted and implemented correctly, provided conditions that could be used to Terrance's advantage.

Waves of Sidhe taint reached Terrance before the driver stopped outside of a small park. Seeing faeries battling in a public parked during broad daylight felt wrong.

It is what it is.

Terrance strode away from the car, duffel in hand. He inhaled the scent of nature, choking on a thick taint that suggested the potency if not the number of battling Sidhe. Stepping into thick brush that parted around Terrance without so much as a snag allowed for enough cover to transmogrify once more.

He drew rock-heavy soil in through his feet and mixed it throughout his body to increase his available mass. Battle gloves of obsidian and granite, quartz and diamond formed on Terrance's arms. He raised one leg and sawed it away mid thigh with a sharp edge of obsidian, grimacing at the pain.

Transmogrified into pure essence, there was no risk of bleeding out from cutting through the femoral artery that wasn't in place at that moment. His unfamiliar balance wobbled a bit, but he redistributed his essence just as he might when filling his nest—or the bottle Dunham demanded be filled—until he'd regrown the missing leg. He kneeled, concentrating and transferring the sacrificed essence into the duffle bag.

I have to trust Anima will sense such a large amount of essence and lead the others here to reclaim it.

Terrance left his bag behind, creeping through summer-dried leaves and undergrowth. The Sidhe battle looked more like an event of the mortal Society for Creative Anachronism. Faerie lords and knights lounged comfortably in tents with sweat-beaded goblets and platters of fine food. Central to the two clusters of tents, lesser faeries battled one another with ferocity the faerie onlookers all but ignored. Mortals undoubtedly in attendance as potential recruits gave the battling Sidhe attention enough to compensate for the bored remainder.

Not ideal, certainly not the situation Dunham described.

Terrance squared his shoulders and marched into the battle field. His clothes had been transformed into body hugging armor modeled in stone after modern designs. "In the name of the Undying Light, I demand your attention."

The half dozen bloody hobgoblins fighting one another abandoned their opposing Sidhe and mobbed Terrance as a man.

Terrance dodged the first short blade thrust and brought his elbow down to break the metal blade. A curved, serrated blade thrust at Terrance's face. He dodged to one side, staying just away from the edge the hobgoblin yanked backward to saw into Terrance's neck.

Terrance slammed a cestus into the hobgoblin's grinning teeth. He twisted his fist as he landed the blow, quartz and diamond digging through the faerie's face like a mining drill. His other cestus knocked away a mace, obsidian edge taking off the hand swinging it.

"Cease this at once. I only wish to speak."

His opposing combatants ignored Terrance, but the observing Sidhe and their potential recruits watched from the edges of their seats. Terrance punched and kicked, spun and dodged. Violet and evergreen blood fertilized the brown grass beneath their feet in a bizarre portrait of gore.

Less than a minute later, Terrance stood alone—the center of a solar system of bodies, body parts and blood.

"Damn, is that what I'll be like if I join?"

Terrance raised his eyes to the speaking mortal. "No, mortal. You will be deceived and used until one of my kind come for you."

An Unseelie elf in elaborate silver and raspberry robes stood protectively in front of the speaker. "Don't lie to the mortal."

"I did not." Terrance said. "Hear me, Sidhe. I am here not to enforce the Articles of Ararat as I might wish, but to slay every single one of you. There will be no escape. I will hunt you down until each of you lies dead on the Earth."

After a short pause one of the elves laughed. His mirth spread to the others.

"This bitch for real?" the mortal asked.

Terrance sighed. The encounter wasn't proceeding as he'd planned. He'd hoped his warning would turn at least some Sidhe on their heels, allowing him time outside Dunham's control while he pursued—as ordered. "Very well, I gave you fair warning."

He chose the mouthy elf as his first prey and waded into the fray.

The elf's gesture summoned a half dozen goblins. They dropped their serving trays, pulled curved knives and charged. Lesser elves followed a moment behind as two Unseelie ogres lumbered out of their chairs to join the fray.

The goblins barely slowed Terrance, but they weren't meant to go toe to toe with a juggernaut. The goblin assault allowed the elves time to summon their magic. Crackling hex bolts slammed into Terrance in threes, their caster trios bracketing Terrance from either side. The magic staggered Terrance, but as with most energy in Creation, ground softened its bite.

Terrance took two moments—one to stud his skin with salt crystals and the other to check on the Seelie—before his haymaker tore up an elf's torso to impale the elf under his chin. He bulled into the elf with a shoulder, spinning to his left to backhand the sharp obsidian edge on his offhand cestus into the gut of the second of three. The elf dodged backward as expected, darting in to gut Terrance only to meet Terrence's right battle glove with his face.

Hex bolts slammed into Terrance's back, but the salt further dispelled the energy, reducing them to horsefly bites rather than the deadly blasts they were intended to deliver. Terrance turned his attention to the last Unseelie spellblade only to take a face full of fire so dark red it was almost black.

Pain seared Terrance's skin, but felt muffled compared to the agony of his melting eyes. His burning hair crisped his scalp. Blades drove into Terrance's back carrying agony spells on their edge.

Blinded both literally and by the pain, Terrance lashed out in a whirl of fists. At least one of the blades broke off in his back and another blast of fire engulfed him.

Terrance mastered his pain, listening to his feet to position the attacking elves. A flurry of punches impacted three of the four combatants. He pushed his essence into the ground, shaking it underfoot to buy time to master his essence. He leapt with all his might.

In an instant, Terrance transmogrified into his phoenix form, snapping two elf heads off with his talons before landing once more in his human shape to glare at the hellfire caster. Terrance drove into the elf like a locomotive before the elf could respond. He shifted a spike of stone out of one heel to pin the elf's foot to the ground and savaged the caster with an avalanche of crystal-edged blows.

He turned from the pulped elf to the last of the elves just as the ogres meandered into the fight. Over their snarls, Terrance heard the Unseelie taunting the Seelie as cowards. His experience with the petulant, almost adolescent nature of the Sidhe pretty much guaranteed the Seelie would join the fight.

Terrance took a sword to the gut, the blade scoring his armor but deflecting off to one side. He turned his head at the last moment as the remaining elf's head exploded violet-grey pudding all over Terrance's arms. He extruded essence down the Sidhe body, encasing it before hefting the elf off the ground. Terrance swung the elf into the first ogre like a cudgel.

He ducked low, dodging a blow he'd felt more than heard. A long quartz spike grew from the center of his right fist. He drove it up into the ogre's groin.

The ogre doubled over, bellowing opera and swinging wildly.

Terrance grabbed the beast's stringy hair and yanked his head down into a newly-grown knee spike.

Massive hands wrapped around Terrance's shoulders, lifting him off the ground. Terrance swung his legs up as he turned the modern shoulder armor into medieval age spiked pauldrons. The ogre released the sudden spikes before they dug into his hands, allowing the momentum of Terrance's kick to flip him upward and upside down. He wrapped the ogre's head in a leg lock and threw his torso weight sideways. Terrance spun a half orbit around the ogre, clapping both cestus into the ogre's ears with all of his strength.

The ogre staggered.

Terrance raked the obsidian edge across the back of the beast's head and threw his weight forward. They both fell. The ogre face-planted dead into the ground. Terrance rolled off the felled Sidhe into the Seelie reinforcements.

The Sidhe forced Terrance to transmogrify and repair himself three more times before they fled in opposite directions. He took a moment to catch his breath before chasing down the mortal and disabusing him of any delusions around his survivability as one of the Fae Kissed.

His duty to Creation discharged, Terrance set out after the Unseelie elf lord that had angered him. Dunham's orders required Terrance to track down the Seelie too, but allowed enough latitude for Terrance to choose the pleasure of vengeance before other concerns.

Dunham

Magic swirled up in a crescendo, coursing through Dunham's quarters like a welcome symphony. Energy coalesced over a giant flat square of stone in a fog of blues and oranges, violets and reds. Depressions at the four points of the compass held blood fresh from the latest company blood drive. Their contents dwindled as the life energy of his employees fueled the opening Arch.

Viviane strode through first. Her naked skin glowed with a vitality that often clung to her after she returned from Faery. The knights she'd broken—Gherrian and Dolumii—entered next, keeping a wary eye on their opposite.

Either would have gladly slain the other in hopes of earning enough glory to escape their shame. Dunham wouldn't allow it. Being out of favor within their Courts made them easier pawns and easier to control.

Dunham pointed. "Stack them there, gentlemen."

Gherrian gave Dunham a look of long-suffering, but Dolumii wanted Dunham's blood nearly as much as he wanted Gherrian's. Each directed an entourage of faerie porters as the parade of equipment taken from the Shield sanctum assembled next to the windows. Both knights lingered near Dunham's caged phoenixes, eyes lingering on runes.

"If you gentlemen are so interested in my spells, I am all too happy to offer you firsthand experience."

"Watch it, mortal," Dolumii said. "Her Ladyship may not favor you forever."

Dunham gathered his power, a litany of silent incantations flashing through his mind. He swept a hand toward the seditious Unseelie knight. Light lashed across him, carving away fine garments to stitch a tortured scar across the faerie's flesh as a replacement.

Dolumii grabbed at his chest, legs folding beneath him.

Disapproval undercut Gherrian's words. "If I am not mistaken, that was divine magic."

"You are not mistaken," Dunham said. "Imagine it hurts worse than the infernal magic your kind performs."

Gherrian offered Dolumii a hand up.

The Unseelie slapped the offered hand away, climbing to his feet and drawing an ornate elven sword. "I intended you to join my bevy of slaves eventually, mortal, but today you have chosen your time."

"Do you really want to die again?" Dunham asked. "Your patron may have excused a death defending her meeting place, but dying again and so soon not to mention when away from your duties. You might not be offered a rebirth."

"You're not even armed," Dolumii hissed.

"I am a druid, elf—the eye of the storm, the balance of forces," Dunham's lips curled into a smirk. "Forgive the cliché, but I am a weapon."

Gherrian placed a hand on Dolumii's sword arm. "He's wielding divine power in addition to what Her Ladyship has granted. I do not think even so honored a knight can prevail in this."

Viviane appeared in an elegant skirt suit fitted in a way that made her more desirable than when she sauntered around naked. She propped a hand on one hip. "Are you boys misbehaving? There's work to do."

"See this thing put back together exactly as you removed it." Dunham crossed to Viviane, lowering his voice. "Your ranks seem less numerous than I recall. Have you assigned them another task?"

Her eyes flashed. "You may recall we are supposed to be thinning the ranks of both Courts."

Dunham gestured to the gear. "This will allow us to better coordinate deployment of your forces and mine."

"You exhausted poor Caelum on your own petty business."

"A test of control, milady." Dunham smiled. "With a bonus. The Terra is eliminating some of your foes now."

Viviane's attention searched the faeries reassembling the Shield's control room before drifting to Summuseraphi. "We need to find the Vitae and recapture Quayla."

"The divine is suitably weakened. I don't think he will be able to challenge his cage again soon," Dunham said.

"Always plan for every contingency, dear boy."

Chapter Eleven

Shifting Pieces

Dunham

Dunham shattered a thirty-thousand-dollar vase against the phoenix's main display screen. The equipment was powered, but it didn't work. To exasperate matters, there'd been no word from the Terra. The driver he'd sent with the phoenix had lost her in the park, only managing to catch up and begin filming after the fight was joined in earnest.

The Terra had torn out after fleeing prey too fast for Dunham's agent to get to his car and follow. Despite losing the Terra who had no choice but to return once her mission was completed, the agent had done the smart thing. He'd called in for support and collected abandoned Sidhe campaign paraphernalia.

Viviane ascended the stairs. She looked at him, then the pottery shards and sighed. "I loved that vase."

"This thing doesn't work!" Dunham snarled. "And your informant should be skinned alive. He said the Sidhe would be fighting, not lounging around in tents."

Viviane's laugh incensed him further, but he grappled his temper back under control. "I'm not amused."

"The Terra?"

"Following my orders. I thought I'd included instruction for every possibility, but it never occurred to me that the Courts would be sitting around drinking in broad daylight instead of trying to kill each other."

"I imagine they were killing each other, just not at the pace you desired. Life's treated differently when you can't die of old age."

"What's the draw of these little war games they play then? Faerie fascination with death?"

"Pretty much. What's wrong with the control center?" Her tone became dry. "Other than the rogue fragments of three-thousand-year-old pottery?"

"The servers have power. None of the hardware has any alert lights showing. Everything is connected exactly as it was, but there's no data. No seeds. Nothing."

"Could they have rigged it to purge the database? Could the automata have initiated some kind of self-destruct protocol when Dolumii and Gherrian returned?"

"It's possible, but if that's the case this junk is useless. Hell, my lowest, entry-level employees have newer gear than this."

"Have you asked them about it?"

Dunham turned his attention to the cages. "Caelum's still in too bad of shape to be very responsive and the Pyri remains stubbornly resistant to control even when I use both his egg and heart."

"Strong."

"Very. I'll ask the Terra when she returns."

"What are you going to do if you can't get this to work?" Viviane's question held an edge.

"If you want me to thin the Seelie and Unseelie ranks, we're going to have to rely on your information sources."

"We need to stay focused, Dunham. You can't use this as an excuse to shift your attention away from the plan."

"Your plan, and I'm upholding my end of the bargain. It's the intelligence from your people that's falling through."

Viviane closed the distance, her voice dangerous. "I'm coordinating a worldwide offensive, boy. Atlanta may be the tip of the spear, but without everything I've been building these past couple centuries—including your little empire—all of this is for naught. You will find a way to force the Courts to concentrate here. The other Queens both need to be convinced they need me and the Anseelie to tilt the balance against the other."

Dunham turned his back on her. She wanted her vengeance even more than he wanted his own. He'd prepared for the eventuality just in case there were elements of the phoenix tech he didn't understand. Looking at it up close, he wasn't sure what he was missing, but even so, there were other ways to keep track of incursions.

Never offer up a miracle until you're sure the client will pay for it.

Quayla

I headed over to a Lowes and bee-lined through the store for the garden section. Searching up and down the exterior aisles offered small fountains, but none small enough to turn into a nest. I eyeballed the edging stones, wondering if I could seal a ring of them well enough to create my own basin. In the end, I picked up a few plastic buckets from cleaning supplies so I could build up reserve essence. The line wasn't moving very fast, so I scanned the impulse buy items. I decided which candy bars needed to go into my bucket and then shifted my scan to the next register to see if there was anything different there I wanted to accompany my chocolate.

My gaze drifted past the third register's goodies to an end cap display under a sign which read: Are you compliant with the new code?

Beneath the sign, a water heater with some kind of sub tank

suspended over it rested on a small aluminum catch pan. My breath caught. I ducked out of line, shoving several goodies into my buckets before hurrying back to the plumbing area. Not finding what I was looking for, I finally stopped an old wafer. He led me back to the right section and left me to gaze down at the water heater catch pans.

"Ani?"

She sounded sullen. "Here, Quayla."

"Is everything all right?"

"Yes."

"You know you can tell me what's bothering you."

"I...I got in trouble."

"Why?"

"For talking to you, but not to Vitae."

My brow furrowed. "Why aren't you talking to Vitae?"

"He thinks I'm just some horrible tech that he resents. He treats me badly, and to be honest, right now I'm scared of him."

I flashed to Vitae wading through the foliage into the entry of the Marriott. The plants recoiled and died around him. Then he'd tried to run me through with both Champion blades.

"Yeah, he's a little scary right now."

"The Isaac managed to get one of the first host sent down to help—"

"What?! That's fantastic. Where is he...she...whatever?"

"Vitae insulted him and sent him away."

My core went hot and cold all at the same time. "He did what?! We need that help, blighted-night, we need an angel more desperately than just about anything right now."

Anima's reply was tiny and quiet. "I'm sorry."

I pushed away my frustration with Vitae and softened my voice. "It's all right, Ani. You're awesome. Thanks to you, we're going to rescue the others and take back Atlanta."

"Dunham took all the control equipment from the sanctum. He's trying to get it to work."

"I can't fathom why he needs the ability to see incursions."

"He can't...not unless I interface with the tech."

"I don't understand."

"I'm his missing component. The control center tech let you guys interface with me in a way you understood, but I'm the one that feels the seeds and feeds the information into the displays."

"Why does it work like that?"

"The old way, the oracles, we had no voice. We showed Shields the incursion locations, but as the cities became bigger and bigger, we had to find a better way to communicate with the Shields. The computer systems allowed us to help better without revealing what we are."

"I don't understand why knowing what you are is forbidden."

"The Isaac will not answer that question no matter how many times I ask. None of the others I've interacted with know either. We just know that we are supposed to be separate, Watchers only."

"I don't want to get you in trouble."

"The Isaac knows. He Sees all. He has not punished me yet."

"Can you tell me more about the Isaac? What he is? How he does what he does? Like the IDs. Why did you have them delivered to the bank instead of waiting for me when I woke up? I know you can materialize at my location."

"The government facilities had to be open to process the requests. It's why some shields work places like the DMV. If you look at yours, you'll see we had your new identification delivered from out of state since you don't have a home here."

I took out my ID and checked it over. Sure enough, I was from Jacksonville, Florida. "You couldn't get me an address on the west coast where the water isn't so dirty?"

Anima laughed.

"All right, back to business. Can you see these?" I picked up one of the catch pans. "Will this hold enough for a rebirth?"

"At your current mass, yes."

"Can we link more than one?"

"If you draw a precedence rune on the basin, it will disappear from the previous basin. Only one nest can be primary."

"All right. Thanks." I tucked the bucket into the basin and headed back toward the front. I stopped mid step as a horrifying thought struck me. "Ani, can you tell when precedence is changed on a nest?"

"Of course."

"Can I?"

"Not instinctively no, but you'd be the one changing the rune."

"After I get this one built, please warn me immediately if precedence changes. I don't want Dunham capturing me again."

"Neither do I."

I exited the Lowes and headed to where I parked my scooter. Digging into the bag, I unpackaged a small container of bungee cords and went to work securing everything.

A subtle taint rippled across my skin like a breeze on a lake surface, tickling my nose a moment later. I yanked the Karambit hilts from my belt loops and turned to look into a Guy Fawkes mask with its nose painted red and an American flag across its forehead. The figure dressed in a tailored suit. He folded his hands behind his back and waited.

"You know Fae Kissed don't normally walk right up to us."

A husky voice escaped the mask "If you ever desire to see Mr. Snyder alive again, you will come with us."

My mind reeled, but before I could even ask a question, he turned his back on me and marched across the parking lot to an old blue panel van. Glancing around for observers, I jogged toward the van. It pulled out and headed for the exit, forcing me to run back to my Vespa. The van pulled into traffic as a pickup older than Terrance's sharked slowly through the parking lot looking for a space.

The Vespa mumbled insults under its breath as I forced it to whip around the truck with all the power it could muster. The van took a left several blocks ahead just as I slipped into traffic.

Aggressive driving and scooters are made for one another. I rode the dotted lines staying watchful of blinking lights on side view mirrors. It took forcing the Vespa to shriek like an asthmatic banshee to cross the heavy oncoming traffic. The van had accelerated to an almost six-block lead. I did everything I could to catch up. Even though the Vespa was doing all the work, my heart thundered in my chest, silent under the roar of the ocean in my ears. Whoever the Fae Kissed was, he had Dylan. The idea that erasing myself from his life hadn't been enough to protect him made me sicker than the faerie taint. We played cat and mouse, my scooter slowly closing the distance between us as stop signs and traffic played in my favor.

I didn't try to overtake them. I didn't assault them. There was no way for me to tell whether or not Dylan was in the cargo van. There was also no way to know how many were involved. I knew one thing—there wouldn't be enough of them and their sure as blight wouldn't be enough left of them to identify when I was through.

The van turn left into an industrial area and turned left again almost immediately, pulling through an open chain-link fence topped with razor wire. It disappeared inside a large warehouse. The garage door rumbled closed behind the van, leaving only an open doorway as an invitation.

You're going to be really sorry you invited me to this party.

I dismounted and pushed essence into my Karambit knives. The fence gate rattled closed, but I paid it no mind. I would leave when Dylan was safe, and the Fae Kissed had been put down.

Vitae

The mortal shield summoned to the accident scene had shown more deference to my cleavage than doling out proper punishment for my damaged vehicle. Since his nethers seemed in charge of his actions, I carefully considered cursing them with something properly punitive or at the very least employing a glamour to convince him of imminent rotting.

The process involved in the damage to my Mercedes stretched on like an ancient Greek epic. The comedy of errors peaked as the little old woman in the crushed corvette repeatedly demanded I pay for her vehicle in a language only I apparently understood while we awaited an official translator.

She refused to understand the translator's explanation of process and fault, dragging out the situation to unacceptable lengths.

I stepped up to her, fixed her with my gaze and pushed my will. "I have no time for your hysterics. You *will* be silent and stand aside."

The translator snorted, but his expression changed to marvel when the woman folded her hands on her lap and leaned against her car.

I turned to the officer and pushed. "You *will* cease ogling my body, make these people move these vehicles, excuse me from further proceedings and complete this process without me."

I turned to the startled translator. "You *will* forget all I said."

"I-I need you to move your vehicles out of the road. Thank you for your patience, ma'am, you're excused."

"What?!" The minivan driver asked. "She pulled into the road out of nowhere. If she wasn't cutting into traffic like she owned the road, I'd never have hit her."

"*Do* as this shield instructs."

They moved their vehicles, and I left their sorry melodrama behind. One of my dwarves would make short work of repairs, beyond that and the present mobility of the vehicle, I had no interest in the entire series of events.

There were far more troubling things afoot, particularly Aquaylae's attempts to go over my head and undercut my authority. It seemed despite my desperation to reclaim the Unseelie

Champion blade, bringing her to heel had to be elevated on my list of priorities.

I'll see her put back on probation, purified and her essence employed to complete oracle construction.

A wafer blared its horn at me as I got out of my car and marched into the government building. The entitled mortal shouted after me about space ownership of some sort, but his opinion of reality didn't remove my vehicle from the parking space.

A weasel-faced man with charcoal, oil-plastered hair nattered at my thrall, brandishing a sheaf of irrelevant documentation. My thrall's eyes shifted to my entrance. A queer expression clouded his drawn features. He dropped to one knee, placing his forehead on the questionably sanitary flooring. "Master, I—"

"What the hell are you doing, Sky? I need all of these documents redone with proper language and none of your weird little hobby speak on them." He rounded on me. "Where's your badge? Who the hell do you think you are just marching into my morgue like the Queen of Sheba?"

"Your better. Begone little man, correct your own paperwork, I have need of my thrall."

The wafer spluttered, looking back and forth between me and my thrall. "I...I don't know what kind of perverted games you two are up to, but this is a government building, and—"

I seized the little man and threw him across the room. "Do as I command, wafer!"

He impacted against the entry door, slid to the ground and moaned. I marched across the intervening distance, seized him by his collars and ejected him from the room.

"I have need of your services. Why have you not returned?"

"You instructed me to ensure things were right here, Master. I swear that I've worked without a break trying to catch things up."

"Have you procured more bodies for my use?"

"There aren't any here."

I followed the scent of death to a wall of drawers and yanked open one. "There are bodies a plenty for my use."

My thrall stiffened. "Master, appropriating bodies who have families awaiting their release for burial won't go unnoticed."

"Notice is not acceptable. You will have to fetch bodies from cemeteries, but first I have another task I must entrust to you. I'd rather not, but my time is too important to be wasted."

"What task, Master?"

"I must rebuild and cast a sentry net over this city. This involves strategically arranging small amounts of my essence throughout Atlanta so that the Oracle can alert me of Sidhe incursions."

"We just need to smear your blood on things?"

"Seeds must be marked with angelic runes and engineered to minimize tampering or removal. Work it out on your way to a cemetery."

My thrall bowed, his voice muffled. "Yes, Master."

I turned my back to him, marching away to handle my next task.

Bradley

Bradley clenched his teeth. "Yes, Master."

He was too exhausted to feel the pleasure transmitted by his obedience. He needed sleep, but he had orders.

Still, she declared drawing notice as unacceptable. It'll be far easier to rob graves at night. That gives me time for sleep.

Bradley dragged his feet to the room's rear and pulled out a body drawer with a cheap pillow and blanket. He climbed feet first onto the tray, pulled the drawer into the wall and drew the door closed with the tile puller attached to the door's inside as an extra handle.

Chapter Twelve

Pitched Battle

Quayla

There seemed little reason to expect anything less than a full ambush, so I closed my left eye and evaluated other options for nullifying whatever preparations they'd made. Armoring up in addition to arming seemed prudent, but declaring war before I'd had the chance to measure their intentions wasn't the smartest thing I could do.

Still, dealing with Fae Kissed, guns seemed likely—something a transmog into liquid form would handle with minimal effort. Rather than change into all water out in the open, I prepared my essence for the change before I stepped through the door. The warehouse lights were shut off with the intent to cause momentary blindness.

Meaning they're going to jump me.

I swapped eyes and scanned the dim confines. Scents of old oil and moderate taint undercut the room.

"Isn't this quaint?" The comment bought me the time intended, allowing a less rushed evaluation of my circumstances.

Four men in suits stood at different points around the open space, using industrial shelving filled with boxes and car parts or—

in the case of Flag boy—the van for cover. Each wore the same Guy Fawkes mask, but decorated in different ways. Two had been painted roughly clown like and the last had red smeared all over the bottom half of Guy's face as if he feasted on the organs of his foes.

An ogre lumbered out of the rearmost darkness, his skin a dark olive made darker by the stark white collar of his tailored business suit. He wore dark hair up in a man bun. Talon scars bracketed his remaining intelligent eye. More scars disappeared into a leather patch with a ruby set into a bronze fitting at its center.

I cast back to one of Dylan's favorite movies and lowered my tone to a growl. "Hello again, Cyclops."

To my knowledge, we'd never met, but I hadn't wanted to screw up the quote just for the sake of accuracy.

"Where's Dylan?"

A deep, melodic tone escaped the ogre's lips instead of the gruff guttural words I'd expected. "Mr. Snyder is not present for this negotiation."

Negotiation? Really?

"I'm listening."

One corner of his mouth ticked upward. "You will surrender to me, and Mr. Snyder will go free."

"What do you intend to do with me?"

"Deliver you to the Courts for a beheading and apology."

"I'm not feeling particularly apologetic at the moment."

He shrugged. "Then we move to Plan B."

I raised my brows. "Kill or capture me then torture Dylan for your trouble?"

The ogre smiled.

I had to admit, the faerie was smarter than most, and his calm confidence was far more threatening than the usual rigmarole.

"May I counter?"

"By all means," the ogre said.

I cast my eyes to the clowns. "You boys surrender whatever

gift you've been granted in exchange for absolution." My gaze fixed at the very large rabbit in a suit. "Then you're going to tell me where Dylan is to stop the pain."

He smirked, turning his back to me and strolling back into the darkness. "Plan B."

Quicker than should have been mortally possible, all four Fae Kissed pulled heavy caliber pistols from inside their coats and opened fire.

I released the transmog I'd been holding on the run, essence rippling out of my core to transform me into water. I threw myself into a forward kneeling slide and leaned back, ducking under probable bullet paths and preparing to bring myself back upright.

My plan went to hell in instants.

Magic-shrouded bullets bent their paths, following me low, and slamming into me with teeth-jarring impacts. Novae of pain exploded through me as the hollow point shells tore out chunks of essence. Mushrooming bullets opened up to release metallic sodium payloads that immediately ignited into blazing orange stars. Accompanying spell energy set the surrounding essence alight.

A rectangle of light opened in the warehouse's rear as the ogre exited, but the agony occupying my thoughts didn't leave room for pursuit. The gunmen fired again and shifted position to maintain a distant, four-pointed perimeter.

I threw myself sidelong and rolled for all I was worth.

The bullets pursued anyway, all four hitting.

I managed my feet, pushing the burning sodium out of my body by sheer, tormented will and bolting for the nearest cover. Their initial assault cost me the blades in my Karambit hilts. I extruded replacements, ducked out of cover and hurled one of the blades at my nearest attacker.

Essence tore away, a spinning s-shaped blade hurtling at the gunman. Separating the blade from my core almost didn't hurt compared to my other pains. My target stepped out of the blade's path, but he wasn't the only one who could control his ammunition.

At the last moment he jerked up his other fist, absorbing the essence blade into his suit sleeve.

Blighted hells!

The four Fae Kissed moved in eerie silence, repositioning to surround the huge industrial shelving I'd chosen for cover. I had almost no time, but I needed a new plan yesterday.

I like to think of myself as flexible, but reshaping myself to include armor on the fly seemed too much to bite off. Even so, I reformed with the thickest tactical armor I could recall from my garage encounter with Fae Kissed.

The gunmen kept to a distance that made thrown blades less of a risk, forcing me to add adapting my attacks to the long list of tasks on my already teetering plate.

Tucking away my hilts, I drew Ignis's hilt from behind my back. I hadn't had time to experiment with it, but I'd seen him launch crushing assaults with the bow he formed. His little blazing star arrows shot faster and farther, using far less essence than my own hurled blades.

Picturing Ignis's ornate, glowing bow I pushed essence into the hilt and focused on my memories of his weapon. I ended up with something vaguely bow-shaped with a string of essence connecting the ends.

Another shot hit me in the back. It hurt like hell, but the essence I'd layered into thick armor stopped the shot from penetrating. Facing Fae Kissed with bullets in my essence form had proven an effective advantage, but the sodium hollow points the Four Horseman of the Clown Factory used cost too much essence —not to mention the exothermic reaction that tried to boil me away one tiny metallic star at a time. I whirled toward the offending clown and pulled back on the bowstring.

The bow bent. The string pulled tight. Arrows, though, didn't just magically appear in the string.

Blight this is complicated.

I leapt through the shelf to dodge another shot, making the bullet impact on an old engine block. I planted my feet and pushed essence from the finger and thumb holding the bowstring, willing an arrow into existence.

Maintaining so much essence outside my body built up the pressure behind my eyes. It was bad enough I'd lost so much to the first bullet volley. It occurred to me I could try to create the arrow shaft in a kind of straw shape, transferring heat from the arrowhead to the back. In theory, the heat shift would create a steam rocket propulsion while allowing the arrow head to harden into a barbed ice spike.

It was an absolutely fantastic theory.

It also failed dismally.

I didn't have enough practice with the bow to build arrows on the fly while dodging magical bullets and aiming a weapon I had very little practical experience using.

Not all of my new ideas were bad.

I sucked back in my essence, shifting myself back to water and pushing out my wings. I'd thought only divine phoenixes could pull off this shape until I'd seen Ignis and Terrance shift their shape that way. I reformed into flesh as a bullet took me through the gut and sprayed blood onto the boxes behind me.

My arm could only flip a knife blade so far and so fast. It was a matter of physics more than strength. My wings however had greater flexibility, reach, and more easily leveraged strength. Shaping one of my wingtip feathers into a dagger of essence, I whipped a wing at the nearest gunman. The feather blade shot out a little off target, but aqua kinesis pushed it back on track.

Two of the gunmen ducked out of cover and took their shots. I batted a wing at the bullets, only being partially successful at deflecting the hits.

Saved myself a little pain.

My target's suit sleeve absorbed the magic feather.

I was in trouble.

Ranged assaults weren't working and every time I tried to

close with one of the gunmen, the other three shot. I'd lost essence. Blood trickled from several wounds that made it past my armor. I turned tail and bolted around the van. Breathing hard with my back covered by Chevrolet, I took a moment to rebalance my essence.

As the roaring waterfall of my blood in my ears calmed a bit, I noticed a low tone. I pushed around the waters of my essence to repair the damage I'd suffered and bolster my armor. The tinny hum intensified, splitting into two sounds a few moments before my assailants came around both sides of the van at once.

The two gunmen opened fire, seemingly unconcerned by the potential for crossfire. I let my essence snap back into flesh, launched myself up and vaulted off the top of the van with a handspring.

The hum vanished.

The tracking bullets tore chunks out of the van. Rather than earning another moment's respite, the two other gunmen fired from where they'd waited.

Both bullets hit high on my chest, breaking my collar bone in at least two places and sending red hot pokers of pain into my flesh. A shift of wing that made exfoliating with a cheese grater before a lemon juice bath sound like paradise turned me sideways to present a smaller target.

Not that it matters when their bullets don't miss.

The twist put me into an end-over-end cartwheel between them closer than I'd gotten to one of them yet. They fired again. I transmogrified into phoenix shape, rebalancing my essence with an agonized battle shriek.

The magic around their bullets fizzled away, and both shots missed. I slammed wings into both of them as hard as I could, willingly risking more broken bones just to score a hit. Thin wing bones shattered as Flag and Bloodface slammed into the nearest shelf full of crates.

The other two fired.

Another transmogrification allowed me to rebalance essence

to mend the broken bones, but it hurt like hell. I cried out once more, landing on one knee with my wings curved around me to protect my head.

Both shots missed.

I gasped breath that seemed the only sound other than my rushing pulse. On instinct, I transmogrified into a watery angel once more.

The hum returned, except it wasn't so much a hum as a kind of harmonic vibration.

I shifted back to flesh, and the sound vanished.

Understanding hit me like a Mack truck.

I'm hearing what they're doing on my essence.

My spare few moments of discovery allowed the gunmen to recover and reposition into their four-sided attack.

They fired.

I transmogrified into phoenix form, shrieked then swept my wings downward in a powerful thrust. The magical auras around the bullets fizzled out again as I sailed over their attack with only a few damaged tail feathers.

My shriek had overpowered or broken the spell harmonics they used to keep their bullets from missing. A dry chuckle escaped me.

I'm facing a Barbershop Quartet from Sweeney Todd.

I hadn't kept track of the number of bullets they'd fired, but I imagined they needed to reload soon. I didn't see any magazines laying discarded on the ground, but it seemed reasonable that Flag and Bloodface had reloaded while they waited to ambush me.

Time to take the fight to these guys in a personal way.

My true form was really too big for the warehouse, but the bird of prey cries had disenchanted their bullets. Wings offered me several maneuverability advantages, but so did the tactical armor. I transmogrified back into a watery form, rebalanced essence and shifted most of the way back to my current body. I kept the wings, and this time kept them essence. I also kept my feathered phoenix head, leaving me a modern-day Horus in tactical armor.

I swept my feet in the fluid circles of Hep-Silat, an ancient martial art taken from Indonesian origins by Egyptian sailors and reborn to honor the river god Hapi.

I beckoned all four with hands and wings. "Come get me, boys."

We fought in earnest—well, more earnest. Their tactics managed to keep me from slicing out any one throat and their suits still absorbed any essence blades I threw their way. The absorption raised niggling questions in the back of my mind. There was no way to tell if driving a Karambit blade into their chests when I finally caught one would actually penetrate their defense.

My change in tactics balanced the fight enough that one on four became mostly even odds.

Both my s-shaped blades and the sharpened feather daggers had been absorbed because they were essence. Shifting heat in the arrows I'd tried had turned them into icicle spike air-water rockets. I hadn't managed to hit them, but the tactic seemed sound.

It seems today is Weird Hybrid Experimentation Day.

I waited until the first of them dropped back to reload. When it happened, both of the clowns I hadn't named reloaded together. The practice motion took only moments, but in that time, I shifted the heat from one wing into my already-fiery core and hurled a trio of frozen feather knives at the first one that dropped his magazine.

The clown's suit didn't stop the ice. Blood blossomed from the Fae Kissed's neck and chest. I shrieked with satisfaction, dispelling the magic on the answering volley of bullets.

The other reloader let loose an enraged scream—the first noise I'd heard him utter—and charged me, emptying his new clip as fast as he could.

I hurled an ice knife barrage at him, but he hit his knees, sliding across the concrete in a move that was sure to shred the skin on his knees. He scooped up the downed gunman's pistol and started unloading that too.

The firing pattern he'd used had been purposefully haphazard enough that several bullets hit me despite my attempts to dodge. Before I could charge the kneeling man emptying his weapons, Flag and Bloodface bracketed him and fired one after another in a coordinated staccato.

I raced for cover, shifting to pure essence the moment I had a spare breath and rebalanced my essence. Neutralizing both their magic bullets and finding a way to penetrate their magical defenses had shifted the battle. The bullets they used were dangerous to both my flesh and essence forms. Up until that last barrage the Clown Quartet had conserved their ammunition and made the most of their shots. Maybe that was one gunman's rage, or maybe I'd changed the battle enough to force them into embracing more aggressive tactics.

Flag and Bloodface came at me from either end of the van. I leapt back onto the top, expecting the twin-gunner to be waiting. Instead, the van shifted under me. I vaulted off the top as a shotgun blast tore a hole through the van's roof. Several pellets hit my wings, and while they blasted their way through, it was immediately obvious the shot included metallic sodium.

The addition of the shotgun upped the stakes. Unfortunately, so did the pair of shrapnel grenades that rolled under the van toward my feet. I dove through the nearest industrial shelving, but not in time to put the crates and machine parts fully between me and the flesh-shredding projectiles.

Killing the gunman had changed the balance. His death had somehow crossed a line, escalating the conflict. I squinted through the pain back at the van to see Flag and Bloodface accept riot shields from inside the van.

Think!

There wasn't enough cover to avoid three explosive wielding gunmen and those shields would stop my newest attack cold. The only way to beat them was from behind, but three on one in the dim warehouse made hiding my approach all but impossible.

Sweat dripped from me.

I'd exerted myself a lot as well as rebalanced internal heat to create ice shards. The exothermic reactions of their sodium ammunition and pure fury added to the heat I was feeling. With all the damage I'd taken and essence I'd hurled at them, I wasn't at prime fighting weight any more.

Fortunately, Georgia humidity was usually thick enough to swim in during the summer. I didn't often try farming the air for water like Dylan's favorite movie hero—some whiny kid on a desert planet.

Moisture's moisture, though it'd be easier if I was drawing on clouds.

My eyes shot to the rafters over our battlefield.

Clouds...water in the air...fog.

My opponents flushed me out of cover. The warehouse was pretty warm already. If I could cool and concentrate the humidity in the air to a higher density, the resultant reaction should create fog. I needed that fog to be thick enough to obscure visibility. Ultimately that meant instead of drawing in airborne moisture to rejuvenate my strength, I needed to push more of my essence into the air, draw in the warmth of the air near the ground and force the fog to form with aqua kinesis.

Sure, no problem.

The next several minutes consisted of me running around the warehouse like a phoenix with his head chopped off, dodging bullets and concentrating the humidity. Fog formed, but since they'd shut off all of the property's water, I couldn't generate enough essence or strength to grow the cloudy bank all the way to the rafters. I settled for about eight feet and hid behind the van. I'd had marginal luck dampening the glow of essence no longer connected to me. I'd never been able to quell the glow of my core essence. So, I transmogrified my wings from water to feathers. I vaulted onto the van's top and into the rafters. The moment I managed my perch, I threw myself over to the other side of the warehouse, trying to obscure my intentions in case one of the gunmen had seen flashes of movement.

I'd used the van because I'd already used it for cover then jumped over it when attacked several times. If the trio of clowns couldn't see everyone in their group through the thick grey fog, they might—might—assume a repeat.

I perched in the darkest corner I could find and slowed my breathing to prevent being heard.

I waited.

The shorter-than-desired fog bank played to my advantage. Gunmen moving through the cloud created swirls and eddies that helped me track them like a shark fin parting water's surface. The clowns were able to use their targeting magic since I wasn't trying to disrupt their hum, but I was pretty sure they had to be able to see their target to guide shots.

I waited more.

I watched.

A flashback of Dylan playing video games that involved hiding overhead in shadows and taking out foes one by one made me smile.

He'd be so proud of me.

The thought immediately stabbed a knife in my gut. The ogre had him, would hurt him because I hadn't just given up. I needed to finish the clowns and get on the strange ogre's trail.

My tactic didn't work precisely like it had for Dylan's video game characters, but I killed the three remaining clowns with only a few new holes in me. When they were dead and I'd scoured them for possible clues, I drew in all the water in the room and power washed their flesh and bones into innocuous grit.

With nothing to lead me toward the ogre and Dylan, I hurried back to Mrs. Cox's apartment complex. I needed to set up my nest in a hurry, but more, I hoped Grynnberry might know something about this particular ogre.

Chapter Thirteen

Sky Conflicts

Vitae

I'd barely pulled into my parking space when Scurith rushed up to my door, ears pitched forward. I rolled the window down. "Yes?"

"Master, we have intelligence of a Sidhe battle not far to the west."

My lips curled. I stepped out of the car, pushing the tome I'd acquired from the willful and misinformed angel into Scurith's paws. I drew my fighting batons from behind my seat. "Excellent. Fetch me a half dozen enforcers. Perhaps I can finally reclaim my swords."

Scurith took the book. His eyes widened and his ears twitched, but both returned to their former position. He scurried into the hotel without another word.

I strode west, hands tightening and relaxing around my fighting batons. Anticipation hurried my pace until I was two blocks from the hotel when my black-painted trollmen enforcers jogged up to bracket me.

"I want prisoners, but if you glimpse the Champion swords,

you are to ignore all others combatants until you've reclaimed my blades."

The once dead bodyguards didn't so much as grunt.

I pushed essence into my hilts as the press of taint prickled hair along my arms and legs. Part of me wanted to connect the bladed batons into a lajatang, but twin weapons offered more flexible assault options.

My pace slowed to allow a confident swagger in my swaying hips. I stepped into the mouth of an alley only to find two forces watching me enter from walls against opposite buildings.

"I told you," a Seelie knight said.

His Unseelie opposite sneered. "I guess we won't get to shed your blood after all."

"By the Undying Light—"

Both groups screamed battle cries and charged me.

My trollmen drove bodily into the enemy, taking up the entire alley's width lined up shoulder-to-shoulder. Gnolls and briarlings, goblins and orcs slammed into my defenders. Meaty greenish fists crushed bones as faerie blades hacked away chunks of enforcer.

Movement along the back of their combined mob drew my eyes skyward. Something combining one part woman and two parts humming bird buzzed into the air. Three long, mosquito-like noses pointed my way and led a diving assault.

Hergies

I spun side to side, dodging thrusting beaks. Following through on my evasive spin, I launched crescent blades of essence in the hergies' wake. I missed one, but my second strike sheered a wing from one of the hergies.

Another trio dove at me.

I sidestepped and spun, axe blade coming down to cleave a hergy in half. An elven Unseelie knight bisected one of my trollmen and rushed through the subsequent gap. Blade to baton, our weapons flashed through elaborate cuts and parries, feints and ripostes.

Hergies dove at me again. I dodged in a way meant to move

my elven opponent into their strafing assault, but the flying fey rolled around the elf's head without upsetting a single hair.

A trollman snatched up his severed arm and hurled it at a passing hergy only to lose his other arm to a briarling's troll blade. The briarling darted in to take advantage of his success, only to have the baby-sized arm regrowing from the sliced side of the downed trollman seize his ankle. The trollman's still full-sized arm grabbed the briarling's other leg and made a wish.

"I want prisoners!"

The Unseelie elven knight renewed his onslaught, driving me back toward the alley's entrance. I couldn't allow our altercation to enter mortal view, so I kicked off a loafer and hamstrung him with a foot transmogrified back into a talon.

His blade drove through my sternum.

For a moment, red-gold filled my vision. Desire to thrust a hand into his chest and tear away his life force blinded my reason for an instant. The sudden agony of an iron spike in my shoulder snapped me out of my rage.

I yanked a rubber band wrapped three-inch nail from my skin, brought the flat of my bladed baton down on the elf and glanced up to a whirl of blazing pixie lights.

A beefy-looking pixie blazed acid green as he spun like an airborne top. Each arm held the ankle of a smaller sprite clutching an iron nail partially wrapped in a rubber band. Three other muscled sprites flew into view, each with two nail-toting helpers.

The concussed elf sliced a curved dagger across the back of my leg. Severed hamstrings released me to tumble. Nails rocketed away from careful grips in a haphazard barrage, peppering my sprawled form.

I transmogrified, rebalanced and launched myself into the air.

Pixies squeaked and darted in every direction.

A hergy drove its rapier-like beak into my back.

Another dove past me only to angle up sharply through my wing.

I transmogrified again, hitting the ground hard enough to twist my newly-repaired ankle.

Gnolls tackled me, driving me to the ground by sheer weight. Teeth shook and tore at my flesh. Trollmen seized the canid faeries. Pained yelps escaped the gnolls' and my own lips as my enforcers ripped locked jaws away.

My palms shoved away the canid faeries, failing to dislodge them until great gouts of fire escaped my hands to set the gnolls alight like furry roman candles.

The elven Seelie Knight appeared, bloodied and disheveled, to drive a thrust at my heart. A bolt of violet power drove through his face, exploding brains in all directions.

I climbed to my feet, eldritch power pulsing around me in time with my seething breath. "By the Undying Light, you will lay down your arms and surrender."

Power washed out of me.

The lesser faeries stopped fighting, weapons tumbling from their hands even as trollmen punched them.

The Unseelie knight cursed me and thrust a blade up toward my groin. I transmogrified my lower half just ahead of the dastardly blow, shifting one leg into a talon and wrapping it around his throat.

Hatred snarled from my lips laced with power. "Surrender or your punishment will eclipse your worst nightmares."

A trollman kicked him in the head before he could answer.

Hergies and pixies took advantage of my distraction to bolt.

It took all of my will not to assume my true form and rip the little vermin out of my sky.

Instead, I turned to my seven trollmen. "Collect the fey and take them to the cages." I gestured to a body regrowing from the shoulder of a severed arm. "Don't forget your body parts."

The Sidhe had banded together to ambush me. They'd used iron against me despite the danger to themselves. I had to answer their ingenuity with cunning.

I must expand my trollmen into the air.

Quayla

Grynnberry was holding a cocktail party when I arrived. Entertaining a strange faerie wasn't really a cocktail party, but he was doing it in what was supposed to be my semi super-secret hide out.

I growled his name by way of greeting. "Grynnberry—"

He exploded to full human size, hands raised. "Whoa, slow your boil, Quayla. This isn't what you think it is."

I drew a Karambit hilt.

Grynnberry gestured. "This is Cember. I'm not real fond of Unseelie, but this one's working for your boy Ignis."

"No one is supposed to know I'm hiding here, Grynn."

Cember exploded into human form too, though his was less playgirl model and more noir detective. "Shield Aquaylae, Grynnberry did not reveal your location. I sleuthed it out on my own as far as the building, then came over to this apartment when I sensed the nymph. He's kept me from leaving for the last several hours." Cember shot Grynnberry a nasty look. "I've already missed one meeting with a new client, so I'd like to get this out of the way while I can."

"Get what out of the way?"

"Shield Ignis hired me to...," Cember shot Grynnberry a sideways glance. "...to find the culprit who stole your Shield's eggs."

I rolled my eyes. "Great, thanks, considering Dunham's already captured most of my Shield and used the eggs to enslave them, that's real helpful information, or would have been a week ago."

Cember pushed a hand into his trench coat pocket, drew out a pixie-sized scroll, handed it over and tucked his hand in the pocket once more. "Even so, I'm required to deliver this information to complete my deal with Shield Ignis."

"Yeah, right," I unrolled the scroll.

A shift in Grynnberry's weight caught my peripheral vision. I looked up from the still-unread scroll and narrowed my eyes. "Grynn? Something wrong?"

"Well, yeah, I've gotten word about your boy toy getting captured and we're wasting time on information you already have."

My gaze sharpened. "You know where they took Dylan?"

"I got word right before Cember showed up. I was about to come looking for you, but I had to keep him from leaving and telling anyone your whereabouts."

A few hours ago. I've known less than an hour.

I glanced at Cember.

His eyes met mine, shot to the scroll and then darted nervously toward Grynnberry. I rubbed the parchment between my fingers, stopping a moment later lest I smear the ink. It was possible Grynnberry had learned of the abduction before I'd been approached. He'd offered me good information on several occasions over the time I'd known him, but usually he had to go to the Courts for information.

"I thought you were laying low here, Grynn."

"Yeah, so?"

"Don't you normally eavesdrop to get information?"

Grynnberry stiffened, clearly affronted. "I have other contacts."

"So, you're not just a conniving sneak thief?" Cember asked.

"Weren't you in a hurry?" Grynnberry asked.

Something wasn't right.

Grynnberry's claims weren't impossible, but they felt askew somehow. Cember had said he was in a hurry, but he seemed unwilling to leave before I read the scroll.

Some kind of inter-Court politics?

I dropped my eyes back toward the scroll. Grynnberry stopped breathing, going fully still. I dropped the scroll, whipped forward and brought my newly-extruded Karambit to his throat.

"Hey, what the hell?" Grynnberry spluttered.

"I don't know what's going on, but I am really not in the mood for faerie bullshit. Where is Dylan?"

"I'm not going to tell you with a knife to my throat. That's not how friends treat one another."

I put all of my anger and hurt, fear and frustration into my gaze. "We're not friends, Grynnberry. You've been a huge nuisance that I've put up with because of occasional tidbits of good information. Problem is, I suddenly wonder if the trouble I had at all the tip locations had something to do with you."

"Quayla, babe, I'm a nymph, not one of the movers and shakers in the Courts. You said it yourself. Most of my tips were from information I overheard, but I gave you the best I had."

On a hunch, I blew into Grynnberry's face.

He didn't fall unconscious, but rather drove a fist into my gut and kicked backward. My slice still drew a bloody line across his throat, but not deep enough to be fatal. Grynnberry reached over his shoulders, grabbing his wings and tearing them away from his body. As he did so, the glamour disguising the twin blades vanished.

"You're going to die for this, Unseelie," Grynnberry snarled.

"You first, Anseelie." Cember drew a pistol from his pocket. "Don't move, Sir Jahriss."

"Sir?" I said over my shoulder.

"Shield Aquaylae, allow me to introduce Sir Jahriss, Knight of the Anseelie Court, Champion of the exiled Wyldfae queen."

Grynnberry launched an assault at me, golden cutlasses hacking through the space my head had been a moment before. My splits dropped me under his cut. I thrust both Karambits into his torso in an upward cut. Cember shot Grynn in the face three times for good measure. Before Grynnberry could react, I swept his legs, dropping him onto the ground. I used the sweep momentum to come up onto my feet and drive both knives into a sideways sweep across his chest and throat.

Cember shot him again, but Grynnberry was already dead.

I whipped around to face Cember.

The Unseelie dropped the gun unceremoniously to the floor and raised his hands. "Not your enemy."

"You're a Sidhe," I growled. "That makes you my enemy."

He rolled his eyes. "World's not black and white, girlie."

I read the scroll he provided, confirming Cember's accusations. "Blight, he was my only lead on Dylan."

"Hey, I've kept my end of the bargain. Can I go?"

I glared at him. "In the name of the Undying Light, in accordance with—"

"Whoa, have a look." Cember held out a stone.

A work visa grant scrolled across the tablet in fiery phoenix essence. For whatever reason, Ignis had granted this Unseelie the right to live in Creation—explaining his insistence in completing his side of his bargain with Ignis.

An idea struck me. "Can you find where they're keeping Dylan?"

The grizzled face he offered the world smirked. "Sure. Tell me what you know, what you need to know and I'll explain my rates."

Vitae

I folded the ancient scroll along long-ingrained creases and closed an ancient leather cover around it. I'd read the tome delivered by the angelic messenger three times.

No wonder He replaced them with us.

Reading the instructions thrice might have been overly thorough, but collecting the ingredient offered enough challenge without being forced to gather them more than once due to ignorance or poor planning.

Scurith bowed into the room. "Pardon, Mist-Master, but—"

"Good, Scurith, I have tasks for you."

Scurith's brows rose. "Yes, Master?"

"We will need several rare components to complete the oracle, some we may be forced to obtain from Faery or the Goblin Market."

Scurith cleared his throat. "Master, after what happened—"

"I'm sure you'll find a way," I let menace enter my voice. "Surely, you'd rather avoid repeating your predecessor's disappointing performance. Wouldn't you?"

"Yes," Scurith squeaked, eyeing me sullenly through his lashes. "Yes, Master. Give me the list. I will see it done."

"Good boy. My thrall has run into trouble acquiring us more bodies to make enforcers. My recent battle worked out a solution on that count, but illuminated a new need for deceased wafers. We're going to need to raid the graveyards for more forces. Start with Oakland Cemetery. You're to focus your collections on obtaining children's corpses."

"Did you say children, Master? You wish us to kidnap waf—"

"No, not kidnap, dig up. Child wafers will be more pliable once reborn. Their smaller bodies will also make flight easier to obtain."

"Flight, Master? I don't understand."

"I must have winged enforcers. Airborne minions will serve me well in the battle ahead."

"I shall see your commands obeyed," Scurith said.

I dismissed Scurith with a gesture. "Be about it."

"Master, begging your pardon, but I bring news you may wish to hear."

I raised my brows. "Go on."

"Word has come to us that a mortal has been captured by one of the Anseelie."

"What is that to me?"

"To you, perhaps nothing, but to the mortal's lover, Shield Aquaylae, the mortal's whereabouts seems of dire consequence."

Anger flashed through me at the sound of my shield's name. The heat of my blossoming temper rose to twice the firestorm as my predictions of the future became reality.

"Do you know where the wafer is being kept?"

"I do, Master. What is your will?"

"Fetch my armor, I shall see about wrenching Aquaylae's paramour from the just dessert delivered on them both."

"You are ever a magnanimous leader, Master."

Scurith scurried from my sight. I rose, setting the precious book gently atop another of my mentor's old Homer manuscripts with a frustrated sigh.

At least rescuing her paramour will bring Aquaylae back into the fold in time to serve my purposes assembling the oracle.

I descended toward the lower depths to collect a few enforcers and make my will regarding aerial forces known to my thrall.

Bradley

Bradley woke, pulling his phone to shed light inside the body drawer. He yawned, shaking off the last vestiges of a nightmare. He always had nightmares sleeping in the drawer, but he'd also dreamed up some of his best ideas sleeping like the dead.

His Master needed to create some sort of sensor grid, connecting small motes of essence in ways that kept tampering and destruction to a minimum. He hadn't charged Bradley to deploy the things—not that it mattered. The hotel he'd found his Master housed enough bowing and scraping fantasy creatures to see the task done.

He checked his bank account. Enough money remained in his account to purchase the items his subconscious had come up with, but he also needed to see about his rent.

I'll need to ask Master about some money to cover my expenses.

He could steal some of what he needed from the morgue's supplies, but he'd been ordered to keep his job. The order gladdened Bradley. He adored his job despite all the bureaucratic bullshit. Instead of steal, he stopped in to visit the office of the biggest prick the coroners had.

Ashley looked up from her desk outside Mercer's office.

Bradley hadn't expected the attractive blond to be at work so late. Her expression flickered before her professional smile rose to the occasion.

Bradley stared at her.

Something wasn't right. She seemed flush and flustered, which wasn't something he'd come to expect from her. One of the buttons on her blouse was in the wrong hole.

"Doctor Mercer is unavailable, Doctor Sky, is there something I can do for you?"

Talking to her had never been easy. Pretty and confident, she was the exact type of woman that glued his tongue to the roof of his mouth. He checked the time on his phone. It was almost seven. Mercer seldom left later than two in the afternoon.

Does he come back after his golf game and work some kind of split shift I didn't know about?

Ashley pushed a hand through her blond bob, fingers tangling a moment. His eyes narrowed at the odd clumping of her hair. It took him a moment for a theory to form. If what Bradley thought he saw was real, then Mercer deserved what Bradley'd planned for him and more.

Master Vitae provided rationed amounts of the blood formula used to create the enforcers. He's been very specific about its use, but he's also insisted Bradley experiment to improve Master Vitae's options. Bradley had brought a small vial of the blood with him to analyze in his office's quiet—though he hadn't gotten the chance.

The formula allowed greater control over the reborn human-trollman—a good thing since Whiskers—Bradley's reanimated roadkill—refused Bradley's commands to attack Master Vitae. Creating the trollmen presented an even greater peril. Sure, the humans had more complex brains than the cat and thus could understand and adopt training better, but they were also more dangerous for the same reason.

Master Vitae's formula somehow forced unquestioned

control onto the trollmen, not only for his orders, but orders Bradley gave on his behalf.

"Doctor Sky?"

Bradley braced himself for what was to come, less concerned about having an actual conversation with the woman than what he intended to do to her. He tucked a hand in his lab coat and worked the top of his serum vial open with finger and thumb. "Good evening, Ashley. I was going to leave Doctor Mercer a message, but if he's in, I can wait."

She paled, blinking at Bradley as if he were the victim of a new and unusual murder. "It would be better if you left a message."

"All right." He strode forward. "I wanted his opinion on this sampl—"

Bradley tripped, splashing her with the bloody serum. Ashley shrieked, trying but failing to jump clear. There wasn't a lot, but almost half of it hit her skin above the misaligned collar.

She shrieked. "You weird, horrible little bastard!"

The intercom keyed on, Doctor Mercer sounding out of breath. "Ashley, is there a problem?"

"Tell him everything is fine," Bradley whispered.

A nasty comment perched on her lips but failed to exit. She looked at the phone. "Everything is fine, Doctor."

"Then keep the noise down. I don't want to draw any undue attention," Mercer's voice became pointed. "Do you?"

She looked at Bradley.

He shrugged.

"No, Doctor." Ashley disconnected the line.

"Obviously something is going on out here and in there, spill."

The words tumbled out of Ashley's mouth and tears followed. Mercer was blackmailing her and at least one other assistant for sexual favors. He'd forced them to do degrading things, recording them without their knowledge and then had doubled down on the extortion.

Bradley listened, heat building in his gut. Mercer was

controlling the women, forcing them to do things they didn't want to do. In the clear moments of thought, guilt stabbed Bradley in the nads. He'd used the serum to do the exact same thing.

"You don't have to tell me, but is Mercer doing anything else illegal?" Bradley asked.

"Prescription fraud. Filing insurance claims for procedures he's claiming happened before the patients died."

Bradley checked the serum vial. There wasn't much left.

How much does it take?

"Are you interested in helping me put him away?"

"I am," Ashley chewed a lock of hair. "But I don't want the things he made me do becoming public."

"I think I can do both, but I'll have to ask you to pretend like we never had this conversation. Would you be willing to do that?"

Ashely nodded.

"I'm sorry about your blouse."

She looked away. "He'd already ruined it."

Bradley offered his best smile. "Don't worry, I'm going to ruin him much worse."

He headed up to his car, leaving Ashley to clean herself up. The further he got from the situation, the more his anger waned and the less important Ashley's situation became. He had to work out the new seed network.

My growing apathy is related to my waning anger. I have to stay angry about this so I can help.

He focused on the horrible things she'd told Bradley. Ashley hadn't been graphic, but he had little trouble filling in the gaps. Mercer had always struck him as an insufferable asshole with delusions of godhood. Bradley just hadn't known how much Mercer had turned delusions into reality.

He pictured the things Mercer made Ashley do, trying to stay angry enough to keep on mission. Ashley's harsh words about Bradley flashed back to mind and in an instant, he pictured her on her knees doing to him what she'd done for Mercer. He was already planning to enslave Mercer with a dose of serum, but another small dose would make her his slave.

Bradley shook the selfish thought away, anger and self-loathing helped clear his mind even more.

How could I think such a thing? Forcing people into things is wrong.

Guilt returned.

Bradley was planning to force Mercer to destroy the blackmail evidence, write the prescriptions Bradley needed and then turn himself in with proof of his other crimes.

That's not the same as making some girl into an object. This is justice.

Bradley got back to the hotel, collected the samples he needed and returned to the morgue. He dealt with Mercer, picked up the boxes of hypodermic needles Mercer prescribed, and headed for the craft store with only a bruised conscience.

He had given Ashely one last order—to forget Bradley's actions—and even though it had been best for everyone, he still felt badly about it.

The cash Mercer surrendered financed a trip to the craft store, buying thousands of self-adhesive googly eyes. Mercer's ill-gotten gains also paid for dollar store roach baits, ant baits and cheap cat collars.

Bradley returned to the hotel, obtained essence from Master Vitae and went to work injecting the essence into eyes and traps with the needles. He adhered some of the filled eyes on the collars. When he'd completed enough to perfect the operation, he enlisted faerie help.

There was a time when seeing all these fantasy creatures was so cool.

Once all of the essence had been exhausted, he sent them out into Atlanta with eyes and traps and dirty needles. "Put the collars on rats and pigeons and the mangiest alley cats you can find. Stick the eyes on those 'we buy cash houses' signs and political signs and street signs."

When the first wave left, Bradley returned to Master Vitae for more essence. At first, Vitae refused, doing something that let Bradley's Master reach out to the seeds. Whatever Vitae found met with his approval. He granted Bradley direct access to the back lab where the essence was kept.

Master Vitae led Bradley to a stone basin marked with runes like some kind of Dungeons and Dragons artifact. "You will never empty essence from this basin, but you may utilize my reserve for the various projects you're assigned."

Chapter Fourteen

Essence of Sacrifice

Dunham

Dunham paced a large square around the caged phoenixes. Heat radiated out of the Pyri's cage. The pentagram restraining the divine dimmed enough to cause concern.

"Problem?" Viviane asked.

"The Terra is overdue."

"I thought you had him under both control and surveillance."

Dunham hated admitting any kind of failure to Viviane. He hated disappointing her after everything she'd done to see him to the brink of success. "She lost her watchers."

"My agents have sold another pair of incursion points. We need to send a shield to the impending battle," Viviane said.

Dunham examined the cages. Both the Vitae and Aquaylae had somehow escaped him thus far. Both their nests had been full when he'd acquired them, but in addition to fueling both pentagrams, he'd employed their essence to strengthen his abilities. He needed essence from all five elements to keep the divine in place. With the essence levels out of balance, he'd had to configure the circle to consume Aero, Pyri and Terra essence at a higher rate.

The Terra had contributed enough additional essence to keep

the divine imprisoned and fuel a rebirth if necessary. Caelum hadn't fully recovered from his punishment, but he'd set by enough essence as well. The Pyri had flatly refused even when tortured. The Pyri's cage hadn't been designed to siphon off essence from an unwilling captive.

Never thought something like that would be necessary.

On the one hand, Dunham needed the Pyri out of his cage and on a mission so that the confinement chamber could be modified. On the other, he really didn't want to have more than one of his prizes absent at a time until he'd successfully proven them safely under control. Moreover, he'd planned on only dispatching one shield at a time, allowing him to avoid splitting his will controlling more than one. The strategy also allowed each phoenix to rest and regenerate essence in the case of deaths.

Dunham focused on the divine. Despite the amount of power Dunham had syphoned off the phoenix, he'd recovered far faster than the others. The stronger the divine got, the more important having essence enough to contain him became.

There's no way I can send Caelum out in the shape he's in.

Viviane watched him, an air of impatience beneath her smug nonchalance. She needed Dunham to act, to send a phoenix out against the battling Sidhe. The Pyri was all he had, but he couldn't risk the Pyri vanishing like the Terra.

I don't have any choice then, I have to accompany the Pyri.

The prospect offered innumerable risks. Of all the shields he'd captured, the Pyri offered the greatest outright physical danger and the greatest amount of resistance to control.

At least, I thought I'd had the Terra under control.

"Summon the Terra back with his egg. I will see to restoring him to his cage while you're away."

Dunham measured Viviane's posture, the set of her face. He'd known her for centuries, a domineering but supportive mother. She'd frequently known the course of his thoughts, sometimes even before he'd known them himself.

"Is there any way to get more life and water essence to bolster our supply?" Dunham asked.

Viviane smiled, sashaying across the room to him. She placed her left hand on his chest and kissed up the line of his neck. "I've already seen to it, sweet boy. My agents will deliver it soon. Do what you must do."

Of course, you have.

Without the duties burdening the other two of the Dark Trinity, she'd been able to focus her resources into other areas. She didn't have underling rulers and their accompanying entour-ages presiding over shires like Atlanta. Wyldfae weren't allowed more than a token voice in the regional councils, allowing Viviane to invest her more powerful faeries to act unchallenged in Creation —often masquerading as a lesser, weaker faerie.

Viviane controlled practically every transaction in the Goblin Markets by simple virtue of having her Anseelie servants serve as the drudge workers gathering resources and the merchants bartering the goods.

A chuckle escaped him. He'd taken her lead and grown a global corporate powerhouse much the same way. Her network of Anseelie had allowed him to acquire resources without respect to borders or border controls.

Dunham crossed to the Terra's cage, bent over the foot and dug his fingers into the imbedded egg. "Return to your cage at once."

He tightened his grip and repeated the command twice more. Thrice ordered, he left the Terra to Viviane's care. He retrieved the ever-burning heart of the Pyri and held the sympathetic ruby in his opposite hand.

"Raise the cage shield."

Viviane didn't move.

Dunham glanced back at her. "Please raise the Pyri's cage?"

She smirked and sashayed over to the control console. A moment later the robotic arms whirred to life. Metal screeched against metal in a squeal like a thousand fingernails on chalkboards as the motors forced the heat-warped metal to move. A blast wave of fire canceled all the effort of the air conditioning system.

An angel of living fire threw itself at the magical barrier, eyes blazing with hatred. The Pyri hit the barrier twice more, trying to bash his way through the magic.

Dunham squeezed both the egg and the Pyri's heart. "That is enough of that. You will be still."

Both the objects in Dunham's hands heated, searing his skin. He kept his grip, wishing he had the option of using silicon gloves instead of having to endure the pain to exert control.

"I like your rage, Pyri. You're going to need it."

"You're going to need two billion SPF sunblock when I get my hands on you."

Dunham tightened his grip and exerted his will. "You will obey my commands, Pyri. You will fulfill the mission I assign without deviation and return directly here for insertion back into your cage."

The Pyri glowered for all he was worth, forcing Dunham to inflict pain through both heart and egg.

"I acknowledge receipt of commands and will obey."

The Pyri's tone set Dunham's hackles on end. "Obey what? Who? I command you to answer truthfully."

"I will obey the mandate given me by my creator."

"In this case you are correct, you will obey your mandate by obeying my commands first and foremost. You will stop an incursion, exterminating all of the Sidhe, correction, all of the Seelie and Unseelie we find. Acknowledge receipt of command and your compliance to obey these orders."

Dunham fought the Pyri's towering will for what felt like an hour, eventually forcing the fiery creature to oath obedience. "You will not attempt to harm me or any of mine before or during this mission. If you encounter one of your other shields, you will subdue, capture and return them here to me. Acknowledge receipt of command and your compliance to obey these orders."

The Pyri didn't fight Dunham as hard as before, but he didn't relent or respond immediately either.

Dunham withdrew a handkerchief and wiped the sweat from his brows. He turned to find Viviane's lips pressed into a thin line.

She's displeased, but why? I won out in a battle of wills against a greater being many times my age.

I folded my hands behind my back and addressed the Pyri. "I've arranged a shower, fresh clothes and a meal if you are amenable. There is no reason for our relationship to be adversarial if you will stop fighting the inevitable."

The Pyri's eyes blazed the orange of hot coals. "Only the end of the world is inevitable, wafer. You will not cage me and my siblings forever." The Pyri's lips curled up in a menacing smile. "Your orders reveal you can't even control those of us you've captured."

"If you'd rather travel caged in a container like a beast than accept my offer of hospitality, then I can accommodate you."

"Bring on the cage," the Pyri snarled.

Quayla

I put the finishing touches on the last rune and stepped back to admire the aluminum catch pan turned nest. Notes littered the area, scribbled attempts to learn runes Anima described but couldn't really show me after the Isaac's reprimand. Even without being able to show me, she'd watched me inscribe the lines and corrected my technique until we both felt I could successfully inscribe the basin.

Apprehension knotted my gut. The runes normally had to be chiseled into the stone basins, but we'd been forced to use Sharpie. If I'd made a mistake, I'd have to try again on a fresh catch pan.

"Well?"

"I am now sensing your new nest," Anima said. "Good work."

Her praise made me smile. "Thanks, but all the credit for this success goes to you."

"You did the scribing, and now you will have to do the even harder part."

Fill the damn thing.

The shallow lip on the catch pan meant standing in the center, hacking off a leg and letting the water fall wouldn't work. Too much essence would escape the basin that way. I sprawled across the floor and tucked my forearm into the pan. It took two tries to transmogrify only my arm, but my control improved with each time I pushed my abilities to a new skill.

Instead of extruding a serrated blade from one of my Karambit hilts, I grabbed the wooden flute that Ignis employed as his weapon hilt. The forward curving blade of a Karambit wasn't suited to cutting inside the pan. I pushed essence out of one end of the alternate hilt until my head throbbed. The resultant short sword didn't reach the length of a wakizashi, but it was the longest blade I'd ever managed. Sawing into my arm cut short my little victory celebration and put a damper—pun not intended—on my day.

There isn't time for any kind of procrastination, not while the ogre has Dylan.

I regrew the arm by rebalancing my essence only to saw it off again. Repeatedly mauling myself was more torture than the hours of tear jerkers I'd used to fill my nest before, but it was much faster. I bent over the basin to ensure my agonized tears dripped into the rapidly-filling basin.

Rebirth essence always had to be concentrated. Otherwise, a nest required enough volume to contain the liquid equivalent of three whole bodies. The shallow depth of my aluminum basin required me to will even higher concentration.

I chugged another pitcher of healing slurry, washing it down with an equal amount of water. It took extreme will not to vomit up both.

My stomach distended enough that had my body been female I would've looked four months pregnant. It would take a few hours for the slurry to replenish my essence. I could dope the water instead of drinking it, but thinning my essence bodily weakened my abilities and diluting the content of my new nest risked rebirth complications like I'd suffered defending the sanctum.

Rebalancing my essence for the last time left me a bit thinner than strictly healthy. "Ani?"

"You will lose mass, but I am confident you will be reborn."

"Let's hope I can stay alive long enough that we don't have to test that." I slid the almost-full nest into a prepared closet, careful not to splash any over the shallow sides.

The chocolate in my bag called to me, but if I intended to risk vomiting, I was better filling my stomach with the last of the high fat, high protein healing slurry.

Really rather have chocolate though.

I rewarded myself with a mini square of dark Ghirardelli and thought positive thoughts.

There's always room for chocolate.

Anima's voice drifted out of the closet rather than the angel figurine. "What now?"

I paced back and forth in front of the closet. I wasn't sure how to answer her. The best course of action was sleep. Without Vitae's essence to speed my recovery, sleep would do the most to rebuild my essence. The problem with that action was the hours it left Dylan at the nonexistent mercy of the Sidhe.

I'd hired Cember to find where they'd taken Dylan. The Unseelie had a far greater chance of ferreting out where the ogre or the Four Clowns of Sweeney Todd had taken my former lover.

Unfortunately, that meant waiting. Waiting meant I should rest, but neither appealed to me. I turned back to the hideous apartment and squared my shoulders. "Clean up."

Staying at the apartment was part of an agreement with Mrs.

Cox to clean up the mess left behind by the last tenant. The sharp, old woman wouldn't tolerate me laying down on the job and I'd never put it past her to check at random intervals. I needed to make some progress to prevent her coming in and cleaning the place out herself—including my new nest.

"You really should rest, Quayla," Anima said.

"I hear you, Ani, but I just can't settle right now."

"But cleaning?" Anima asked. "You've never seemed naturally drawn to tidiness."

"Yeah, but I need to do something."

"Then you are in luck," Anima said. "I've detected a large amount of Terrance's essence. I cannot be sure, but it seems he's left some behind for retrieval."

My pulse quickened. Getting Terrance back meant help on so many levels. It meant not having to carry the burden of the entire territory on my shoulders. It meant having an older, wiser shield to help me plan my rescue of the others.

Viviane

She pursed her lips as Dunham escorted the specially-designed mobile cage he'd built. The battle of wills between the captured Pyri Ignis and Dunham remained far too close for her purposes.

The boy had always been strong willed, but Ignis's temper proved Dunham's superior. Without both the egg and Ignis's heart, Dunham would've lost, costing her decades of preparation.

I'll have to see what I can do about that.

A thought struck her.

Did Dunham invoke the divine essence he consumed? If he didn't, then the only reason for so close a battle of wills was his own hubris.

A flicker of anger kindled in her heart, but she willed it down. The boy was pliable if handled correctly. She'd see that he employed all of his resources next time he ordered Ignis to a task.

Viviane strolled to the dumbwaiter installed in the small kitchen, pulling open the door to flood the room with the aroma of garlic, herbs and grilled rabbit. She shifted the trays onto a rolling cart and wheeled them over to the control console.

The robotic arms raised Caelum and Terrance's cages. The air phoenix's eyes flicked open, and he inhaled stealthily.

A smile curled her lips.

Little Caelum is playing the little lamb.

She let free an exasperated sigh. "As adorable as your attempt to deceive us is, Caelum, if you are in the state you're portraying, you aren't strong enough to eat, so I might as well enjoy your dinner myself."

Caelum made a show of struggling up toward exhausted attentiveness.

Viviane rolled her eyes and gave him slow applause. "You do realize I can command you through your egg too, do you not?"

Caelum's feminine voice was pretty, birdlike, but with the steel behind it, that bird was all raptor. "I didn't know that, Viviane."

She picked up the half rabbit, hot grease sizzling on contact with her fingers. She muttered a spell as she approached Caelum's cage and pushed the roasted carcass through the barrier.

Caelum threw a fist at her through the wall of magical force just above where the rabbit penetrated, shattering the bones in his delicate hands.

Viviane shook her head, tsking and licking her fingers. "I'm a bit smarter than that."

He snatched the hot, greasy meat from his naked lap with one hand while his arm blurred to a cloudy, swirling essence from injured fingers to shoulder. Moments later, the arm solidified, and both brought the hot flesh to pert bowtie lips.

"Eat up. You'll need your strength soon."

Viviane left Caelum to his meal, muttering the spell twice

more. She deposited the rabbit into Ignis's and Terrance's cages under the ravenous watchful eyes of Summuseraphi. Summus had recovered well thanks to the double portions she fed the divine, but she'd been forced to feed him only occasionally to prevent Dunham from learning of his special treatment.

Without all five shields available to provide balanced essence, Dunham wouldn't want Summus's strength returned so quickly.

She had plans for the divine's strength.

Viviane rolled the cart over to the summoner's stone and carefully positioned the two rabbit halves. She stripped off her clothes and stepped onto the stone. A slight laugh escaped her.

Dunham's poor performance has me distracted.

She crossed to the Arch created for travel into her special pocket of Faery. She'd been exiled from Faery proper, but her rivals had allowed her the simple, little sanctuary since it served to remind her of all she'd lost. Little did they know that while she'd never left her tiny island, she'd created plenty of ways from her sanctum throughout all of Faery.

"Pardon me, my Queen."

Viviane turned to find a coyll on the top stair to Dunham's quarters. Her brows rose. "You're not supposed to come here, Scurith."

"I know, Your Majesty, but I have news I thought best in your hands while the chance offered itself."

"Speak."

Scurith related Vitae's desperate search for the other Champion swords, his hatred of Aquaylae and his newest designs. Viviane listened, astounded at the Vitae's temerity as much as his cleverness. The mortal thrall the life phoenix had enlisted seemed almost heaven sent, a troubling possibility she'd rather not have considered.

"Convince him Dolumii's failures will make him reluctant to enter Creation," Viviane said.

"You wish him to pursue the blade into Faery?"

She shook her head. "I don't want the others to have him before I am ready."

"What would you have me do?"

"Play your part, Scurith. Whisper rumors of faerie magic freeing prisoners from the Champion blades. Stoke his hunger for the blade tempered with cautions that make him desire more Sidhe magic."

"He's becoming unstable, Majesty."

She smirked, withdrawing four small vials. "I expected that. Dose his nest with these, two now and one with each rebirth."

"When these are used up?"

Viviane gave him a bright smile. "Vitae's hubris will take over from there, Scurith. Everything is falling into place."

"May you reign soon and long."

She dismissed the coyll and turned back to the Arch. Will and power fueled the gateway. A shimmering gateway opened. Her assorted servants waited on the other side—one more than she'd expected.

Yarque rested on a nearby stone in Zwiesel-style attire, the diminutive old faerie made larger by the eggplant atop his head acting as a hat. His legs dangled from a stone bracketing a runed amphora filled with Terrance's essence. Oshyn and a pair of his brownies toted smaller, wax-sealed vessels full of Caelum's essence. Thatch balanced two jars hung from a staff across his diminutive shoulders, each filled with life essence taken from a distant Shield. The surprise however was her Champion—Knight Jahriss, standing bold as a brass brazier in his true form.

Her brows rose.

He kneeled beside a large cider jar of watery essence. "My Queen. Shield Aquaylae discovered my true identity."

"I thought you said she was too dense to look beyond your pretense," Viviane said.

"The Unseelie refugee Cember revealed me."

"I assume you've killed him?"

"Not yet, my Queen."

"Did you reveal to her the purpose behind the animal thefts?" Viviane asked.

"I did, my Queen, though I have not been able to work out your reasons for letting such important intel reach her—especially without cost."

"She hasn't the resources of a Shield any more, Jahriss. She is young and impetuous. Knowing what we're doing with those animals will pierce her bleeding heart, bringing her to me."

"What if she lets the cat out of the bag to the other Sidhe?"

"How much damage do you think she can do revealing something we're doing openly?"

"Your wisdom rivals your beauty, my Queen."

Viviane rolled her eyes.

She motioned the other faeries into Dunham quarters, stepping aside until Yarque stepped through the Arch. "A moment of your time, Yarque?"

The Kobold glowered at her. His words dripped power, hatred and contempt. "This is the last payment, Lady. With this our debt is square and my service as your gopher is complete."

"You have my thanks, powerful Yarque. I wonder if we might enter an agreement of continued cooperation."

Yarque spat at her feet. "I'd rather be turned into a sex thrall by one of your sisters than spend a single unnecessary moment in your presence."

Anger roared in Viviane's ears. "Watch your tone, Kobold. My star is ascendant."

A cruel smile lit his features. "Think you so? Shall the Morning Star's least servant dare rise higher than he did?"

The other Anseelie tensed.

"Take. Care. Yarque."

"Rise higher or not, the impact of your fall will shake the Earth almost as much as mirth will rattle my belly." Yarque backed through the portal, his container left at her feet.

Viviane glared at the amphora. "This is all you have for me? All you've stockpiled after all this time?"

"This fulfills our bargain."

He's holding out on me.

Viviane held her temper for all she was worth. Yarque was a Power, not as strong as one of the Dark Trinity perhaps, but neither was she as strong as she should have been.

Now is not the time to engage in uncertain contests.

"Your debt is paid." Viviane turned her back on the Kobold. "Be gone and let our dealings be done."

Her servants hurried to the standing stones, all but Jahriss's head lowered into their collars. They poured or scooped essence onto the eggs, refilling the basins enough to bolster the pentagram.

"Not too much, Dunham must not sense the difference."

Once they finished refueling the circle, they hurried the essence containers back through the portal to her pocket of Faery.

Sir Jahriss stopped on the Arch's threshold. "What orders, my Queen?"

She considered. It would have been more beneficial to keep him near Quayla, but that broken trust could not be repaired. "Where is she hiding?"

"The same apartment complex, merely one door over."

A laugh escaped Viviane. Quayla had gall. Hiding beside the first place a hunter would look and cloaking her presence beneath the shadow of the essence seeped into the building from her long residence was brazen and brilliant.

She is everything I thought she'd become, now to enlist her.

"Leave her to me. Prepare my forces for stage three of my plan."

Sir Jahriss bowed his way through the Arch, closing it after himself.

Viviane returned to the summoner's stone. "I'm terribly sorry to keep you waiting, Summuseraphi. I had to ensure you couldn't break free of your current lodgings."

"I will escape eventually, demon."

She smiled, kneeling down to touch a hand to each rabbit.

Power rushed through her limbs, seeping into the carcasses as she muttered the incantation. Both rabbit halves vanished from her circle, appearing inside the one containing Summuseraphi. He fell upon the meat at once, not bothering to keep an eye on her.

She waited until he'd consumed most of the first quarter, anchoring her power firmly into him. She rose, sweeping hands upward. Her circle blazed to life. His ignited brighter than an acetylene torch.

Summuseraphi doubled around his gut. His knees buckled, and he crashed to the stone beneath him. Power flooded into her. Dunham had stolen Summuseraphi's essence. She'd led him to the scrolls, fed him the truth in small enough bits to make him think he'd found a great treasure without her knowing.

Except I only gave him most of the truth.

Summuseraphi wasted away in his cell, his rejuvenated strength crashing into her like a tsunami.

We shall see who is the least, Kobold. We shall see.

Chapter Fifteen

Wyld Revelations

Vitae

I entered the lab area of my hotel basement. Long lines of my smaller minions busied themselves, bent over the bizarre yet extremely effective seed crafting designed by my thrall. I stopped, closing my eyes to the buzz of work to feel my ever-expanding network of sensors. The vast sea of stars made up of my essence spread outward from the new Shield sanctum. Some of the seeds moved, disorienting at first, but brilliant in that moving seeds weren't so easily removed.

Enthralling the queer little man has served me well.

My thrall wasn't among the workers. I found him in the restricted area, staring off into space over my nest toward the rear-most doors with a hard look on his face.

"Thrall."

A flurry of blinks cleared the haze from his bloodshot eyes. "Forgive me, Master, what can I do for you?"

"What were you about?"

"I was trying to calculate which tasks your reserve essence would enable and prioritize the tasks for when more essence became available."

"I have a task for you which is of the utmost priority. As this will require additional essence, I shall create you more. Summon four of my enforcers."

My thrall nodded, exiting the chamber. I strolled to a small cooler, drawing out prepared glasses of healing slurry and setting them on nearby metal tables. Underneath the table, a shelf supplied an industrial kitchen pot.

My thrall entered with the requested enforcers.

I removed my armored robes. "Excellent. While these creations have been very useful, certain aspects of their appearance make them troublesome in certain situations."

A shift of will transmogrified my arm. I halted the change before it transformed into the pure life plasma that, while powerful, deteriorated far faster than the simple blood essence.

The blood essence mixes better in any case.

Sharpened fingers tore the arm from my shoulder socket, dropping bloody essence held in shape until I dropped the limb into the stainless-steel pot. "You also mentioned some of the adults are more stubborn about following your orders, perhaps children will be more pliable. As such, I have ordered the collection of child corpses from Oakland Cemetery and Atlanta's other cemeteries."

I glanced over, finding my thrall's horrified expression locked where my arm had once been. Another nudge of will shifted me fully into life plasma. "Did you hear me, thrall?"

He stared as I rebalanced my essence to replace the lost limb. I'd restored myself to flesh before his eyes flashed up to meet mine.

All color had drained from the already sickly pale mortal. "Master, did you say children?"

Perhaps I should infuse some essence into him to ensure I do not lose his services until I can find a replacement.

I picked up the cup of slurry, opened my throat and pitched back my head to down the gloopy concoction.

"Yes, I have in mind a slightly different design for these new, smaller soldiers."

"Children?"

"Dead children which we will restore to life so that they may defend humanity from the vile Sidhe."

"Like the Sidhe you have in your service?" he asked.

My hand planted a red print across his pale face. "You will not question me, thrall. I know what is best for your people."

His eyes glassed over. "You know what is best for my people."

"Better," I slid back into my robes. "I would like to limit the troll marrow to that necessary to giving the new guard regen-erative abilities. You will need to experiment with winged Sidhe to give the resurrected mortals flight capabilities. Follow me."

I led him to the rear door, entering my own access phrases before configuring the doors for his entry. Once I'd confirmed he could navigate into my holding area without me, we entered my prison.

A stench of blood, unwashed bodies and hopelessness clogged my nostrils. "Use the enforcers to select the specimens you need. Take what you need from them, but try not to kill any unnecessarily. Do you understand, thrall?"

"How many Sidhe do you have in here?"

I shrugged. "Several score, perhaps upward of a hundred. You will want to ensure you use your meter to mix equal parts Seelie and Unseelie elements at relatively even power levels with the pure essence I provided. An imbalance should be avoided wherever possible."

"Yes, Master."

"Be about it. My new aerial force will not create itself."

I left him to it, only small misgivings lingering in my mind. It was possible he might inadvertently release one of my captives. I stopped by a group of idle enforcers in the outer lab. Grabbing three that had stood along the wall for uncounted days, I ordered them to prevent any Sidhe not sworn to my service from departing.

Shifting my attention to the remaining trollman enforcers, I gathered their attention with a snap of my fingers. "The rest of you will assemble in the foyer and await orders."

Dunham

Dunham trudged up the spiral stairs from his office, hands tight around the Pyri's egg and heart. His skin stank from the healing concoction smeared across his face and arms. Every limb moved slowly, almost audibly creaking under the flaking goop applied to heal burns from a very near miss.

The Pyri fought him over every step. The phoenix's conniving expression grew more smug with each groan that escaped Dunham's chapped lips. The Pyri's footfalls scorched wood and burned carpet in a long trail starting in the lobby.

He wasn't aflame, but leaked enough heat to maliciously vandalize Circlestone headquarters.

"Get in your cage," Dunham spat through gritted teeth.

"Problems?" Viviane asked.

Turning his head raked Dunham's neck in fiery agony. "He did the job, more or less."

Behind her, Caelum hunched in her cage eating a rabbit. The Terra's cage was back in the sealed position and the divine slumped unconscious in the center, haggard and wasted nearly to bone.

"Terra is back?"

"In his cage," Viviane said

"What happened to the divine?"

Viviane shrugged. "Divines use their essence to empower everything, including escape attempts. Are both war squads dead?"

"Burned beyond recognition."

Viviane sauntered over to him, holding up his progress to the control console with a hand on seeping third-degree burns.

Dunham winced.

The Pyri chuckled.

"Dunham, dear, do you recall why we went to all the trouble of capturing their divine?"

The realization of his own stupidity washed over Dunham like the flames that had almost 'inadvertently' incinerated him. He took a moment to cool anger that intensified the pain of his burns and tapped into the divine essence.

"On your knees, Pyri!"

The phoenix's face bent stubbornly for a moment before he dropped to his knees.

"You will stop causing damage to my building. Acknowledge command and compliance."

The Pyri struggled another moment. "Command acknowledged, wafer. I will comply through no choice of my own."

Tightening his grip on the egg and heart split the burned skin on Dunham's knuckles, but seemed to hurt less than the agony inflicted on the willful shield. "You will call me 'master' and you will give me your name and the name of your shield mates."

The light in the Pyri's eyes blazed with hatred. "Ignis, Master. Terrance, Caelum, Vitae and Aquaylae."

"What about the divine?" Dunham demanded.

Ignis fought him. "Summus—Summuseraphi."

Dunham shuffled over to the control console, setting aside the egg and heart. "Get in your cage, Slave Ignis."

The effect of releasing the artifacts was immediate. Ignis's will flared to life in opposition to Dunham's own, but the divine power he'd absorbed overpowered the phoenix if not with ease, without a prolonged battle of wills.

Good. Putting the divine essence out of mind until the coming confrontation with Vitae and Aquaylae was a mistake.

"Were they any witnesses?" Viviane asked.

"Yes, and both Courts had Fae Kissed present."

"What did you do with them—the witnesses?"

"Your mass hypnosis spell held them until your dream weavers arrived." Dunham raised Terrance's cage and fought through the pain toward the circled stones. "Why are we still wiping memories? I thought you wanted more forces to help destroy the others."

"The only thing humans reproduce faster than garbage or themselves is gossip. The more mortals aware of the Sidhe, the greater the chance the Plague of Knowledge will begin, strengthening the other queens." Vivian slipped under his arm, helping him across the distance. "Besides, the phoenixes aren't the only ones keeping an eye out for Faery touched."

"Corrupting humanity to give you and your sisters reign over Creation was supposed to be the idea."

"True, but only after I've secured my position once more."

Shifting his fingers through the motions to lower the magical barrier containing Terrance hurt, but was worth the short-lived torment. "Rise, Terrance, and step from your cage. You will refrain from any action that might cause harm to me and mine."

The beautiful black woman rose, offering a seductive smile. The temptress act might've put Dunham off his guard if not for his time with Viviane. He fought stiff limbs to remove his clothes.

"You will remove my clothes and treat my burns with your essence."

"For someone whose commands whisper divine power, your healing salves should have cured any burns."

"Ignis's fire proved more potent."

And I didn't think to add divine essence to the cure.

"Ease my pains and explain why you took so long on your mission."

Terrance reached for Dunham. He fought the instinct to flinch away. The earth phoenix's soft hands settled gently onto Dunham's burns. Soothing coolness drew the fiery pain from his skin.

"The Sidhe fled in separate directions. It took some time to hunt them down, kill them and destroy their remains."

"Did you encounter Vitae or Quayla?"

"I saw neither," Terrance moved from Dunham's arm onto his shoulder and then slid his hands around Dunham's throat.

"Are you considering strangling me?"

"I considered it," Terrance said. "But I can feel your grip around my egg and would rather avoid punishment from a fruitless attack."

Dunham turned his repaired hand over, one finger inserted in the ring of metal that chained the set emerald connected to the Terra's egg within in his palm.

Terrance nodded absently. "Yes, that and your Sidhe master stands ready to wield my actual egg against me if I damage her pet."

I squeezed my fist and dug nails into the stone. "I'm not her pet."

Terrance grimaced. "Forgive my misinterpretation of the situation, Master."

Dunham caged Terrance once more after the earth phoenix had drawn out the pain and spurred regrowth of the damaged skin. He turned to Viviane. "I still think that we're hurting the campaign by surrendering recruitment opportunities."

"And I think the slow progress would be mitigated if you started sending the shields out in groups."

"Do you have intelligence of another pending incursion?"

A wicked smile bowed her cerulean-painted lips. "We're about to release more portal points for two rather large forces."

"How is your animal supply?"

"Unfortunately, the bloodthirstiness of my kin worldwide is denting my supply, cursed spay and neutering campaigns."

Dunham scrutinized the emaciated Summus. There seemed little life, let alone fight, left in the divine phoenix. He kneeled next to each basin, evaluating the essence levels. He arched an eyebrow at Viviane.

"I managed to find a little." Viviane smiled. "I assumed you'd want it employed to help keep Summuseraphi."

"Thank you."

"Thank me by taking advantage of this boon."

"Of course, anything for you." Dunham crossed to the control console and went through the motions of commanding them to refrain from attacking himself, Viviane or Circlestone. Once done, he raised all of the cages, releasing all three phoenixes at once.

Ignis tried to take advantage of his split attention, but Summuseraphi's essence made putting Ignis on his face simple.

"Terrance and Caelum, you will be stopping an incursion that lovely Viviane has uncovered. I'm sure performing your duty will be satisfying. While you are cleaning up, I will see security procures tactical gear so that you can communicate with one another and keep me updated on what you are doing. Once the Sidhe are exterminated—Terrance will explain—you will contact me immediately." Dunham focused on Terrance. "If the Sidhe split up, you will radio in immediately. With night coming on, you should be able to utilize your phoenix shapes, but you are to minimize revealing yourself to mortals."

"Why are you doing this?" Caelum asked.

Viviane stepped forward, traipsing her fingertips down Caelum's body. "All part of the big picture, Caelum dear."

Caelum slapped her hand away. "Don't Caelum dear me, Sidhe demon."

Viviane smirked at Dunham. "Do you think I'm a she-demon?"

Dunham nodded. "Yes. Caelum's right, you are."

Viviane pouted her way off to one side.

Dunham put her out of his mind and glowered down at Ignis. "Since you like burning things so much, you're going to do me the great favor of torching several of Atlanta's important houses of hypocrisy."

Viviane scowled.

"I will enjoy sending you to answer for your crimes," Ignis said.

"Our crimes, Pyri. Don't forget, you're part of the team." Dunham shifted his attention to all of them. "Get to it."

Bradley

Bradley stared into space, barely seeing the menagerie of imprisoned faerie creatures. Master Vitae wanted him to create an air force by desecrating children's graves. A deep fury burned bright around a core of repulsion.

Children.

He couldn't believe it. His benefactress, the giving, gentle—Bradley raised a hand to his cheek.

No. Not giving and gentle. Look at these poor things.

Cages of various designs held the faerie creatures he'd read about, dreamed about, drew in childish, immature sketches. Some cages were so crammed the creatures barely had enough room to avoid touching the iron bars. Some of the prisoners' skins showed marks proclaiming they hadn't avoided the antagonistic metal.

Eyes watched him, but not with hope or even revulsion.

Resignation. How long have they been captive?

The reality of Bradley's situation was that the length of their incarceration didn't matter. His will had been conquered by whatever Vitae was. There'd been flashes of clarity, like when he'd learned about Mercer, but Bradley couldn't remember the last time his head had felt so clear.

Children.

He couldn't look at the Sidhe anymore. He couldn't face the shame of what he had to do next. He wished Vitae hadn't revealed the existence of the room before him.

But I have to do what he orders until I can get out of here.

Bradley trudged back to the lab for his portable detector. He didn't hurry. He didn't want to become the ghoul so many people had called him over the years. When at long last he found the detector, he wasn't sure how he should feel to find the gases used to identify the kinds and strength of magic inert.

He frowned.

He had to figure out what he was looking at in the cells. He had no idea what creatures were what and doubted the pages of monster manuals he'd memorized could be trusted to sort Seelie from Unseelie or measure inherent power.

Bradley trudged back through the security doors. He walked among the cages until he found a glass cage of Tinkerbelle-like creatures with wings on forearms and calves in addition to their backs.

"I don't want to harm you, but I need to run some tests on you. Please don't resist." Bradley turned to the nearest enforcer. "Bring two of them into the lab."

A trollman stomped forward.

"Gently," Bradley amended.

If the trollman heard him, it made no sounds of compliance. He picked a goblin and a willowy elf, having the enforcers relocate them while causing a minimal amount of harm.

Bradley returned to the lab, gesturing the waiting trollmen to bring their captors over to the massive detection chandelier from his morgue. He hadn't used it much since discovering the three types of magic. It wasn't as well calibrated as the rattler, but its gas globes still indicated magic types and concentrations.

The first test lit up all three kinds of magic.

The little winged woman had been caged for ages. There was no way she had residual magic from two kinds of Sidhe.

Bradley slapped his forehead. "Give her to me. Please be still, miss."

He brought her beneath the chandelier magic-o-meter. This time only the Seelie gas illuminated. He nodded at the results.

The trollman was infused with troll magic and Vitae's essence. The presence of both creatures confused the meter.

Bradley motioned over the trollmen. "Please put her gently back into her cage."

The little woman wailed and started sobbing.

Cracks shot through Bradley's heart, but he turned his attention to the goblin. "I just need you to stand under the detector."

The goblin nodded like the effort took all of his energy. Bradley helped the weak faerie half-way over to the chandelier before the creature sprang at his throat. Dirty nails tore into Bradley's skin. He covered his head with both arms, screaming at the trollmen to help.

The enforcer jerked the goblin off of Bradley, dangling him in the air by one hand like a naughty kitten.

The workers filling Vitae's seeds looked up at the commotion, but none came to his aid. Bradley snapped at the nearest, a rotund pig-faced creature with bat ears. The bumbling Sidhe reminded Bradley of the villain's minion from the Disney's Gummi Bears cartoon, earning him and the rest of his species the nickname Toady. Bradley'd dismissed this Toady from lab work twice over accidents. "You, get me handcuffs or something."

Bradley massaged his sore neck, wincing when fingertips brushed the cuts in his neck. He fetched the first aid kit, disinfected the wound and bandaged himself the best he could.

Toady offered him shackles.

Bradley wanted to snap at the creature, berate him for not taking the restraints to the enforcer still holding up the struggling goblin. He pointed. "Put these on the goblin and get him under the detector."

Bradley checked his bandages in the mirror and followed the clumsy Toady. The goblin put up a fight until a trollman fist stole his consciousness. Bradley pinched the bridge of his nose and waited. Toady threw the manacled, unconscious goblin over one shoulder, crossed to the testing area and slapped the goblin down with a head cracking smack.

The noise prompted Bradley to look up from behind his fingers.

One of the globes in his detector burned bright green. The

green globe had never reacted with anything Bradley had inspected with it.

Bradley rushed over to the detector, excitement countering his dissatisfied malaise. The light faded quickly, leaving the blue light to identify the goblin as a relatively weak Unseelie.

"Hey, come back here."

Toady looked up at him like Bradley were a Mack truck and the faerie a stubborn doe daring the truck to hit it.

"Get back over here, now."

The response of the enthralled Toady was immediate, but Bradley's normal sense of guilt stayed quiet in the face of possible discovery. As soon as Toady stepped close enough to the detector, the globe burned green.

Great Gygax, there's a fourth kind of magic.

Bradley's brow furrowed, creasing his forehead in an acre's worth of crooked farming rows.

Vitae said the essence had to be used in balanced quantities—equal parts Seelie and Unseelie to prevent bad consequences.

He stared at Toady. "What are you?"

"A noggle, wafer."

"No, Seelie or Unseelie."

"Wyldfae."

Wyldfae?

"How does that work? I thought there was just Summer and Winter, Seelie and Unseelie. Are you guys a blended species?"

The noggle darkened, snarling out his answer. "No."

"He's an Anseelie," the captive elf said.

Anseelie?

Bradley's brow furrows deepened.

The elf continued. "Anseelie are a separate race, children of the once third leader of the Dark Trinity."

"You're all descended from a different...mother?"

The elf's head inclined slightly.

"Three Queens of Faery, not two?"

The elf's tone hardened. "Two, mortal. The Morning Star's third queen is gone, never to return."

Toady hissed something in a language Bradley had no chance of translating.

"Elf?" Bradley asked.

"He disagrees with my statement."

Yeah, vehemently from the sound of it. Three queens under a king, this Morning—holy shit!

Bradley rushed up to the elf. "Morning Star? As in Lucifer?"

The elf smirked.

"Wait, but that would mean the Sidhe are the children of…"

"We are the Creation of the Fallen, wafer, just as you are the Creation of the Ultimate Creator."

"Wait, then what is Vitae?"

"A bastard bird playing a game that will have his kind cast down just as we were," the elf said.

Holy hells, I'm working for the next Satan.

Chapter Sixteen

True Colors

Dunham

Dunham surveyed the ballroom of assembled clergy. Eyes flit from pastor to priest, minister to rabbi. Many of Atlanta's religious leaders' heads hung from slumped shoulders.

Time to dribble a little hope and lead them to slaughter.

"Welcome, gentlemen and ladies. Looking out at your faces, I am reminded that this month's brunch isn't the cause for celebration it normally is."

Heads nodded.

Lips murmured ascent.

"Many of you have lost churches—buildings and parishioners —to freak storms and fires in recent days." Dunham brightened. "But even in this dark time there is hope in what we have built over the years. Our camaraderie, our setting aside petty squabbles about denominations or manners of faith have paved the way for helping one another in these dark times."

Viviane stepped up beside Dunham, a pert smile on her coral-painted lips.

Dunham gestured. "My assistant Viviane has been put at your disposal to assist coordinating worship schedules in each other's facilities. She will ensure every congregation has a place to discover truth."

Clergy glanced around at each other.

"In addition, I will be renting Mercedes-Benz Stadium and bringing in renowned evangelist Sebastian Jahriss to preach to your combined congregations."

His audience glanced around, brows furrowing as they shared whispers.

"I will of course cover all the costs. Entrance will be free, but proceeds from concessions and a special offering will be split between the devastated congregations to help in their rebuilding." Dunham beamed. "Who knows, maybe I'll be a witness to one of your famed Acts of God."

Dunham's face clouded, a hand reaching up to scratch his head. "You know, from a layman's perspective it's almost as if God were punishing you for something."

An awkward chuckle escaped Dunham. "Forgive me, just the random thought of a nonbeliever." He shrugged. "After all, what would a simple philanthropist know about God's will?"

Brunch ended an hour later, several guests wrapping left-overs in napkins to take on the road. Viviane stood over him in silence until the door clicked shut behind the last exiting clergymen.

"Laying it on a bit thick, weren't you?"

Dunham smiled. "Just planting seeds. Speaking of—"

"Yes, visiting congregations will 'discover' incriminating evidence in their host churches."

"What about vice versa?"

"I'll take care of it assuming you focus the shields on my adversaries rather than destroying more churches."

"Our agendas enjoy a more than satisfactory balance."

She frowned. "I don't agree."

Dunham rose and strode out the door. "Agree to disagree."

Vitae

The ogre that had stolen Aquaylae's pet mortal set up his shop far outside of Atlanta—though not so far as to be outside the borders of my authority. He'd co-opted a fairground used to host a renaissance festival attended by wafers like my thrall.

Due to the open visibility of the fairground's parking, I scouted the position alone. Temper rose as the uneven, unpaved area jostled me and muddied my Mercedes. I parked just in front of the closed entrance, glowering at poor reconstructions of medieval age architecture.

Lazy, incompetent wafers.

Taint lingered near the entrance, but the relative weakness of the scent indicated that few if any of the Sidhe utilized the entrance. I transmogrified, opening up my essence to better detect the taint. There was some risk that mortals driving by on the rural highway would spot me, but the distance involved would confuse what they saw enough to mitigate the risk.

Wafers only see what they want to anyway. In this place, they'll make lazy assumptions and go on with their willfully ignorant, insignificant lives.

The taint led me to a side area, essentially behind-the-scenes offices and warehouses. I strode toward the largest concentration of taint, not bothering to push essence into my fighting canes. Seeing to the Anseelie ogre and his minions would be laughably simple.

Doors opened, admitting me to a warehouse converted into an audience chamber nowhere near as grand as my own. A dark olive-skinned ogre in a tailored suit lounged on a massive throne. Long dark hair was piled up atop his head in a topknot wound into a bun. Talon scars seared into the flesh bracketing a single intelligent eye indicated he'd run afoul of Ignis or another fire phoenix. Another set of scars lanced beneath an eye patch decorated by a large ruby in a bronze setting. Countless nymphs of every stripe littered the area around his feet, their bodies expanded ogre-sized to serve him.

"Ah, if it isn't Atlanta's infamous Shieldheart, looking both dangerous and particularly fetching."

"I've come for the mortal you captured. Surrender him at once and I will allow you to slink back into Faery with your skin in place."

The ogre's booming laughter shook the metal building.

I raised a single brow. "Do you really intend to make me thrash you, Sidhe?"

The ogre snapped his fingers with a particularly loud crack of thumb against the meaty flesh of his palm. Four men dressed in tailored suits and panda head masks slipped into view from behind the ogre's throne. The taint in the warehouse intensified and the scent of oiled metal and acrid black powder mixed with Sidhe magic.

Doors around the warehouse opened, allowing in a wash of hot wind carrying an aroma of citrus and prickly pear blossoms. Three covens of five filed into the room, magic licking their bodies like an enthralled lover.

"Charming, but I recommend you dismiss your witches and your posse of very endangered pandas."

"I think not. As you can see, Shieldheart, I have more than enough Fae Kissed to deal with you."

Another snap of fingers opened panels in the warehouse roof, piercing the gloomy interior with summer sunlight. Gnoll crossbowman curled lips enough to expose sharp, yellow canines.

"Shall I snap my hand again?" The ogre asked. "I assure you, I am more than ready for a single shield, even a Shieldheart."

"You prepared for Aquaylae." I offered him a serene smile. "In other words, your preparations are vastly insufficient to the task of facing me, but please, allow me the pleasure."

I snapped my fingers.

Trollman enforcers appeared in a dozen trios all around the warehouse as the elven swordsman glamouring them from sight dismissed his magic and leapt blade drawn onto the roof poised to assault the gnolls. I gave the ogre a smile and a shrug. "Your little hidey hole reeked so thickly of taint, I knew you wouldn't notice a little more."

The ogre paled. "Peace, Shieldheart. I will surrender the wafer."

"Release him. Kill him. I care not at all. What I care about is the disrespect you've shown me. Bow before me, ogre. Beg forgiveness and I might still let you slink off to Faery with your tail between your knees."

Pale ogre flesh purpled. "Neve—"

I willed my thralls to attack.

Quayla

I leaned over the duffel bag, marveling at the amount of already-concentrated essence Terrance had left behind. With the exception of my desperate attempt to fill the water heater catch pan, I'd never extruded that much essence in a single day.

The slurry, lots of water and stopping at nearly every bakery and coffee shop on my way to the cache had bolstered my strength, but I wasn't anywhere near full strength.

I didn't stop at every bakery, but most of this mass will finish out my nest when I get back.

I eyed Terrance's essence. I could use some of what he left behind to bolster my own nest. Earth essence wouldn't work anywhere near as well as life essence, but every little bit helped.

No, I need to go about this the other way around. I need to build up enough earth essence for Terrance to be reborn in freedom.

I hefted the weighty bag then dropped it when Cember exploded to his full-sized wafer detective right in front of me.

I grabbed my chest. "Blighted hells, Cember."

"Yeah, get over it."

"What do you want?" I asked.

"I found you boy-toy, but you're not going to believe it."

My heart went from racing to escape velocity. I held my breath, waiting for the news that would launch me into action once more. Cember's gruff appearance remained passive and silent.

"Well? Where is he?"

"Started thinking you weren't interested in the info."

"Maybe I was just busy weighing the benefits of power-washing that smug expression right off your face."

He chuckled then rattled off an address.

"Ani? Why does that address sound familiar?"

"It is the location of your Johammer," Anima said.

Cember watched my eyes, gaging my expression as he delivered another surprise. "Yeah, well it's also the unofficial Shield headquarters and Palace of Lady Vitae of Atlanta's Queendom."

I stared.

I'd heard the words that had escaped the disguised Sidhe, but they didn't seem to be in the right order. They swam and wove, too slippery for my mind to manage a firm grip. They slowed eventually, but rather than remedy my confusion they seemed to demand answers to new questions.

"Did you just say Queendom and Vitae in the same sentence?"

"Yeah, so you want to pay up now or what?"

"Vitae has Dylan?"

"Yeah."

"The ogre whose Fae Kissed tried to kill me worked for Vitae?"

"No, Vitae's goons raided the ogre. He got away, slippery sod that one, but they rescued your mortal."

Vitae rescued Dylan...why?

"About my payment?" Cember asked.

"I-I have the cash, but I left the rest back at the apartment."

Cember grinned. "No problem, I'll just let myself in."

He was gone before I could object. There wasn't much he could take from the apartment of value beyond the essence in my nest. Cember had delivered Dylan's whereabouts even if he'd been right about my inability to believe the information.

"Quayla?" Anima asked.

It took me a moment to answer. "Yeah."

"Do you intend to pursue this matter immediately?"

"What?"

"Are you going to risk Terrance's essence by taking it with you to that hotel?"

Shit.

Anima had a really good point. There was no way to guess what was in store for me in Vitae's so-called palace. We were both shields, but something told me that simple reality wasn't so simple anymore. I could not risk Terrance's essence no matter how much I wanted to rescue Dylan.

Maybe I shouldn't bother. Dylan's safe and Vitae won't want him around. He'll just release him, won't he?

"Won't he?" My stomach flip-flopped.

"Won't who what?" Anima asked.

"Won't Vitae just release Dylan? Vitae wouldn't want him around and Dylan doesn't know me anymore. I guess he might wait until Summus or Vili can erase Dylan again."

"You don't wish to see Dylan?"

"Yes? No? Both? Neither?"

"I am glad you have cleared that up," Anima said.

Laughter bubbled out of me, joyous, then hysterical in short order. I could see Dylan, make sure Vitae let him go or I could just trust in the life phoenix's nature and focus on finding a way to rescue the others.

Vitae could help me. Surely, he'll want the others free to do their duty...then again, he could try to kill me again.

"I don't know what to do."

"I did not sense Vitae when we were there last, but now that we know his location I could See within the walls."

"Maybe Cember is lying."

"I seem to recall you threatening the Sidhe."

Another laugh bubbled out. "Yeah, I remember that too."

"Do you think Cember would remember?" Anima asked.

"Yes."

"Then there is little likelihood the faerie lied. Vitae rescued Dylan and has him inside his...new sanctum."

"But why?"

Anima didn't answer for several minutes. Deep down, I knew I needed to move, to act, but I just listened to the white noise of surf hitting the shore while I waited for her answer.

"Vitae probably intends to use Dylan to draw you to him. He will leverage your mortal to force your cooperation or at the very least an opportunity to reconcile without an altercation."

"What if he tries to kill me again?"

"You must choose whether or not to take on this risk."

I thought of Dylan—wonderful, warm, loving Dylan with his golden tongue. A tingle spread between my legs, evoking a body-wide stretch and an erection that forced me to adjust my jeans. My nest contained enough essence for a low mass rebirth. I had to see Dylan again, ensure he was safe—even if it meant seeing Vitae. Whether or not I actually liked Vitae, doing my duty meant at least trying to reconcile so we could rescue the others from Dunham.

I pulled up the nearest storage facility on my phone.

"One of Caelum's caches is closer," Anima said.

I hefted Terrance's duffel over my shoulder and adjusted my jeans once more. "Lead me there."

Vitae

Scurith brought me news of Aquaylae's approach as I settled into the plush chair centered in my audience chamber. The dwarves had overdone it, claiming me deserving of such lavishness. I appreciated their adulation, but worried too much luxury would soften my resolve.

"Let her approach, guide her here and fetch her paramour."

Scurith bowed out of the room, replaced almost immediately by my thrall.

"Pardon me, V-Master. Did you know there are three types of Sidhe?" he asked.

"Of course I knew, mortal. The third is of little consequence. Tell me you have done as I commanded."

My thrall hid his face. "I've tried serum variations on a dozen bodies. I imagine one will provide what you desire."

"You have documented all of the experiments meticulously?"

"Yeah."

"What?!"

"Yes, Master, all is as you command."

I scrutinized my thrall. He'd often forgotten formalities when distracted by a problem.

Perhaps Aquaylae's approach has me on edge, has me seeing sedition where there is none in effect.

No sooner had I pushed away thoughts of my thrall escaping my will than Aquaylae appeared at the room's entrance.

She wore tactical armor and had both her Karambit knives to hand. "Vitae?"

I weighed her, trying to keep her last act of treachery from igniting my temper. While taking her life might serve my immediate pleasure, it did not serve my long-term goals.

The longer I watched her, the more apparent the changes come upon her since the ungrateful whore had killed me and robbed me of my glory.

Calm. Patience. A wise leader does not kill his children.

"Vitae?"

"I greet you in the name of the Undying Light, Shield Aquaylae."

"What the hell is this place? Why aren't you at our head-quarters?"

"Our other sanctum was compromised. I built this place to replace it."

"The place is full of Sidhe."

"Servants of the Light, Aquaylae, converted to our purpose."

"How—you know what, never mind."

Her petulant attitude beckoned my anger.

"I'm told you rescued Dylan from that ogre, is that true?"

"It is."

"May I see him?"

"I think some gratitude would be the first respectful order of business, don't you?"

She closed her eyes, shoulders relaxing. The blades drew back into her hilts. She tucked them away. "You're right. Thank you for rescuing him."

"It is my duty to protect mortals, though my higher duty is to protect our Shield and its purpose."

Her eyes started to roll, but she caught herself. Likewise, I caught the sudden spike of fury, pushing it aside in response to her attempt at civility.

"May I see Dylan now?" she asked.

"He has no recollection of you."

Aquaylae's face fell. "I know. I'm the one who requested him rewritten, remember? I just want to see him safe, then I'll go."

I was on my feet. "You will do no such thing. You are part of my Shield. You will bring your nest and resume your duties."

"Vitae, this whole place is filled with Sidhe." She gestured to a nearby enforcer. "And what is that? It smells of Sidhe and you and mortal decay."

"My enforcers, Aquaylae. Fallen mortals protecting Creation in my service."

"Your service? Not in service to Him? The Undying Light?"

"Shield Aquaylae!" Rage paced my gut like a caged tyrannosaurus. "Have you not been paying attention out there? Covens of Fae Kissed are rising all over the world. Atlanta's been plagued by fires and storms and earthquakes that have slaughtered mortals and destroyed Churches dedicated to the Undying Light."

"Those things happened because Caelum, Ignis and Terrance are Dunham's prisoners."

"You must focus on rising to the occasion as I have, take your place at my side as we work to build the greatest Shield in all of Creation history!"

"Vitae, please set aside this...." She gestured around her. "You need to come out of hiding and help me rescue the others. We can discuss your...vision once we're all back together."

"We will free them when it is time to do so."

"We need the whole Shield together to protect Atlanta."

"We don't. Me and my thralls can protect this city."

"Then why do you need me?"

I stopped, withholding her answers. She was a willful child, too stubborn to understand greater thoughts in any case. "You are a phoenix assigned to Atlanta's Shield. You will pledge yourself to me and obedient observance to your duty."

She tensed. "Just let me see Dylan, and we'll discuss it."

For a moment, I considered denying her, but preventing her from seeing the paramour used against her as I had predicted would rob her of a lesson she so desperately needed to learn.

I seated myself once more. "Of course. Scurith should be down with your paramour in a moment."

Quayla

The Vitae on a throne and his vehement demands left my mind spinning on the brink of being swallowed by Charybdis. I couldn't believe what had escaped his mouth.

He'd be of no help with the others.

His words claimed he wanted us together, demanded I join

195

him, but in my heart, I knew he wanted me for little more than an audience to his perceived greatness. I scanned the Sidhe, the human standing to one side.

Thralls he called them. That's what he wants, me as an obedient cheerleader.

Dylan's appearance at the door didn't erase my horrible tailspin so much as freeze the tempest in the moment. After everything I'd been through, after the words that had escaped from Vitae's lips, seeing Dylan was like simultaneously plunging me into agony and orgasm. I forgot about rewriting his memory. I forgot about the new body from the death I'd died since he'd been erased.

I rushed to him, wrapping my arms around him and pressing my lips to his. He stiffened, but only for an instant. Remember me or not, his subconscious or his soul remembered me. His lips answered back with soft caressing kisses that launched my heart soaring to the heavens. I poured my love into him, feeling my rising desire answered by his matching hardness.

We had the whole world in that moment. All of Creation was right, exactly as God intended it. Warmth washed over me, then Dylan's lips stopped moving and pulled away.

I opened my eyes, seeking whatever emotion had stopped his end of the kiss.

No emotion lurked in Dylan's blue eyes. They gazed blankly ahead as the top of his head slid away and tumbled backward, replaced by a wash of blood driven into my eyes by the last few beats of his heart.

Vitae stood behind Dylan, a glittering emerald essence blade coated in Dylan's blood.

The soprano escaping Vitae's lips caressed my ears with soft affection that hit me like a battering ram. "Now you are free to serve, Aquaylae. This mortal will never be leveraged against you again."

The body in my arms went limp.

Sound died.

Warmth fled.

Fresh snow cleared away the taint clogging my nostrils.

The taste of tears and Dylan's blood faded from my tongue.

A tsunami of rage exploded in my chest like a sun going nova.

I wanted, no needed to tear Vitae's head from his shoulders. I needed to hunt down his nest and kill him again and again, adding my own essence to his so that I could murder him once more.

I didn't.

I didn't kill Vitae—not because of mercy or compassion or forgiveness or anything else.

Killing Vitae meant letting go of Dylan.

It meant releasing his body to fall to the floor.

I couldn't.

I just couldn't.

"Now pull yourself together, shield. There's work to be done."

I transmogrified, screeching my agony until it felt like my lungs might tear. I seized Dylan's body in one talon and his head as gently as I could in the other. I threw myself upward, somehow blasting my way through the ceiling and the ceilings beyond that until Dylan and I were above the clouds—as close to heaven as I could carry him.

Chapter Seventeen

New Alliances

Bradley

Bradley'd watched Vitae and the oddly-named Aquaylae argue.

He'd looked on with shock when handsome Aquaylae had kissed the man Vitae'd rescued—Dylan something. Bradley's abject horror had nothing to do with their homosexual embrace or public display of affection.

He stared at the debris littering the floor from Aquaylae's departure peppering a pool of Dylan's blood.

Vitae had interrupted their kiss by decapitating Dylan.

Rather than bow to Vitae or attack him, Aquaylae had transformed into a phoenix of raging water and taken away Dylan's body—the decapitated remains of a man Vitae murdered in arctic-cold blood.

Dear God, what just happened?

Bradley bolted from the room, shoving Sidhe out of his way and battering open doors in his headlong flight from the hotel. He paused only a moment outside the door to track the glowing blue bird carry Dylan's corpse into the sky.

He grabbed a white motorcycle from the extra vehicles parked in the lot, cranking the key left in the ignition and following the fleeing phoenix the best he could.

Not like I can fly.

Once he was safely away from the hotel of horrors, he parked and watched the sky. He had to help Aquaylae. He didn't know why or how, but he absolutely had to do something—not so much to make things better, but something to help.

Thunder cracked overhead.

Rain deluged the world.

Quayla

Dylan hung from my talons.

I transmogrified so I could hold him in my arms and stay aloft. I tried to hold his head in place to hide the wound, but the high winds buffeting me made keeping it in place all but impossible. Nothing I could do with Dylan's body would be right, but I couldn't think of anything that was right. I couldn't let him go, but no Divine Ones came to fetch his body. I shouted out for help, but only heard a whisper over the roaring which refused to diminish.

"Ani?"

"I'm so sorry, Quayla."

"Help me."

"There's nothing I can do. I cannot bring him back."

Fury shot through me like lightning. "Isn't that what Vitae's doing with his creatures?"

"No, not exactly."

"I erased him, Ani. I tore him out of my life. That was supposed to protect him from harm."

I'd been too involved in the situation to recognize the smells I'd scented at first, but I knew that Vitae had somehow resurrected dead mortals. He'd been arrogant before, but his delusions of superiority never approached false worship of himself.

All that has changed.

"He's playing God with mortal bodies, Ani."

"I know."

"You knew?"

She didn't answer.

"You knew!"

"I hadn't dared get too close, but I Saw, Shield Quayla. Now I have Smelled."

"He smells more Sidhe than phoenix now."

"It is a close thing," Anima said.

"Close my feathered ass, he's not only playing God with mortals, he's been trying to recreate himself. You heard his rant, he doesn't need the others because he's made himself into something he thinks can protect Atlanta all by himself."

"Is that not what you're trying to do?"

"Only because I haven't found a way to save the others. I don't want this, any of this. I've been putting myself last, just trying to get through all this. That's why I erased Dy—" My voice broke, but I forced myself through choking sobs. "That's why I erased Sabrina, M-Mrs. Cox and...and Dylan."

Dear God, what if Vitae's done that to Sabrina too? He wouldn't have much patience with her opinionated forcefulness.

Four short, dirty-looking not-so angelic men floated down on neon orange wings.

"Ani?"

"I did not contact them," Anima said.

"We've come to take him Home," Rusti said.

I stared at the putti. I knew I should give Dylan over to their care, knew I couldn't take him where they could.

"We will care for him like a mother her babe, Shield Aquaylae," Rusti said. "You have my word."

I squeezed my eyes closed and relaxed my hold. The putti

eased Dylan from my grip, taking his head last of all. I didn't open my eyes until they'd been gone a long time.

"What will you do now?" Anima asked.

"Pray for answers."

Bradley

Bradley stared at the small bronze statuette just beyond the motorcycle's handlebars. The motionless Angel peered up at him just above her hands. He couldn't believe what he'd heard escape what he thought was an ornament.

"I-I might have some answers."

"Who is this?" Asked the man whose boyfriend had been beheaded.

"My name is Bradley, Bradley Sky. Is this the man named Aquaylae?"

The woman's voice returned. "What are you doing on Quayla's motorcycle?"

"I was trying to follow the phoenix that took the dead man's body away, but my car was on the opposite side of the hotel. So, I grab the first thing I found with keys in the ignition," Bradley said.

"You said you have answers?" Aquaylae asked.

"Are Quayla and Aquaylae two names for the same person?" Bradley asked.

"Yes," the woman said.

"And who are you miss?" Bradley asked.

"Her name is Anima, and you can call me Quayl," Aquaylae said. "Now that the introductions are over, how about those answers?"

"Sure, can we meet?"

Anima gave him an address.

"On my way." Bradley plugged it into his phone, glancing back at the hotel before pulling into traffic.

Quayla

"I've isolated him from our conversation," Anima said.

"Thank you."

I wasn't sure what else to say. Anima had sent the stranger to Caelum's cache where we'd set aside Terrence's essence. I can't say I wasn't glad that Anima was doing the thinking because the only thought circling my brain was Dylan's final appearance.

No matter how many centuries I lived, I would never be able to get that image of him out of my head. Thanks to Vitae, seeing Dylan's decapitated corpse through the spray of blood on my face would shadow every good memory.

I landed in the highest building near the cache, transmogrified, and headed down to meet the stranger offering answers. It wasn't hard to pick him out of a crowd straddling my baby. Bradley didn't look particularly comfortable on the electric jellybean, but there was no way to be sure whether or not he was even comfortable in his own skin. When I approached, he started to bow then aborted the motion to extend a hand only to hesitate halfway to offering the handshake.

A nervous chuckle escaped him. "I'm sorry, Kale, I have no idea how I'm supposed to address you. Do I call you master or something?"

Niagara Falls roared in my ears.

Master? That arrogant son-of-a-bitch!

I took a deep breath and offered Bradley a firm handshake. "Like I said, you may call me Quayl—Quayla if I am reborn female."

Bradley's answering handshake was a little clammy. A queer expression crossed his face. "You can change gender?"

"Yes."

Delight washed the rest of his expression away. "Do you change gender at will or does it have to do with rebirth?"

"I thought you were the one providing answers."

"Yeah, sorry. Master, I mean Vitae doesn't answer questions."

"I imagine Vitae barks orders and insults."

Bradley ran a hand to the back of his hair. His eyes shifted away from me. "Yeah. You know I'm really sorry about what he did to your boyfriend."

The waterfall returned, fed by a hot spring of volcanic heat.

"Quayla, your Johammer is not exactly inconspicuous," Anima said. "Perhaps we should move this discussion out of public view."

"Why does she get to call you Quayla while you're male?"

I rolled my eyes and opened up Caelum's cache.

"Nice place you have here," Bradley said.

"It's just a supply cache. I'm not exactly spoiled for options."

I dragged Bradley inside and closed the door. I would've brought my baby in too, except there wasn't enough room. Caelum's wall of weapons sent Bradley's jaw to the floor and drew his fingers as if each firearm had a gravity of its own. I indulged him as long as I could stand it before demanding his story. Despite being inside a small concrete room without any windows, Bradley whispered his tale.

When the obviously intelligent medical examiner finished, I just stared. The whirlwind of unbelievable actions taken by the always proper Vitae left me tumbling through a tornado with a broken wing.

"You know thinking about it, you might be able to use Vitae's old warehouse. We didn't leave much behind, but he owned it outright and I doubt he'd expect you to hole up there," Bradley said.

"He may have a point Quayla," Anima said. "I'm not sure how Vitae purchased the property considering I've been the one to facilitate most of Vitae's financial transactions. However, it seems based on Bradley's timeline there is a high probability our inability to locate Vitae was due to cloaking runes around Vitae's warehouse."

The world still felt as if it were in a tailspin, but even if we didn't take over Vitae's old warehouse, I wanted to see it. "Take us there."

Bradley made no objections to riding bitch on my Johammer. A tactical headset allowed us to communicate on the move, hoping to escape police notice since we didn't have a second helmet.

We found the warehouse unlocked and the security system offline. A hook near the door held keys, and a giant pentacle drawn in blood dominated the center of the warehouse.

Taint and dust vied for aromatic supremacy while something unsettling prickled my skin. It took a moment to realize I'd plunged into an eerie hush that extended not just to my ears but to my other senses. I wasn't blinded or deafened but in some kind of sensory deprivation bubble that protected occupants from the outside world.

Bradley started to play tour guide. I hushed him with a gesture and drew both my Karambit hilts.

Several cages in the back held the rotting remains of faeries left behind. They'd been drained of blood and probably magic. Even out of his blight-loving mind, I couldn't imagine Vitae being wasteful. The side workroom contained a smaller version of the lab Bradley had described filling the hotel basement. Scratches on the floor of a walled-off area suggested what was once a bedroom.

Most of the warehouse was a shock, but the back dock held a surprise too. A shrink-wrapped pallet contained half a dozen stone basins. I didn't have the tools or the talent to carve new nests but Anima assured me Rusti and his ilk could do the job for us.

I struggled to take joy in the bit of good fortune, but the horrors of the day left no room for anything other than sorrow.

We re-entered the main warehouse to find someone just inside the outer door eyeballing the pentacle.

Detective Sabrina Foxner looked up and my heart skipped a beat. Relief washed through me—at least until she drew her gun and pointed it at us. "Hands up, both of you."

Dear Creator what next?

"Bradley Sky you're under arrest, charged with criminal trespass, grave robbery and misappropriation of bodies from the morgue."

Anima

A firestorm of essence drew Anima's attention away. Ignis rampaged through a huge combination church and university, sending mortals running for their lives.

Earth essence shook another part of the city, drawing her to the eastern perimeter in time to see Terrance's earthquake demolish a civil war era church and the neighborhood surrounding it.

Tornado alarms brought her to Caelum as his winds shredded an old synagogue.

Atlanta's faithful ran screaming from the wrath of a mortal madman. Anima had no idea why the Fae Kissed druid forced her shields—the city's protectors—to attack places of worship, but she needed to return to Quayla.

Together they could find a way to stop the carnage.

We have to stop them.

Anima shifted the city beneath her until she'd centered over Vitae's warehouse once more. A police detective slipped inside.

Anima turned to a shimmering mirror, speaking through the angel network to warn Quayla, but Quayla didn't reply. Whatever Vitae had done to the place to keep her from finding him before, seemed to prevent Quayla from hearing Anima through the statuette.

She had to warn Quayla, not only about the detective, but the destruction caused by the other shields.

Those radios. Maybe I can enter ethereally and speak into one.

She grabbed the edges of Atlanta and dragged herself closer to the warehouse. At first, the spirit building resisted her. The barrier was enough to keep her out if the barriers weren't her focus, but she had strength enough to penetrate the fortress ward if she focused.

Chapter Eighteen

Old Allies, New Enemies

Quayla

My relief at seeing Sabrina Foxner alive and well vanished, replaced by the realization she'd cornered me in the same building with caged corpses. Sabrina wasn't the kind of woman to be forgiving. Even the revelation that I was a phoenix or that I'd entered Howell Mill Humane society to save animals hadn't dissuaded her from putting me away.

Only fighting and bleeding together in the Lady's trap had brought her around, and I'd had our ordeal in Faery erased from Sabrina's memory.

She'll take one look back there and throw the book at both of us. I can die—hopefully—but without Summus to rewrite her again Bradley is stuck.

"Sabrina stop—"

"Shut up, hands where I can see them," Sabrina said.

Bradley raised his hands, looking sidelong at me with a soured milk expression that told me he hadn't forgotten what was hidden in the back room either.

I stepped away from the young doctor, splitting my focus

between gathering my essence and meeting her eyes. "Sabrina, please."

"Detective Foxner," she snapped. "Stop where you are or I *will* shoot." The hard set of her eyes confirmed that she would put a bullet in me if I didn't start cooperating. "Sky, on the ground. You, hands up, stop moving and kneel."

I transmogrified my torso and unfolded my wings with as much glow as I could manage. I hoped to all that was holy she'd follow training, shooting me in my center mass instead of in the face. "My name's Q—"

Bullets ripped through my torso.

I fought against showing her the pain that came with them. She wouldn't aim for my torso the second time if I didn't convince her I was invulnerable to her bullets.

She wasn't convinced.

I transmogrified the rest of me, becoming a winged man made of shimmering, glowing water. "Sabrina. My name's Quayla."

She shot me again, this time through the face.

I kept speaking, rebalancing my essence to repair the holes. "You have helped me before."

"I think I'd remember meeting something like you," Sabrina said, the venom in her use of 'something' stinging like acid.

"You first encountered me investigating the break-in at the Howell Mill Humane society. You thought I'd done it, so you staked me out when you couldn't find anything searching my apartment."

Her eyes stayed on me, but a slight wrinkle to her forehead told me she was fighting a doomed battle to fit what she did remember of those events with my story.

"On stake out, you witnessed goblins abduct a woman from the apartments. You followed, but—"

"I remember that," Sabrina interrupted. "But the perps sure as hell weren't goblins. They were gangbangers, some kind of sick cultists. She was dead when we arrived. They'd sacrificed that woman on a makeshift crucifix built in the middle something a lot like that."

I shook my head. "They lost you behind Whole Foods. I helped you track them to the rundown apartment complex west of Georgia Tech—you can't remember the fantastic parts because I had your...memory rewritten—to protect you."

"Convenient story." She turned the gun on Bradley.

I threw out a hand to catch her attention, "No, stop. He's mortal. You'll have enough to explain expending rounds with no evidence of a target."

Her gaze narrowed. "What the hell are you?"

"I'm a phoenix—"

"Everyone knows phoenixes are made of fire."

"Only some of us. We are God's protectors on Earth, shields like yourself but here to protect you from the supernatural."

"The devil can look like a saint." She jabbed her chin at the blood circle. "That doesn't look like a holy roller picnic to me."

"We're here investigating—"

"Bullshit. We've got Sky there wheeling bodies out of the morgue, a video of some Igor-looking fuckers digging up children's graves at Oakland Cemetery and loading them into the coroner's van he checked out."

I shot Bradley a look.

He opened his mouth, but I cut across him before he got himself shot. "Bradley was forced to do those things by the person who owns this warehouse."

She charged toward me three steps. "Hands up, on your knees and...get back in human form so I can cuff you."

I let a little of my exasperation into my voice. "You are the most frustrating woman I've ever met."

"Good thing I don't date men then, on your knees or I shoot Sky over there."

I snorted. "You're a good cop, Sabrina. You won't shoot him so long as he complies no matter what I do."

Sabrina looked as frustrated as I felt. Her hand hesitated over her radio. Backup wouldn't solve the problem raised by facing a being of pure water, but if push came to shove, we'd be gone before her reinforcements could arrive.

"Dispatch, this is Foxner."

Static.

"Dispatch?"

She pulled out her cell phone and swiped a thumb across it to unlock the screen, eyes flicking back and forth between the screen and me.

Whatever Vitae had done to the place had killed all in and out communications. The only question was whether or not I could reach Anima through the bronze statue on my person.

I dropped my voice to a whisper. "Ani, please tell me you can get me a divine."

"What are you saying?" Sabrina snapped.

A chuckle escaped me. "I'm asking dispatch for a supervisor."

Anima didn't bother whispering, her voice reaching me from the tactical headset rather than the statue. "I'm afraid no one is available, Quayla. You will have to act on your own discretion."

It took me a moment to realize that since she apparently couldn't penetrate whatever barriers Vitae had put in place, she'd tapped into the device like we'd discussed once upon a time.

The whole situation couldn't go much worse. I'd known from the moment Sabrina raised her gun that turning her to an ally was a doomed proposition.

I spread my wings and hands. "Look, I don't want to hurt you. I'm out in the cold here, and I could sure use all the help I can get right now. Please don't make me fight you."

"If you're some kind of supernatural cop like me, how are you out in the cold?"

"Other than a supervisor who covers the southeast only five of us protect Atlanta. I'm the last one in any condition to do the job."

"That's bullshit. Look at you. How could anything harm you?"

"You fight your criminals, we fight ours. We're in the middle of a supernatural gang war heading from bad to Armageddon. Our headquarters is gone. All I've got is what I'm carrying and one mortal caught up in this against his will."

I saw the 'bullshit' forming on her lips. Hating myself for doing it, I jumped her. She fired several more times, the bullet's lancing through me and bouncing off the concrete floor behind me. Pulling my punches forced me to hit her a few extra times to knock her out.

"Shit," Bradley said. "You realize how bad this is, right?"

I sighed. "Yes. She will have called in her position outside before coming in. If she doesn't report back in within a reasonable period, this whole place will be teaming with police."

"Actually, I meant about losing my license, but that's bad too."

I owed Sabrina a lot for rescuing me from the Lady. She'd lost a lot of time in the timeline of that slice of Faery. Summus had been able to reweave things together to keep her from losing her job, but without a divine to clean up after me, anything I did to her damaged someone who really didn't deserve it.

"We'll take her car out to a friend's place and hope I can reach a divine to remove all this from her memory."

He climbed back to his feet and came over. "There's a way to help her remember again?"

"No. They don't rewrite memories so much as reality around people so they live the whole scenario over in a different way."

"Kind of like Marvel alternate timelines."

Bradley's resemblance to Dylan made my heart ache like a missing limb.

"Hey, what are the chances the brain remembers both, accounting for stuff like déjà vu?"

I shrugged. "Never been rewritten."

"Have I?"

"Yes, several times."

He didn't look too happy about that, but I was just too tired to lie. I headed toward the exit.

"Um."

I turned to find Bradley resembling the three-year-old standing over the shattered cookie jar.

"I could use Vitae's serum to tell her what to remember."

"Vitae can't do that. Not only shouldn't but just plain can't."

"He can and so can I with the stuff he gave me. I think it's a side effect of the Sidhe blood he's mixed in."

Light save me, can things get any worse?

"No," I said with all the vehemence I could muster after everything else that had happened. "Enthralling her with faerie magic isn't the answer."

I took Sabrina's keys and exited through the big door.

Bradley followed. "Then what do we do?"

"You pack your things and get the hell out of Atlanta. Anima?"

"I want to help you," Bradley said.

"No. My job is to protect mortals, not risk their lives."

"Quayla, perhaps he could help us learn what's wrong with Vitae," Anima said.

"No mortal could live long enough to catalog everything wrong with Vitae," I snapped.

"I'm a passable biochemist," Bradley said. "I could at least try."

"No, you're safer just leaving. I'll deal with Vitae when the time comes."

Bradley's expression turned shrewd. "You can't rewrite her memory, so you can't rewrite mine either, right?"

The conversation wasn't getting me any closer to finding a way to deal with Sabrina. "So?"

"So, you can't use faerie glamour to enthrall me either, right?"

"Of course not! I'm a phoenix, not some Sidhe from the pit."

He smirked. "Then you can't force me to do what you say."

My irritation must have shown in my eyes, because he took a

step backward. "I can break your legs and fly you to the next nearest territory."

He stopped retreating. "I don't think so. Vitae needs to be stopped. I'm going back. If he's one of the good guys, I'm going to find a way to bring him back to your side."

"I don't want him on my side!" Anger shook me like an earthquake. "He k-killed D-Dylan. I-I want to rip his h-head off and use it to replace t-that stick up his ass."

"I'm going back. It's my experiments he's using to enforce his will on others."

I looked at the odd little wafer, really looked at him. He didn't seem like much, but he had a fire in his belly that reminded me of Ignis. He was right that I couldn't control him. If he was going back anyway, maybe there was a way he could help.

"Fine."

"Quayla, he might fall under Vitae's influence again. You can't let him return to enthrallment. You need to protect him."

Blighted hells, Vitae wielding glamour.

Anima was right. She was trying to do what was right, but the wafer was right too.

It isn't my choice.

"Quayla?" Anima asked.

"You heard him, Ani. I can't control him. Maybe he can tell me things that we can use to fight our way through this."

"Maybe I can tip you off so you can kill Vitae," Bradley said.

I fought off the roar of Niagara Falls once more.

Bradley fidgeted under whatever he saw in my face. "I mean, that would stop him for good, and he did murder your boyfriend."

Bradley's story gave me the impression that he'd freed himself, but there was no way to tell which would win in a war between cumulative anger or Vitae's glamour.

Such a rare mortal deserved a long life, not to be sent back into the lion's den to dodge who knew how many teeth.

Maker, protecting free will sucks.

"It's your choice, Bradley."

"He's digging up children." The young doctor tightened the fists at his sides. "I'm going back. Someone has to find a way to stop Vitae."

I shoved my Johammer keys into Bradley's hands. "Go get nose plugs, something that filters out pollen. I'll modify them to filter out faerie taint. Hopefully that will help you resist any attempts to enthrall you once more."

I drove Sabrina's car into the garage, taking care not to hit her or park atop the blood circle.

If I can't convince Sabrina to help, I'll just have to die again.

"Ani, can you or the Isaac scrub any video from the car? Ani?"

Guess Vitae's ward is cutting us off again.

I closed the big doors once more and went to work pitting both my essence and my hatred of Vitae against his sins.

Vitae

Isn't that a fine How Do You Do?

In typical Aquaylae fashion, the selfish, miserable excuse for a shield disobeyed my instructions and launched her fully transmogrified form into the sky without concern for exposing herself before the public.

That is the last straw.

I'd tried to embrace her after her betrayal. I'd tried—against my better judgment—to bring her back into the fold until such time Vilicangelus removed her. I'd even rescued her paramour from unimaginable torments.

She should be grateful.

Hadn't I'd given him a merciful end—quick and relatively painless? Hadn't I freed her so that she could perform her duties without having to fear Sidhe leveraging her addiction against her?

She's beyond redemption. It falls to me to do what should have been done centuries ago.

A lazy thinker, it seemed reasonable that she would return to comfort and familiarity. I took my Mercedes into Cobb county, heading for her former apartment. I wasn't disappointed.

Her essence tingled at the edges of my awareness.

I drew my fighting canes and marched into the old three-story walkup. There wasn't any need to feel for her essence in order to confirm my suspicions, but I did so anyway. When I arrived on the third-floor landing, my senses turned me aside from Aquaylae's old residence to the next-door apartment.

Better, but still lazy.

"Where do you think you're going?" Mrs. Cox asked.

I turned to the geriatric woman, something about her perfume burning my nostrils. "I've come to visit A-Quayla."

Mrs. Cox scowled at the canes in my hands. "Quayla's out of town. You're going to have to come visit some other time."

I met her eyes and pushed my will into the frail old landlady. "You will let me into this apartment here."

My nostrils burned.

Mrs. Cox smiled. "Oh, of course, dear."

She shuffled forward, pulling a massive ring of keys from her large purse. She unlocked the desired apartment, pushed the door open and stepped aside. "Anything else I can do for you, dear?"

"Stand aside."

Mrs. Cox stepped to one side of the door frame and pushed her keys deep into her bag.

I ignored her, the feeling of Aquaylae's essence heady.

What power would mixing her essence with mine provide my next body?

I stepped into the apartment, sweeping my gaze over the atrocious mess.

Just moved in and already a pig sty.

A ferocious battle cry offered me only enough warning to twist around. A small sickle slammed into my side, piercing a kidney and burning like molten agony. "Try to enthrall my mind, will you?"

She jerked the sickle through my gut, ducked an answering cane with shocking agility and hacked into the arm holding the weapon that barely missed her.

"You won't get one over on Hadley Sage Cox, Faerie!"

I reeled, backpedaling from the mad little berserker. Despite the added pain, I would have normally rebalanced my essence to repair wounds without a full body transmogrification. Considering her shrieking accusation that I was a faerie, I shifted my body to pure essence to restore myself and extrude the half-moon blades from my fighting canes.

"Two weapons against one, huh?" Mrs. Cox dug a handful of something from her bag. "I don't think so!"

I charged her only to have a handful of flung rock salt slam into me like dozens of tiny flaming comets.

That's not possible.

She dug an old combat knife from her bag as I recovered, kicking her bag so that a handful of Edenberries rolled out of it into recesses across the floor.

My eyes fixated on the fruit.

I licked my lips.

Her sickle hacked my hand off at the wrist. The little woman leapt, bringing the Rambo knife down at my chest. "Die, faerie scum!"

I backhanded her with my stump.

The little woman left a dent in the drywall and slid to the floor, no longer a threat.

Even so, her knife had cut an eight-inch gash along my torso. Being in essence form, it shouldn't have done anything but passed through with the essence filling back in automatically. Instead, a charred laceration scarred my liquid body.

I willed the wound to fill.

It refused.

I forced my essence to regrow the lost hand.

The stump burned but didn't sprout a new hand.

I pushed my essence to the higher plasma energy state and tried again. My injuries refused to mend. My plasma ignited, fury burning with the same heat as the agonizing wounds.

Glaring at the broken little woman filled my mouth with the taste of hot blood. The impudent wafer had attacked me in the course of doing my duty. She would hurt for it, at least as much if not more than the injuries she'd inflicted.

I stalked across the intervening distance, raising my bladed fighting cane.

The closet door exploded outward, Anima's voice thundering in its recesses. "Shieldheart, stop!"

Quayla

"Quayla, Vitae's going to kill Mrs. Cox!"

Panic shot through me. I'd only partially finished the cleanup meant to protect Bradley from getting arrested for Vitae's warehouse, but I had no doubt he'd kill the little old lady just like he had Dylan.

If I transmogrified, I still couldn't fly across town in time to save her. That didn't absolve me from trying, but if Foxner arrested Bradley, Vitae was as likely to abandon the mortal as kill him too.

I dropped what I was doing and sprinted across the intervening space. I scooped up Foxner on the fly and shoved her into her passenger seat, leapt into the car and drove it backward through the garage doors.

Ani will just have to send the putti to finish up for me.

I hit the sirens and broke every law I could in my haste to rescue Mrs. Cox. Slapping my thumbs on the steering wheel wasn't enough to salve my fury. If I'd been a fire phoenix, the steering wheel would have melted beneath my grip.

If Vitae killed my landlady, I was going to steal his egg away from Dunham, stomp it to little pieces and kill Vitae and keep killing him until he stopped coming back.

Caelum

Caelum curled around the rotisserie chicken thrown at his feet just before Viviane closed him back into his cage. Up to his own devices, he'd have avoided eating another bird. His hunger insisted birds of prey ate what they wanted, even other birds. After being forced to destroy churches and fight Sidhe with almost no rest, his conscience was in no shape to go three rounds with primal instincts.

He'd managed to escape death thus far, but he was exhausted enough that the thought of filling his belly nauseated him.

Dunham descended from his bedroom and strode across the intervening distance. Caelum's old boss didn't waste time with the intercom, instead triggering the robotic arm on his way to Caelum's stone.

"Put that aside, I have a task for you."

"I may not be human, but I still need time to rest and recuperate," Caelum said.

"I see." Dunham drew out the control key chain and deactivated the spell keeping Caelum penned. The grip of Dunham's hand wrapped Caelum like the hand of an iron Colossus. He drew a large caliber pistol from within his suit jacket and shot Caelum in the face.

The free essence of his former body eased Caelum's fight to reform against the control valve at the stone basin's bottom.

"New body, no fatigue," Dunham said. "Problem solved with the bonus that you now resemble your old self somewhat."

Caelum dug nails into his palms.

"Now, a conflux of major incursions is about to happen—

something about an old blood debt being settled, but the thrust is that two large Sidhe forces will converge here in Atlanta to settle their differences. You'll slay both groups."

Caelum seethed. "Yes, Master."

"Excellent, see to it."

Chapter Nineteen

Dire Choices

Vitae

I turned toward the closet and froze in shock.

A not quite substantial being like the Isaac, but not, hovered over a pathetic, trailer trash version of a nest. It was child-like, a hybrid of cherubim and the baby angels people misname cherubs. Light even shone from the shimmering kaleidoscope of colors captured in fog.

Everything from the eyes on her hands and wings and tips of her fingers was right, except a Watcher could not manifest in Creation.

Illusion then, meant to deceive me, to rob me of my conviction.

"You will stop, Shieldheart," Anima said. "You will employ your essence and heal that mortal this instant."

I refused to be fooled, even by the false effect of cleanliness wherever the light shone. The so-called entity over Aquaylae's nest employing our automata's voice was a masterpiece of glamour, but as was the very nature of the Sidhe, they took the illusion too far.

The Watcher sported a rainbow of gemstones in its forehead, each matched to a shield's element.

I will not be fooled.

I redoubled my determination and stepped forward into the glamour. Strength surged into me, restoring weariness and somehow filling me with wholeness—God rewarding my conviction. Clarity and wisdom trailed her cleansing aura. I'd been deceived, but not by glamour. The automata had lied to me.

"How dare you deceive me! I am Atlanta's Shieldheart!" Aquaylae's correction burned through my mind like a hot knife. "And you told her? That insignificant, incompetent traitor?!"

"You will master yourself, Shieldheart."

"You don't tell me what to do, *automata*."

Even as the word escaped me, I knew it was wrong. Anima was a Watcher, younger than the Isaac, but still one of the Creator's Overseers.

"You're the Watcher that old angel meant. You were the one that summoned a First One so that he could try to order me to serve Aquaylae."

Her voice softened but her expression did not. "Vitae, you are not acting like yourself. Look at what you've done to this mortal —your charge."

"She attacked me. She's obviously Fae Kissed."

"Why does your wound not heal?" Anima asked.

"She used a faerie weapon on me."

Anima's many eyes narrowed. "The weapon near her body is iron, Vitae. Cold. Iron."

"Preposterous."

"Are you sure, Shieldheart?"

She's stalling me with all these lies, but why? Aquaylae!

I sneered at Anima and strode toward her. "Very good, illusion, you almost had me deceived about your identity. This is all a distraction to keep me from claiming Aquaylae's essence and rebuilding my oracle. I will not be fooled."

I reached through her.

Vast fathomless infinity swallowed me. Time slowed. Scintillating colors swirled in clouds surrounded by stars brighter than the Star of David. Creation sprawled out before me, hurtling toward me like a runaway comet. I was plunged into a sea of life both separate and interconnected.

Old man's words echoed out of eternity. "This is not the path, Vitae."

Peace and wholeness shattered around me. Battlefield after battlefield filled my world—Sidhe and phoenix, mortal and angelic.

A great Arch opened to swallow me, vastness concentrated into shadow to blight out all around it. Three figures strode toward the rend's opening—three Sidhe queens emerging from left and right to stride behind a third marching down the middle. Behind the third queen, a massive being of darkness-shrouded light and beauty marched toward Creation unchallenged.

The man's voice returned. "Sacrifice is the only redemption."

Life and strength vanished in the blink of an eye—simple as snuffing a candle. My heart stopped, frozen for eternity without end.

I shook off the sensation, lifting Aquaylae's nest and marching from the building.

Quayla

I tried to take the apartment staircases in two bounds per flight, but my wings were too wide for the old building construction. The door to my temporary apartment hung open. Mrs. Cox lay just inside beneath a deep dent that made me want to kill Vitae a few extra times. Blood stained a line from her lip.

"Mrs. Cox?" I kneeled next to her. "Hadley?"

Mrs. Cox groaned. "Don't take kindly to being addressed in the familiar, young man."

Relief washed through me. If she was strong enough to

correct me, she'd probably recover. "My apologies, Mrs. Cox. Are you all right? Do you need a hospital?"

She nodded. "Faerie was tougher than Nana gave me to expect. Not sure what she was after, but if you can, we need to get word to Quayla."

Faerie?

I glanced to the empty closet. "Don't worry about that. I'll see to that, but we need to make sure you aren't hurt."

"I'll tell you this for nothing. Even if she did knock me out, I'm not anywhere near as hurt as that witch with a capital B— pardon my spelling—after I took cold iron to her."

Despite her bravado, my little landlady was lucky to be alive. A flash of Dylan's lips falling away from mine squeezed my chest like Vitae held my egg.

I have to get her out of here, but where?

Mrs. Cox struggled onto her feet.

I helped her up. "Easy. You know, it might be best if we got you out of town, maybe you could take a trip or we could just check you into a hospital so they can keep an eye on you."

Mrs. Cox stabbed a finger into my chest. "I'll have you know, young man, that Hadley Sage Cox does not run from ruffians, not even faeries."

"He could come back—"

"I wasn't accosted by a man, Kale," Mrs. Cox shuffled toward the door, her motions pained. "Begging your pardon, but while those of the male gender have the muscles, the spawn of Lucifer have no fury greater than that of a woman riled."

Truer than you realize.

"He or she, I don't want you where you'll be in danger if they come back," I said.

Mrs. Cox turned, cupping my cheek and patting it. "You're a good boy, Kale. Wasn't sure you were Quayla's kin at first, but you've both got the same heart."

I needed to get her out of the apartment building. Considering I wasn't sure how far back Summus had rewritten Foxner's timeline, I also didn't want the cop to escape the trunk and tie Bradley into the Howell Mill misunderstanding.

"So, you'll take a short trip?"

Mrs. Cox snorted. "Not hardly, dear, not Hadley Sage Cox."

"At least see a doctor? Please?"

"All right, but I'll make an appointment. Emergency rooms are highway robbery, actually worse than being robbed on the highway. Bandits at least let you keep your shoes on."

Once I'd helped her down to her apartment, I hurried back up to search my apartment once more. It had seemed as if Vitae had taken my whole nest, water heater catch pan and all, but I had to be sure.

He took everything.

I had to start over from scratch.

Well, not scratch exactly, I have the basins back at his warehouse.

The problem with going back for the basins was two-fold. If the police had gone back and found that crime scene, the location would be locked down. If they'd focused instead on the GPS in Sabrina's government-issue vehicle, I might have time to return, but I had to have some place to go first.

"Ani?"

"Yes," Anima said.

I cradled the cringing bronze angel in both hands. "Can you tell me if the authorities have raided Vitae's warehouse yet?"

"No, but your prisoner is working her way out of her restraints."

Great.

I felt bad about what was to come as I trudged down to Sabrina's car. I didn't want to knock her out again, but I didn't have any choice. I reared back a fist and popped the trunk with her key fob.

Sabrina shoved the lid open and pointed something at me.

I threw the fist forward, grabbing her rather than punching as

I transmogrified my essence. A Taser she'd hidden in her trunk sent its charge through me, down my arm and back into the detective.

The Taser came out of her unconscious grip with ease. I shifted back to human, closed the trunk on her once more and looked up at the bay windows fronting Mrs. Cox's apartment. There wasn't any sign she'd been at the window or seen what I'd done.

Maybe it would be better if I showed her what I am. Maybe she'd let me hide her then.

"Quayla!" The alarm in Anima's voice sent another jolt of electricity through me. "Caelum needs you."

"They all need me."

"No, Caelum just reached out to me through one of his old seeds. He needs your help."

"Give me directions while I drive." I leapt into the car and cranked both the engine and the sirens to life. What I was doing probably wasn't wise. First, running the sirens in a stolen police vehicle with the owner in its trunk was apt to draw attention one way or another. Still, getting across Atlanta without lights and siren, meant fighting the whole populace for right of way rather than the three quarters too self-centered to make way.

We made good time out I-20 west. A foreboding grew in my gut as the tall rollercoasters of Six Flags rose in the distance. "Ani? Are we heading to the amusement park?"

"He's a few blocks from there."

I let out a relieved sigh.

"I'm sensing one, no, two massive incursions."

"Another pair...let me guess, inside the park?"

"That's correct."

I took the offramp too fast, missing the light and maneuverable Johammer I'd sent back with Bradley. Tires lost their grip, leaving us to spin almost a whole three-sixty through oncoming traffic.

We jolted to a stop without hitting any of the other cars.

Thank God.

I waved out the window, muttering apologies as I got the car moving once more. "Ani, where's Caelum?"

When she didn't answer right away, I glanced into the passenger seat. The bronze angel cowered, hands over its head and wings pulled protectively close around its body.

"Give me a break already, you're metal." I blew out another breath. "Ani?"

"Up and on the right. He's inside."

I looked at the small yellow building and shook my head. "How's my guest?"

"Still unconscious."

There wasn't any smoking allowed in public restaurants, but an age-old cigarette taint pressed against me. Caelum sat at the bar, shoveling food in as fast as he could under the disbelieving glare of an old, blue-haired waitress.

"Caelum?"

He whirled around and threw himself into my arms. "I'm sorry, but I had to call you out. I need your help."

"Slow down. How did you get free of Dunham? When did you die?"

The waitress's scowl worsened.

His head shook. "I'm on mission—one I can't manage alone. I know bringing you in is bad, but like it or hate it, we have to succeed."

The waitress scowled and slapped a bill on the counter. "If you gentlemen are going, I thought you might like the bill. No hurry."

The tone of her last words didn't match her claims. A police cruiser pulled into the parking lot and I tensed.

Caelum grinned at me. "You do have money, right?"

"What?"

Caelum tilted his head toward the cash register. "Dunham's not exactly trying to make me fat, and I'm going to need all the essence I can muster for this fight. Do you have money to cover the bill?"

I dug the cash out of my pocket, trying not to tense on the outside as much as I cringed inwardly as the police entered.

"Problem?" Caelum whispered.

I shook my head, hoping he'd take the hint and shut up. I dropped a five next to Caelum's plate and turned toward the door. A hand came down on my shoulder.

"Just a moment, sir."

I froze.

"What's the problem, officer?" Caelum asked.

"Your friend dropped a twenty in front of the register."

I turned to look, forcing a smile as I brought the bill up and extended it toward him. "Thank you, officer. How about you and your partner have lunch on me?"

He smiled and took the bill. "Appreciate that."

"Not a problem," I hurried out to the car.

Caelum sat on the statue with a yelp, but I was already in motion so he adjusted in a hurry. "Ani, doll, thank God you were listening to the seeds."

"Pleased to be of service, Shield Caelum."

We glanced at one another, simultaneously asking one another what was going on.

"Stolen cop car," I said. "She's unconscious in the trunk."

Caelum whistled. "Not your normal dating method, but effective."

"Cut the crap, Caelum and tell me what's going on."

"I'm ordered to capture you or Vitae if I encounter you."

I tensed. "So, this is some kind of trap?"

"No, I genuinely need your help. Problem is, when we're done, I'm going to have to capture you," Caelum smiled. "Unless you kill me in the process."

"You just died."

"And I'm low on essence, but I have enough for another rebirth."

I fought streaming foot traffic running from the park and pulled the car to a stop in front of the entrance to Six Flags behind another two police cruisers.

"We're never going to be able to rewrite that many people."

"Don't worry, Viviane is handling that part."

"What do you mean?" I asked.

He jabbed a thumb over his shoulder. "She'll have some kind of Sidhe road block so she can rewrite the minds of any witnesses. She doesn't want the mortals knowing what's going on any more than we do."

"That doesn't make sense. You and the others have been tearing up the city."

"As disasters, not as phoenixes."

"But the Sidhe want to usurp Creation."

Caelum shook his head and leapt from the car. "Not this time."

I scooped up the statue and ran to catch up, abandoning Sabrina in her trunk. Caelum veered to the left and leapt the wrought-iron fence in a single leap. I followed, not clearing the spiked tops with quite as much space. "Explain."

"Dunham and Viviane are working together—sort of—but Viviane doesn't want any press right now while she's thinning out the Seelie and Unseelie troops for her own power grab," Caelum glanced sidelong at me. "Grynnberry is her creature."

"I know," I said. "He's her corpse now. Now what's the plan?"

"If they're where they're supposed to be, then we take out both armies easy peasy."

"Armies?"

"Caelum's description is apt," Anima said. "There are large forces of both Courts fighting from cover just up the hill from the Great American Scream Machine attacking each other and slaughtering any mortal that goes too near."

"Near the Ninja?"

"Closer to Superman." Caelum chuckled. "Been a while since you went to the park, huh? It's the Blue Hawk now, not Ninja."

"Whatever, how does that make fighting so many faeries easy?"

Caelum smiled. "The lake. You and I are going to teach them why they shouldn't cause a ruckus in the south."

We made our way through the crowds along the foot paths. With faeries erasing memories and considering Caelum's plan, I'd rather have transmogrified and flown. Caelum convinced me that a stealthier approach was to our advantage.

We passed the Blue Hawk and edged up the hill toward the Scream Machine. An involuntary gasp took my air away. I'd never seen so many Sidhe in one place, let alone out in the open in the mortal world.

If his plan doesn't work, we're going to have a serious fight on our hands.

Caelum led me away from the fight proper toward the water. We parkoured over safety rails, through employee-only areas and down to the water. Overhead, grey clouds darkened the sky.

No wonder he was shoving food down so fast.

Wind gusted over the lake, spraying the not-quite-fresh water in my face. Caelum grabbed me by the shoulders and turned me to face him. "Remember, Quayla, if one of us goes down for the count, it has to be me."

No kidding. If I die, I'm stuck going back to Dunham. Thanks, Vitae.

"If I'm still standing, I have to attack you and mean it." Caelum winked. "Surely there've been moments you wanted to kill me. Now's your chance."

Caelum transmogrified. His phoenix wasn't too different from mine in basic shape. Rather than being composed of shimmering water in a thousand shades of blue, zephyrs swirled around a bank of dark vapor shot through with little sparks of lightning. I'd seen his form before and knew the storm clouds at his core were synchronized with the clouds above. They could be white and fluffy too, depending on his mood.

I transmogrified to my true form after a moment's hesitation.

Caelum was right in that even two of us together would have a hard time wading into the battling Sidhe and coming out with our necks intact.

His wing brushed against mine, and a cry escaped his beak. "Come on, old girl. Let's see what you've got."

"Call me 'old girl' again and I'll thrash you," I screeched back.

"Good," He shot into the sky, twitching a pinion to rise with a slow spin.

I joined him with several heavy beats of my wings, taking a position above him with effort and matching his spin.

A funnel of wind whirled into existence around us, the mouth skimming the lake until thick mists rose up the funnel's walls. I reached out to the water in his storm and sent my essence to meet it. Lifting the water vapor through wind and will, we raised a hurricane.

By time we had the storm formed, we definitely had the Sidhe's attention. Both of us cried a simultaneous challenge—mine roared the loudest no matter what Caelum said.

We pitched our position toward the Sidhe and hit them with a storm mortals would tell stories about until the end of time.

Lighting lashed around the hurricane, lancing into Seelie and Unseelie alike. Our storm's path took us across the Scream Machine. Wind and water weaponized the splintered old wood and metal bracings in moments.

Sidhe threw their magic at us. Elves tried to ride the winds and bring their blades to our throats.

Talons greeted them with death.

When the Sidhe ran, we both went opposite directions for a moment, almost collapsing the storm. Caelum screeched at me. We coordinated the assault under his direction. I hefted the water weight, and he employed his essence to lash the faeries with blast after blast of lightning.

In a very few moments, the main body of Sidhe had been reduced to a combined total of three faeries. Caelum collapsed under the weight of our onslaught and I knew in that moment that he'd intended to incapacitate himself to protect me.

My Karambit knives slew the last three. I returned to my transmogrified, unconscious shield brother, laying my knife across his neck.

No, there has to be a better way.

I threw him over my shoulder and ran for the park entrance. No one stopped us when we neared the line of police and security hunkered under the eaves of the park's entrance. Sabrina's car sat where we left it, trunk still closed.

I dropped Caelum into the passenger seat and drove away, a suspicious knocking sound coming from behind me.

"Quayla, Caelum said you had to kill him," Anima said.

"I know."

"This is dangerous."

"I know, Ani."

"Where are you going?"

I'd given that question a lot of thought. There was only one place I was pretty sure I could go. True, Dunham could have been watching it, but out in the country, watchers or mercenaries would stand out like a sore thumb. The well-armed locals weren't likely to put up with them either. That meant I might have one last bastion of safety.

"Terrance's house."

Dunham

Viviane paced in the background until Caelum headed down to the gym, but she didn't wait a moment longer to express her obvious discomfort. "That was wasteful, Dunham."

"He claimed he was too tired to perform the task, so I remedied the situation."

Her lips pushed together into a thin line. "He was right. You've been pushing them hard, splitting their energies trying to accomplish two missions at once."

"I don't feel my goals are any less important than yours, and I do not see why my priorities should suffer when we can pursue both."

"You wasted essence."

Dunham scowled. "Give him extra food then. Killing him made your mission possible."

"I am not sure Caelum is the best choice for facing so many Sidhe. You should've sent Ignis."

"He's busy."

"Exacting your vengeance against those that tried to drown you, I know, and that's exactly my point." Viviane put a hand on his shoulder. "What did I tell you was the key to getting this far?"

"Focus."

"Exactly, singular focus, but now that we're here you're splitting your resources. Our goals suffer because of this."

"I do not agree."

"Agree or not, I am older and wiser."

"Says the," Dunham made air quotes. "'Exiled Lady'."

Viviane darkened. "You should be grateful. I wouldn't be in this situation if it weren't for saving you."

"I might have been the last straw with your sisters, but that's hardly my fault." Dunham gestured at the standing stones caging the phoenixes. "You wouldn't have them without me either."

"Capturing a Shield was a way to achieve both our goals—one at a time. I'd hardly have needed you if I pursued only my priorities."

"If you say so, but I'm not sure I concur."

"Do you agree that without me—even if you'd somehow managed without my help to eject the water from your lungs—that you would have died a century ago from old age?"

Dunham folded his hands behind his back. "It is impossible to say I would not have found a way to tap into my abilities without you because that is not the course of events which occurred. Was there any other point of guilt you wished to address or perhaps something else you wished to blame on me?"

She darkened and stormed down the stairs without another word.

Chapter Twenty

Incursions of Wisdom

Vitae

I'd barely gotten the junkyard nest secured to prevent spillage while I drove when taint tickled my senses. I swept my gaze around only to realize the taint had entered into the area of one of my seeds.

I needed to get Aquaylae's essence back to my sanctum so I could finish the oracle, but an incursion had to take precedence. With no answers from Vilicangelus and that imbecile Summus sleeping on the job, the Sidhe had to be stopped without the mortals seeing.

Not that I need either to compel the wafers to see what I wish.

Selfish wafers attempting to thwart my rescue split my focus. With what remained, I felt my way across Atlanta, using pristine seeds around the tainted to estimate distance and direction. Unusual as it was in a mortal, the sentry net my thrall created exceeded expectations. Fortunately, the incursion wasn't too far from Aquaylae's apartment.

Confederates of hers no doubt, if not lovers.

I pulled off the road in sight of an old airplane marking the edge of the Cobb County Air Force Base. Seelie and Unseelie fought one another across the open field, oblivious to the traffic on nearby highways.

No time for subtlety.

I shifted to essence and lopped off my arm above the unhealing wrist wound. Once cleared of the damage, will regrew the missing hand. Satisfied in my superior solution, I transmogrified into my true form, life plasma flickering gold on the burning scarlet, reflecting off of my armor. I dove into the fray without warning. Bladed wings cut imps and hergies from of the air. My beak snapped orcs and hobgoblins as talons tore into elves and ogres.

The Sidhe turned their attacks on me, forgoing their former rivals.

I changed back into a human shape, whirling my canes like a living combine. An ogre seized me from behind, but I swung both canes backward and stretched my crescent axe heads into short scythes, impaling his skull with essence blades. Sidhe ichor hooded me in a flood as he dropped my soiled form to the grass.

I took a moment to rebalance my canes and interlock them together. I launched myself at the surrounding faeries like a mad dervish. The whirling bladed staff cut down the Sidhe.

The devastating attack didn't come without a price. Hergies pierced one shoulder and one wing. An elven blade sliced one thigh, and a hobgoblin sank teeth into a calf. An ogre fist's glancing blow staggered me an instant before I severed his head from his almost nonexistent neck.

I stood bleeding, gasping and seething amid their slaughtered remains. The battle had taken too long for someone of my skill. My present body had reigned supreme through many battles, but the pains creasing my flesh suggested my triumphant body needed replaced with a stronger, deadlier version.

The Sidhe should've cowered at my feet, ready prisoners to fuel my quest for perfection. There should have been elves begging to reveal the whereabouts of my swords.

Neither remained.

Both forces were dead, victims of intemperance and weakness.

I must become more.

An act of will extended my senses, pushing tendrils of my essence to their bodies. Each of my extensions sank figurative fangs into the body parts strewn about me, guzzling their essence down en masse.

Power surged through me.

Strength strained to be unleashed.

Cut after cut wove closed—except the chest wound delivered by Quayla's feeble, geriatric landlady.

No point in cutting the wound away. I need a stronger vessel to wield my power. I'll return to the sanctum, set aside the lion's share of my strength and discard this body for a new one.

"Master, you must see this!"

Scurith beckoned me from the nearby overpass traversing South Cobb Drive, jogging part way to meet me and escort me over to whatever he wished me to see.

"Why are you here, Scurith?"

"I caught sight of you a few miles back and decided to postpone my task and offer you my services." He led me under the overpass. "When you engaged the others, I noted strange magic and felt it better to investigate rather than interfere with your sport."

I must get a grip on myself. I've wasted so much thought of the false automata and that treacherous Aquaylae, that I thought ill of my loyal servant—reason clouded by unfounded suspicions.

I didn't apologize to Scurith. There wasn't any need. The coyll knew nothing of my suspicious thoughts nor did apologizing to an inferior set the proper tone.

"I see. What do you wish to show me?"

He drew me up to a ledge that reeked far in excess of the tainted blood splattering my robes. Torn jeans and a green US army jacket wrapped an ancient mummy. The corpse clutched a squirming, wheezing cat. The death grip around the animal wasn't the cause of its distress as much as its shrunken, partially undone collar.

"What am I looking at, Scurith?"

"I believe this is the source of the incursion points and the reason we've been unable to better pin down where the Seelie and Unseelie would fight next."

Scurith undid the collar but didn't release the cat. "These markings are—"

"A leech spell," I said. "The others are for a portal creation. Why would they be on this animal's collar? Is it some witch's familiar?"

"Possible," Scurith's head bobbed. "There is a seed of magic in the clasp, but it's not mortal magic."

Primer for a spell?

I looked at the animal and the apparently homeless corpse. The body was in horrid shape, but the cat looked better cared for than I'd have expected of a stray, particularly one owned by the indigent.

Breaking the man's fingers allowed me to draw the cat to my nose. It raked my face with its tiny claws. Snapping its neck stopped its struggles. I inhaled deeply, scenting Seelie taint, Anseelie that wasn't Scurith and mortal chemicals—flea shampoo.

"I believe this creature may be one of the animals stolen from shelters by your kin."

Scurith tensed. "You think that could be true?"

I rounded on my assistant, transmogrifying my hand into a claw as I sent him flying. "Did I not just say so with my own lips?"

Scurith glared for half an instant before remembering himself and returning to a proper subservient attitude. "I offer my apologies, Master."

"So you should."

I stared at the broken animal, unwilling to accede the possibility that it evidenced proof of Aquaylae's suspicions.

She probably knew because she was colluding with the Wyldfae.

"How may I serve you next, Master?"

I dropped the dead cat and restored my hand to its proper shape. "You will teach me more about the spells on this collar—how they work and what they're meant to do."

"My spellsinging is not so advanced, Master, but I shall endeavor to give you all you deserve."

"Good. Dispose of those remains and return to the sanctum."

Quayla

I left Caelum in the passenger seat and Sabrina in the trunk, pulling my hilts as I exited the car. Opening myself up to sense Fae Kissed and Sidhe brought something to me, but I wasn't sure what. The overpowering aroma had the faintest tickle of rot, like meat thinking really hard about going bad.

Sage and earth scents rode an undercurrent on what I was still convinced was Sidhe essence. They matched what I would have expected to find in Terrance's home, but instinct warned they had little to do with my older brother.

I approached the house, cutting left up a driveway and then hooking into the back through open accordion doors to an empty parking pad. A Japanese garden dominated a small depression of a filled-in swimming pool. The garden sat between a wooden deck and a glass wall looking into the house proper. Beyond a second wall of glass in Terrance's central atrium, a small figure sat in a meditative pose.

The outer sliding glass doors weren't locked. I let myself into a living area decorated in a sparse-but-tasteful manner. Two halls led around either side of the square atrium dominating the square house's center. I took the left, passing by sliding wooden doors closing off possible ambushers my nose told me weren't there. Nostrils open to my surrounding, my eyes kept to the small figure with an eggplant on his head sitting cross-legged on the rock.

I opened another sliding glass door, entering the house's tiled foyer and turning right toward the otherwise open atrium.

Round yellow eyes opened. "Good evening, Quayla."

I pushed essence into my hilts.

"Child, you would be hard pressed to defeat me that way. Besides, it is poor manners to attack someone waiting to help you."

"You're a Sidhe."

"In the strictest sense of the definition, I am not, but that is only a small matter of semantics. I am Yarque, a friend of your Terra and Power of old. Speaking my name thrice while touching the earth, you may conjure me if you have direst need."

"I've had all the help I need from Sidhe lately."

Yarque reached behind him under a cleft in his rocky seat.

I tensed.

He drew out a small alderwood box inlaid with tarnished silver and set it gently on the ground between us. "I kept this from Viviane's pet and his thugs. I tried to prevent the theft of Terrance's nest too, but they overwhelmed me."

"I thought you said I wouldn't be able to beat you. If a bunch of Fae Kissed were—"

Yarque held up a hand. "I said you would be unable to defeat me with your knives—strong as your element is, and said they overwhelmed me."

"What's the difference?"

"Direct assault versus overwhelming power. When facing one of us, the latter is the only way to defeat us." He quirked a grin. "Remember that."

Right, like he'd tell me how to defeat him.

"I was a putto once—the greatest builder Heaven ever created," Yarque's expression grew distant. "As you can imagine, I had quite the ego, but I digress. You have an injured air phoenix in your vehicle and a most determined wafer about to escape you."

The doors behind me opened.

"I will wait while you settle your affairs."

I eyed the small box, cursed and hurried out to the car just as Sabrina climbed out of the trunk. She saw me coming. Dropping into a fighting stance, she lifted a tire iron and glared a double-dog-dare that I come at her.

I hurled the blade of my Karambit at her chest. She ducked as I softened the s-shape blade into a glob that splatted against her shoulder. Had I left the blade as it was, she'd have lost the arm.

"As attacks go, that one's pretty limp," Sabrina said. "You're under arrest, whatever you are."

"I really don't want to do this again. You can't handcuff water." I split my focus between circling with her and the essence spreading across the shoulder of her blouse as any amount of water is like to do. "I need your help."

She lunged at me before my essence had done the job I'd been concentrating on. The tire iron shattered my forearm and her foot shot out, hooking me behind the knee. I went down with an explosion of air. She followed through with the fist wrapped around the metal iron.

I transmogrified.

Her fist slammed through what was my head. The suddenness of my change gave her little time to correct and shock stole it. She slammed her fist into the concrete behind me with pops, sounds like snapping celery, and what we'll just call a warrior's battle cry.

My essence finished its trip up her neck and slapped tight across her mouth and nose.

Sabrina grabbed at the water with one hand. She had the sense to keep hold of the tire iron despite the pain. When clawing at the water didn't remove it from its barricade of her air passages, she wailed on my watery form with the tire iron. She hit me once in the chest. The second, slower blow went for my head. The third hit my gut with the force of a toddler's swat as she fell over unconscious.

Damn she's tough.

I repaired and reconstituted my body while shifting the essence on her face off of her nose. I threw her over one shoulder and Caelum over my other. My juggled objects were winning until I expanded my wings to help cradle the two bodies while I grabbed my bronze statue.

Yarque was still on the rock where I'd left him. He smirked at the detective already struggling on my shoulder. "She's a good choice—for a mortal—reminds me a bit of Michael."

"Caution," Anima said. "The entity before you is extremely dangerous."

"She's right of course." Yarque smirked. "Watchers have excellent vision."

"Why are you here?" I asked "What do you want?"

"I owed Viviane a debt of honor now paid, but I owe Terrance a debt of friendship. I want to help him." Yarque unfolded himself and crossed the distance between us. He touched Sabrina's flailing leg. "Sleep, mortal."

Sabrina went limp in my arms.

"To help Terrance, I must help you free him."

"I don't trust you."

"Good," Yarque said. "Don't. What do you need?"

"It's not a short list."

Anima's tone screamed a warning. "Quayla."

I weighed Anima's warning against the possibility of help. I had no shortage of things I needed done. This Sidhe didn't smell right, but without Terrance to ask, I had to go with my own instincts.

Verify his willingness to help without agreeing to anything?

"Let's start with the easiest item," Yarque said. "What are your intentions for this mortal?"

"I don't know. She used to be an ally, but she's been rewritten. Right now, she's a danger to the only ally I have left. I guess my best choice is to get her rewritten again."

Yarque turned around, picked up the box and offered it. After a moment, he set it down at my feet and offered to take Sabrina.

Had he offered to take Caelum I'd have objected outright, but he'd put Sabrina to sleep when she was becoming a problem. There seemed little doubt he could've done far worse to her. Despite his size, I let him take the police detective.

Yarque set her gently on the tile at my feet. He picked up the box and presented it to me cradled in both hands. "I will hold it so you need not relinquish Caelum."

"Quayla," Anima said. "I don't like this."

I shook my head. "You could make off with the feather."

"True." Yarque handed the box to me and took three steps back.

I juggled the box and Caelum until I could hold both while touching the sapphire embedded in my chest. Under the circumstances, I skipped closing my eyes to keep them on Yarque. "In service onto death I swear this life unto the Undying Light."

The words sent pulsing shivers through my body and the box vibrated. Light gleamed from the seams of the little treasure chest, fading a moment later. I turned it over, dumping a silver-dipped feather pendant and chain into my free hand.

"Now you can summon your rewrite," Yarque said. "I will wait."

"Anima? Any indications of an Arch or more Sidhe that could ambush Vilicangelus?"

"None yet," Anima's tone hardened. "But I am watching."

"Vilicangelus. Vilicangelus. Vilicangelus."

After several minutes of nothing, Yarque spoke. "Perhaps you should place Caelum in Terrance's bed while we wait? My kin are keeping your kind very busy."

It wasn't a bad suggestion. I settled Caelum in the nearby master bedroom and returned to find Yarque in the exact position I'd left him in. I didn't trust the whatever he was, but he'd provided the box and the ability to summon a Divine One once more.

I lowered my voice. "Ani, can you hear me?"

"Yes."

"Is this pendant genuine?"

"Yes."

Yarque rolled his eyes.

"Why isn't Vilicangelus answering?"

"I don't know," Anima said. "Perhaps he just expects Summus to answer."

"Didn't you tell the Isaac that Caelum said Summus had been captured?"

"I did," Anima said.

"Then shouldn't Vilicangelus be answering? He's still over us."

"He's over the England shires too," Anima said. "Yarque is correct in that all Shields have been heavily engaged. I will reach out to the Watchers over Vilicangelus's Prefectures."

"In the meantime, perhaps I can assist," Yarque said.

"I am not going to let you muddle her mind, you could enthrall her like—" I cut off the sentence with a click of teeth.

"Like your Vitae is doing?" Yarque asked. "That one needs to learn from history."

"Right, well, I'm not letting you do that to her."

"What if instead, I unraveled her previous rewrite?"

"That's not possible," Anima said.

"Did I not tell you I was once putto?"

"Ani's right, once reality is rewritten there is no way to undo it."

Yarque shook his head. "A rewrite is like a patch sewn onto a garment to fix a rend—though these days they are used more to cover over a stain. The new reality—the patch—exists in parallel with the old reality—the stained fabric. Mortals are made in the image of God, they exist in all the times and places they've ever been. All I have to do to reconnect her with that timeline is make it possible for her to see the cross-section."

"You're going to let her see both?" I asked.

"I cannot remove the new reality without damaging her, but when He created mortals, He connected them to the cosmic consciousness. She still remembers the old. I need merely give her a chance to remember the mental terrain that lies beneath what has been bridged by the new memories."

"Ani?"

"I-I don't know," Anima said. "His explanation doesn't conflict with what I know about rewrites. It certainly explains how some mortals unravel them."

"But don't those mortals go insane?" I asked.

Yarque lowered his voice. "Are they insane or are they navigating two realities without someone to guide them?"

Having Sabrina back as an ally would be a huge boon, but risking her mind wasn't something I really wanted to do. On the other hand, I was running pretty short of allies and if I didn't do something, she was going to make Bradley's life a living hell—though come to think of it, being enthralled by Vitae might've been worse.

I can't be selfish. I can't let this Sidhe screw with her mem—

Before I could make my decision, Yarque bent over her and touched her temples.

"Stop!"

Yarque's voice was strained and his eyes never shifted from the middle distance to focus on me. "Now that I have begun, stopping is certain to cause her damage."

"If you damage her—"

"You cannot kill me until you've learned your lesson."

Ghostly realities rose like movies projected on fog around Sabrina. Summus's rewrite had been extensive due to the sheer amount of time being redesigned. He'd fretted over the amount before starting. As I watched Yarque examining the two timelines, I had to wonder if the length of the bridge covering the old might not help Yarque in the end.

"Dammit, Quayla!" Caelum's voice proceeded his furious charge out of Terrance's bedroom. "I told you to kill me."

I turned away from Yarque to face Caelum. "I'm not just

going to surrender you back to Dunham. I found some basins. If we build you a new nest—"

"He still has my egg!" Caelum snarled. "As long as the spell he has over it remains, I have to do what he commands—including his order to apprehend you."

Caelum attacked.

His sudden assault swept me up before I could react. Wind stole my footing, and a lightning-shrouded fists slammed into me as I went down.

"Caelum, stop!"

Dunham's voice escaped Caelum's mouth, chilling me to my core. "You've thwarted my plans for the last time, Aquaylae."

"I don't know what you're talking about."

"Hedingham, Essex 1863."

A hurricane of ice shredded my insides. Torchlit faces swam around my memory, fading to line after line of fresh graves now over a century old.

Caelum's hands tightened around my neck. "You murdered my family."

The words escaped in a whisper. "I didn't mean for anyone to be hurt. I was just scared."

"Scared like a little boy watching his family be drowned one by one?" The vehemence exiting Caelum's mouth bent his features from flippant playboy to malevolence. "Scared like a little boy waiting his turn for stones to be tied around his legs? Waiting to be thrown into the lake?"

"I—"

"You could've saved me. You were the water phoenix set to protect us!"

My head shook, hurling tears to either side.

"She was put under house arrest while the divine investigated," Anima said. "She couldn't have saved you anyway. We're not allowed to interfere with what mortals do to one another."

"Every death, every burning and drowning and beheading was Aquaylae's fault." The rage in Caelum's voice eased, though the murderous expression grew even more demonic. "You're right though, Watcher. She was the catalyst, but human beings were the actual problem. Hypocrites spouting commandments, then claiming God's will to violate them."

"The churches," I gasped. "That's why you're attacking the churches."

Caelum's smile sent shivers through me. "Yes. They will pay. Hypocrites and intolerants, my Shield will wipe away the ignorant, superstitious, self-righteous masses in this city and then the rest of Creation—after they show their true colors and turn against one another."

"If you kill Quayla, you won't have a full Shield," Anima said. "Without all five phoenixes, you'll never be able to keep a divine phoenix caged."

"She will be reborn here." Caelum fixed me with mad eyes. "You will let me kill you or there will be a reckoning."

Yarque edged into view. "Pardon me?"

Caelum's head shot up in time to meet the spike of Yarque's pickaxe. Before I could do more than scream my objections, the body atop me unraveled into wind essence.

"Catch it, we need to catch his essence," I lurched up, but it was too late. Without a nest designed to keep his essence or some other vessel to capture and keep the wind of Caelum's body, there would be no way to keep his essence from dissipating in the air.

"I am a creature of earth," Yarque said. "I have no means to capture wind."

I rounded on the Sidhe. "Why did you kill him?"

"Better to return Caelum to capture than let Viviane's toy capture you." Yarque helped me to my feet. "Caelum, Ignis and Terrance are enslaved to the spell on their eggs. You are the only free shield in Atlanta. The Exiled Lady must not have you."

"Vitae is free," I shot back.

"Is he?" Yarque asked.

"What's going on here?" Sabrina held her head, blinking as if trying to push away double vision.

"The mortal has been reconnected," Yarque turned to her. "Sabrina Foxner, this is the phoenix you remember as Quayla. A death has changed her form, but she remains your ally."

"Ally?!" Sabrina scrambled to her feet and decked me. "You bitch! You had me rewritten despite my objections!"

Chapter Twenty-One

The Blood Phoenix

Caelum

Caelum's body reformed back in Dunham's cage. His former CEO towered over him, purple with rage.

It took a moment to realize that not only was the bell jar lifted out of position by the robotic arms, but the magical barrier keeping him on the stone was gone. He tensed to kill Dunham only to freeze as phantom fingers crushed down around him, holding Caelum immobile.

"You failed me, Caelum."

"I brought her in to complete your mission." Caelum gasped as ribs cracked. "As soon as I was conscious, I attacked her, tried to apprehend her as ordered."

Dunham shook his head. "You purposefully used too much essence attacking the Sidhe. You set things up, so that you complied with my orders without any chance of success."

"No, I—"

Dunham squeezed. "Don't lie to me."

Bones popped.

"I've been watching," Dunham held up the egg. "Listening.

You know, despite the fact that you represented everything I hated, I really liked you."

"Dunham—"

"Where was that location? Where is she hiding?"

Caelum struggled against the spell on his egg.

"Tell me!"

The egg won.

"Terrance's house, out in Dallas."

Dunham squeezed once more, whispering over the egg.

Pain and brute force put Caelum on his knees, not writhing on the stone in agony thanks only to the spell that held him still.

The Fae Kissed strolled over to the next cage. "Ignis, I have a mission for you."

"Go screw yourself, *Master wafer*," Ignis spat.

"You will go to the Terra's house in Dallas and slay Aquaylae."

"Help you cage her?" Ignis snarled. "No chance in Creation."

"You will do as I command." Dunham returned to Caelum, drawing a pistol. "Or I will punish you."

Dunham put the gun to Caelum's temple. "I considered using the vacuum chamber to suffocate you so I could collect your essence. Problem is, I am not sure an air phoenix can be suffocated."

"Dunham," Viviane rushed up the stairs. "Stop. He doesn't have enough essence."

He pulled the trigger. The egg in Dunham's hand flared with light as Caelum's essence dissipated for the second time.

"What have you done?" Viviane demanded. "We needed him."

Dunham met Ignis's gaze instead of Viviane's. "He failed to obey my orders even after I warned him."

"Fuck you," Ignis said. "Trading this little zoo for my egg is no threat."

Dunham's brows rose. He strolled toward the balcony.

"Dunham, there's a way to hurry him to rehatching. You need

to stop before you make things worse," Viviane said. "We need five phoenixes to keep the divine."

"We're doing all right with three." Caelum's former CEO pushed open the balcony door, walked out to the edge and stopped. He peered into the yellow topaz and celestial silver egg, searching for some sign of the phoenix within. "I really did like you. I imagine there's nothing you liked better than the feeling of flight."

Dunham dropped the egg over the side.

Viviane lunged for the egg.

Dunham seized her, yanking her back before she could catch Caelum's egg. "One last flight as a severance for all his hard work."

Once the egg had tumbled beyond her ability to catch it, Dunham shoved her away and marched toward Ignis. He withdrew the phoenix's crystalized heart. "You will go to Terrance's house. You will attack Aquaylae with everything you have. You will kill Aquaylae. Acknowledge command and your compliance."

Anima

Pain lanced Anima's forehead, the yellow topaz in her forehead burning like a star only to die in a sudden supernova of agony.

Caelum! No!

She reeled, eyes wildly searching the phantom, spirit-world soul of Atlanta for answers. She found none. The agony of Mare's death had been different, but no less torturous. The Unseelie sword so blithely wielded by her Shieldheart after the egg thefts had ripped Mare's soul away, tearing its connection to her egg and to Anima in a devouring hunger.

That he could stand to touch the blade that had pierced both he and Mare should've signified something desperately wrong.

The sword welcomed him, changing its shape to suit him, but why? Mare? The taint in his blood? Has the blade a taste for his blood?

Mare had thrown herself between the Unseelie Champion and Vitae. Still, the blade drove through her heart into Vitae's back.

When it stole her soul, did it steal something from him, too?

Anima pushed away the past to focus on the present. Wings spun her around, oriented within a storm's eye of mist and magic, Creation and Infinity. She peered beyond swirling nebulae filled with pools of Eden-born spring water, not to other such islands and her fellow Watchers, but toward the beginning, the Isaac.

Surrounded by the constellations of her Shield's seeds, Anima dipped an eye-tipped finger into a mirrored pool of cosmos. Another like her, but scarred and ancient, appeared

"Anima," the Isaac said before she could announce herself.

"Caelum has been Destroyed."

"So I See."

"Our divine remains captive. Aquaylae is doing all she can, but she needs help. We need another Aero."

"There shan't be one." After a moment, the Isaac continued. "There are none to send."

"She needs help."

"He sent the Messenger."

"Vitae turned Gabriel away," Anima said.

"So be it."

"So be it? Is that all you have to say?"

"I See. The Beginning of the End. The End of the Beginning. What was. What is. What shall be."

"I already know that."

"You know, but do you Know?" the Isaac asked.

Magic yanked at Anima's core.

"Your Vitae calls."

Vitae

I poured Aquaylae's essence into the pool and invoked the mantra to activate the runes. Atlanta shimmered into view in the pool, seen as the phoenix flies high above. Tiny dots appeared around the city. Most of the dots represented my seeds, but some represented Ignis, Terrance and Aquaylae.

Caelum's are all gone. I really shouldn't have expected more from him. It's a shock Aquaylae has any remaining.

"Oracle, hear my call."

Silence.

I put power behind my voice. "Oracle, answer my call!"

Anima's voice emerged from the water. "I have nothing to say to you, Vitae."

"How dare you use this oracle to speak to me, automata?"

"I was your oracle before I was your automata," Anima said. "Before you turned your back on your Shield. Before you stole Aquaylae's nest and attacked a mortal you were supposed to protect."

"I do what is necessary to fulfill my duty, and I will not be lectured by the likes of you. Now do your duty or I shall—"

"Shall what, Vitae? You have no power over me."

My voice tore from my throat. "Do your duty!"

"Behold the seeds upon the waters. Thus is my duty."

"This is insufficient. These seeds are too small to zero in on their location."

Anger undercut Anima's voice despite the impossibility. "That is why the oracle was upgraded, Vitae. When the city grew too big for the oracle, the divine adapted to the times just like your shields did."

"You will curb your tongue and do as I command."

"I do not answer to you, Vitae. I have filled this oracle with this Shield's seeds. That is my duty. If you want more, you will purge the Sidhe taint from your essence, apologize to Aquaylae, and join her in saving the others."

Each word of the disrespectful automata pumped the bellows fueling the glowing forge of anger in my gut and sent molten blood thundering through my veins. "I don't need the others. I am Atlanta's Shield."

Sarcasm dripped disdain into my ears. "Great job protecting the city, Vitae."

A roar filled my ears, drowning out the thundering of my heartbeat. "I will show you. I will show the world how to protect a Shield and deal with the Sidhe once and for all."

"Goodbye, Vitae."

"Wait," I did my best to rein in rampaging fury. "You're right, I should apologize to Aquaylae. Tell me where she is and—"

"No."

I slammed both fists into the water. "Tell me!"

Ripples spread out across the oracle pool, bouncing off the sides, rippling back and eventually calming. The city and seeds remained in the waters exactly as they had been, granting me a view of a silent Atlanta.

I stormed downstairs, killing the first three faerie servants that crossed my path. I spluttered through my passcode, so spitting mad that uttering the pronunciation correctly took three tries.

My thrall worked at one of the experimentation stations. He turned as I approached, offering me perfect line of sight to his throat. I seized him, lifting him from the ground. "Where have you been!?"

He met my eyes for a split second before dropping his gaze respectfully. He tried to choke out an answer, forcing me to let him down that he might speak. "Doing as you ordered, Master. I was delayed at the old warehouse by Atlanta police. I had to lose them before I could return here so that they didn't bother you."

"What were you doing at the old warehouse and why were the authorities bothering you?"

"Cop was after me for stealing corpses from the morgue," Bradley said. "She caught me at the old warehouse searching for...something that could help."

"Help with what?" I demanded.

"You did want me to work on flying warriors next, didn't you?"

The impertinent automata had unsettled me too much. She'd defied me, Atlanta's Shieldheart. The wafer cowering before me hadn't been defiant. He'd offered the proper deference and had produced everything I'd asked since enthralling him.

I took a deep breath.

"You are correct, but I must change your priority."

He bowed. "How shall I serve, Master?"

His deference sent warmth blossoming in my chest. "Scurith will be showing us a spell that will help our cause."

My thrall set the items still in his hands down on the counter and turned back to me. "Lead and I shall follow."

Scurith entered as if on cue, saving me the trouble of summoning him. He dropped a dead cat on the table side by side with the one he'd brought back from the overpass.

My thrall looked from Scurith to the carcasses and back.

Scurith removed the collar from one of the animals. "I've confirmed with this second animal that these collars use the cat's life to power short-term Arches. The runes here leach the power out of the animal, passing it to the secondary runes that allow a Sidhe to open a portal from Faery into Creation using this third set of markings to zero in on the collar."

My thrall pulled the collar off the second cat.

"Hey, this is just like the one Whiskers was wearing when I found him." A frown wrinkled my thrall's forehead. "Is there anything magical about the runes?"

"Not per se," Scurith said. "The clasps contain faerie essence much like Master's seeds—a catalyst to fuel the spell initially."

My thrall snickered.

I raised my brows at him.

"Cat...catalyst?" He dropped his eyes, face straightening. "Sorry, Master."

"Would any Sidhe essence suffice?" I asked.

"I imagine so," Scurith said.

A frown of my own grew as I considered the animals and their collars. By some miraculous accident of fate, Aquaylae had been right about the shelter thefts.

"Scurith, could an Arch be opened using the spell from within Creation to bridge two points?"

My thrall brightened. "You mean like a long-distance dimension door spell?"

"I suppose it's possible," Scurith hedged. "Some tests would be prudent."

"On it!" My thrall volunteered.

This could prove an effective means of visiting an impudent druid with a squad of enforcers.

A quick instruction held my thrall from rocketing off to test the collars until Scurith had demonstrated how the spell worked. The spell was simple enough, so easy in fact that my thrall managed to evoke it twice—draining life from the grendlings holding the collars.

Scurith must've sensed my concern. He dismissed my thrall to gather construction components for more collars before confiding, "The spell is meant to be used by goblins and their like, Master. The magic is in the collar's essence and the life consumed. Your mortal isn't Fae Kissed and I doubt he has the innate magic to work such magic on his own."

"Thank you, Scurith. I'd hate to be forced into destroying him. Please go monitor the oracle for incursions."

"If I witness one?" Scurith asked.

"Send enforcers to capture what Sidhe they can and bring them back here for processing."

"As you wish, Master." Scurith bowed deeply, but hesitated.

"Something else?" I asked.

"There are rumors, great Master, terrible rumors that in the Court's fury Vusolaryn and Mariena have empowered their Champions. Begging your pardon, but I fear for your safety. What if you no longer have strength sufficient to slay them?"

"I am touched by your concern, Scurith, but all is in hand."

Scurith inclined his head and hurried off on his task.

When he'd gone, I took my thrall aside. "Prepare two enforcer squads and provide me the spell encoding to activate a collar placed with each."

My thrall kept his eyes on the floor. "Of course, Master."

Bradley

Bradley watched Vitae leave, waiting for a ten count before exhaling. He'd kept his head and acted well enough not to be subjected to any more enthralling magic.

The Arch spell hadn't worked as well from place to place as it was supposed to between Faery and wherever. Scurith had pointed out that the difference was one of life energy consumed to create the initial link. He'd also claimed that a Sidhe coming over would brace the Earth side of the portal with faerie magic and let the energy of Faery fuel the other side.

Still, this could be seriously useful—especially if I use an enforcer or some other trollman to fuel the spell since they can't be killed.

He jotted down all the instructions and notes, ran a quick Xerox and turned his attention to creating additional collars. The first two he built with troll blood in the clasp, but the second pair he seeded with Vitae's essence.

Bradley packed one of each into a priority mail box with a copy of the instructions and addressed it to his house. He put the parcel in the hands of one of the grendlings and ordered the feral, oversized Smurf to ship it off.

Vitae

My thrall interrupted my reading with the details of the two collars I'd requested. I dismissed him and turned to a pair of covered bird cages. Removing the covers revealed a selection of pixies from each Court.

Their little bodies were emaciated, and the colors had drained out of their wings. None of them looked fatter than the others and the shriveled remains of berries cluttered the floor of their cages.

Curious. I'd think they'd eat if hungry.

Pixies had never struck me as more than the most adolescent of the Sidhe. Selfish and flighty with the attention span of a middle-school mortal, they'd been of use in my Sidhe blood experiments only at the very beginning.

Since then I'd collected the ones captured in the two cages, unsure what to do with them until that moment.

"I'm willing to free two of you—"

Several of the pixies started chattering high-speed, high-pitched pleas to be selected. A few of them didn't even raise their heads. Concentrating on the power in my essence, I spoke a word of command. "Freeze."

Silence returned to my study. I reached into the cages one at a time, selecting the weak, lethargic pixies that hadn't volunteered. My essence could restore their vigor, but even that wouldn't help with their broken wills.

I covered the cages, silencing disappointed groans and hurled insults. A pair of Edenberries liberated from Aquaylae's landlady and filled with my essence rested on two china saucers.

"I would have your oath of a single service, payment of your debt for freeing you." I set the two pixies down next to the plates. "Once given, we will celebrate the bargain."

"What service?" the Unseelie pixie asked.

"I don't care what the service is," the Seelie pixie said. "I oath to perform one service for you, Shieldheart, to square the debt of you releasing me."

I nudged the Edenberry over to the pixie. He gobbled it up,

rallying visibly. With his obvious improvement, the Unseelie pixie offered his oath. I pushed on my essence, exerting my will to ensure they would obey. I handed them each a small strip of paper. "You will activate this spell for me where I release you and when I command it."

I had barely finished preparing my two new confederates when Scurith burst into the room. "Master, an incursion, a huge one out near Sugarloaf Mills mall."

About time the automata came to its senses.

"I suppose it is time once more to show the Sidhe they cannot simply penetrate my Prefecture?"

"Yes, Master," Scurith grinned. "It is time for a lesson."

Vitae

Before I left for the incursion, I sidelined to my bedroom. I removed two bottles from a wine cooling device in the closet near my nest. I stripped, setting aside my clothes, and poured the concentrated essence of two elven knights into my nest.

Stirring the violet and emerald blood into the almost black blood in my basin sent power thrumming up my skin. I'd had to kill the knights, but I'd saved their essence until I was ready to wield it.

They think me too weak to deal with their enhanced Champions? I shall remind them who is God's cherished.

Retiring to my bathroom, I secured the whirlpool tub's drain plug, seated myself and severed my femoral arteries. My nest was too full to catch my essence, but the tub would contain it until it could be concentrated and mixed with Sidhe essence for rebirth or wherever else I needed it employed.

Consciousness faded as blood pumped in slowly weakening spurts.

I awoke a moment later as my essence wove a new body into

existence within my nest. Power thrummed through me like never before. Every cell of my essence tingled, but more, the power possessed a harmony other combinations hadn't provided.

I felt like myself for the first time in ages, even though a quick glance proved my body a pale-skinned female with long hair so black as to be hued blue.

Scurith stared up at me, terror alight in his eyes. Tail tucked and ears flat, his voice emerged in a squeak. "Mistress?"

"Master." No rage backed the correction, rather the calm of a dappled pool.

The coyll shook himself then started bowing. "Yes, Master, apologies Master. Your car awaits you."

"Lead on."

Chapter Twenty-Two

He's Got Balls

Quayla

Sabrina let me regain my feet. "I'm sorry. I only did what I thought was right—you know, following the rules?"

The Atlanta detective's jaw tightened, and she didn't meet my eye, but she offered a single nod.

"Things are bad, so much worse than when you were rewritten. I really need your help."

Sabrina pinned her bottom lip with her teeth. "I don't know, Quayla, I'm already in a lot of—you know it's not right calling you by a female name."

I shrugged. "You can call me Quayl."

"Can't you just become female?"

I shook my head.

"But you're water, couldn't you reshape yourself or something?"

"This body's DNA would remember what it's supposed to be, forcing me to expend energy staying in a shape foreign to its makeup. I could die again and be reborn, but Vitae stole my essence. For now, this is my last and only life."

Sabrina's face hardened, summoning a blossom of warmth in

my chest. Male wiring responded a moment later, but I pushed it from my mind.

"Quayla, watch out!" Yarque grabbed Sabrina and me, throwing us to the ground in Terrance's foyer as the back half of the house exploded in a fireball.

A moment before the back glass crisped pitch black, I saw Ignis rise from one knee and transmog into human form.

My heart caught in my throat. The fury Dunham had spat through Caelum's lips left little doubt about Ignis's presence. I shot a look at Sabrina. "Get out of here."

"I want to help."

"You can't, not against Ignis. Go back to the warehouse and fetch the stone basins. That gets you out of harm's way and still helps."

"Only if you're here to take them when I get back."

I squeezed her hand, leapt up and drew my Karambit hilts.

"I am here to kill you, little sister."

I'd known Dunham sent him to get me from the moment he'd firebombed Terrance's kitchen, but hearing my death sentence from his own lips chilled my essence to ice.

"Can't we talk about this, Ignis?"

"No," Ignis snarled. "I have been ordered to kill you, to use every ounce of my ability to murder you without mercy. Dunham killed Caelum for failing to capture you—True Death, Quayla. He would not hesitate to do the same to me if I do not slay you."

I frowned.

Ignis was being awfully informative for someone ordered to do his best to kill me.

He has to be trying to help me somehow. Think...Yarque!

I whipped toward where the Sidhe had stood only to find the place empty.

Ignis strode down the right passageway, blackening the glass as he came. "You cannot stand and fight me with any chance to prevail, Aquaylae."

I ducked out the other hall. A strong scent of smoke clogged my breath, but I held in the coughs as I rushed toward the back yard. I'd barely leapt over the shattered glass of Terrance's back wall when a searing pain latched onto my wrist.

The intense heat of Ignis's grip flashed essence to steam in a moment. I wrenched myself away, glancing back to see he'd retrieved one of his hilts from somewhere.

Dunham wouldn't have given him one. Terrance must have kept a spare for him. Does that mean Terrance has some spares for me, too? Focus.

A sudden jet of flame shot out of Ignis's human fingers.

I dove sidelong, his fire igniting my pant legs. Fire shot past me, setting Terrance's back fence aflame.

"You have to do better than that, Aquaylae."

"I'm thinking."

Ignis shook his head. "You're doomed."

He threw another gout of flame. I dodged, barely, leaving Terrance's carport to burn.

Why would he miss? He can surely bend fire like I can water.

"You can't win. You never learned enough about your fellow shields." Ignis lifted his hilt, extending a bow from its center and drawing back an arrow. "You don't understand your element well enough to prevail, Quayla."

Quayla? Why did he change?

I transmogrified a feather's breadth ahead of his arrow. It passed through me, radiated heat flashing nearby watery essence to steam. The arrow hit the neighbor's wooden fence, exploding in a starburst of fire that ignited the wood as if had been dry kindling.

"You cannot fight fire with water. You only have so much essence. Water clings to its own, but fire...fire likes to grow." Ignis lifted his hilt to his lips. A flowery tune floated out of the little instrument. Flames rose around us.

I stared in horror as the growing inferno grew even bigger. A moment later, the fires split from one another, forming humanoid-shaped flames that jumped from fences and the roof to encircle me.

Shit. He's right. I can't beat him. Ignis has me totally outclassed. Think!

Had we been in Atlanta, I might have sliced open a hydrant, but out in the edges of Dallas—essentially out in the sticks—there were none. Firefighters had to bring water with them. There weren't even any sewers where Terrance chose to live.

But there will be water. Well water!

I transmogrified into human, throwing myself through the flaming linebackers getting ready to tackle me. Pain lit my skin, but better to burn flesh than lose more essence.

I ran around the house, hoping to find a front spigot and doubly hopeful Ignis hadn't killed the pump somewhere along the way.

I found it by spotting the yellow hose curled up in a cradle against the house. I extruded a blade in preparation to cut the hose away from the spigot only to find it already disconnected.

Terrance, you're way too conscientious.

I sliced the spigot away from the house. Water spat out onto the ground only to slow a moment later. It never ceased, but if the minimal flow were anything to judge it was coming up because of a syphoning vacuum.

"I destroyed the pump." Ignis said.

Right, he has to do his best. Well, a little water is better than nothing.

I drew water from the ground around me and faced him with a Karambit knife in each hand.

Ignis shook his head as he sauntered across the crisping lawn. He lunged in a flash, hilt extruding a long, curved blade as he rocketed toward me.

I caught his sword on my knife and whipped an s-shaped blade into Ignis's gut.

My blade held his off, but my assault evaporated in an angry hiss.

I cursed, extruding another blade just in time to fend off a flurry of sword strikes. Ignis angled his blows so that even when I caught it between two knives, the length sliced hair or cloth or skin.

"You're dead, Aquaylae. You can't win," Ignis smiled. "Certainly not in a hand-to-hand fight."

My will threw the feeble stream of water into his face. It couldn't hurt him, but the sudden cloud of steam let me throw myself backward. I transmogrified, spun and launched myself skyward.

A backward glance caught a smirk as Ignis sucked in his flame men and transmogrified to follow. He caught up too fast, larger wings and thicker muscles granting him a faster climb.

Movement at the corner of my eye caught Sabrina's car leading firetrucks toward Terrance's home. She was supposed to have cleared out, gotten to safety, but I was glad I wouldn't be responsible for burning Terrance's house to the ground.

A long, wide strip of blue caught my eye.

Gore Lake.

I pivoted my course, beating my wings to drag me higher and higher. I reached out to the thin cloud cover, sliding left and right to collect any clouds that passed close enough. I was starting to feel really good about my chances when a fireball slammed into my lower back.

Agony blinded me. Essence flashed to steam as the fire burned away my tail, talons and everything below my pelvis. I spun out of control, the world going topsy-turvy, upside down and sideways all at once.

Ignis had burned off all I'd drawn into myself and more.

Shit. I really am dead.

I was alone.

My bronze statuette lay on the tiles back in Terrance's foyer.

My divine token was a watery lump in my breast feathers.

I couldn't call to Anima.

I couldn't call for reinforcements.

There were no other shields, not even a divine to call upon.

I was moments from splatting all over the countryside far short of a lake that might give me a chance.

Another fireball hit my wing.

Agony and vertigo made me their bitch.

A powerful screech filled the wind. "It's over, Aquaylae. I won't let you reach the lake."

I wanted to cry, but couldn't waste the essence. I focused on my essence with every last shred of my will, reforming and rebalancing a much smaller body. A peregrine falcon wasn't all that big, but it was deadly just the same. I had to be the peregrine, but without forgetting that mass to mass, Ignis could flash me to cloud without suffering major losses.

My flight leveled, but the moment it did, I slipped left, rolled and dove. A fatal fireball barely missed me as it careened through where I'd been just a moment before.

From the corner of my eye, I saw Ignis transmog, extrude a bow, launch three arrows and reshape into his native form.

I rolled through his shots even as their courses bent in to catch me. A flash of blue passed beneath us.

My heart quickened.

I dove, wing tips flicking back and forth to create a wild, reckless dive for the below swimming pool.

Ignis transmogrified and fired twelve arrows in mere instants.

Flames rocketed from the end of their shafts.

I dodged wildly, barely slipping between his speeding missiles.

Relief flooded out of me in a breath.

He missed.

The arrows hit the pool, exploding in a firestorm. Their inferno consumed the chlorinated waters in two blinks.

I cursed, not caring, but rather hoping my blasphemy might catch God's ear and eye.

Foolish or not, I maintained my dive, heading into the flash-evaporated water vapor. As soon as I felt its leading edge, I banked hard, pulled up and drew in all I could manage. I wasn't able to recharge the way a whole pool's worth of water would have allowed, but my wingspan and body swelled toward normal size.

An arrow burned away one wing.

I shrieked my frustration, rebalancing as I careened into the ground. Impact and road rash dragged essence along the hot asphalt. Several hard wingbeats and a quick transmog of talons into legs let me change a drag into a breathless sprint. I folded wings around my human body in thick armor all too aware any one of Ignis's arrows could deliver debilitating wounds.

I poured my strength into my legs and ran a serpentine flight like Lucifer himself was on my heels. I wasn't even sure where I was going, only that I had to find some way to slip my dogged pursuer.

Arrows rained down around me, melting and igniting asphalt and setting cars and one lawn mower ablaze. I leapt a hedge to dodge through a Slip-N-Slide, leaving some poor kid to awful plastic burns as I raced away with all of the yard toy's water.

Houses grew more frequent, alerting me to my location. Dallas proper lay ahead, filled with buildings and mortals.

If they haven't seen us already, there's nothing I can really do to keep things quiet if I want to survive.

Guilt twisted my gut, but luckily Ignis's steady barrage kept me too busy to worry about it. He circled, transmoging and firing arrows in an attempt to herd me away from town.

If he wants me out of town, then in town is where I want to be...unless he's using reverse...screw it. There's plumbing in town.

I spotted a hydrant and bee-lined for it.

Hair along the back of my neck all stood up so fast it almost plucked itself from my skin. I threw myself backward, extending wings on pure instinct and back-winging as hard as I could.

Ignis crashed down in front of me, talons burning twin craters right where I should've been. He turned, repairing himself and reshaping into a human with his Katana in hand.

The red, iron hydrant peeked through his legs.

I hurled an-S-blade at it.

Ignis cut the projectile and sprinted forward.

Blades shot out of my hilt. Sword and knives flashed and clashed at inhuman speeds. Ignis drove me like a man possessed, but there was no rage in the glowing coals in his face.

Dunham wasn't behind his eyes.

Ignis was a calm, cool, killing inferno.

A screech of tires and the sound of rending metal almost cost me my head. Sabrina's sedan wrapped around the hydrant, an air bag keeping me from seeing through the shattered windshield to her condition.

Water, God-sent glorious water rained down all around us.

Even as my heart ached to know the mortal shield's condition, I pushed my attack. Raining water popped and hissed against Ignis's skin, dampening his heat as it strengthened me.

This is it. I've got him.

Ignis spun, turning his back to me as he hurled a massive gout of fire at Sabrina's sedan.

I drove both knives into his fiery human shape even as terror stole my breath. The sedan burst into flame, its metal engine melting over the broken hydrant.

All time seemed to slow.

Ignis, my brother shield who was trying to kill me, was vulnerable for only a few more instants. Once the hydrant's rain vanished, he'd have the upper hand once more.

Those same instants were all that stood between Sabrina and her vehicle turning into a raging inferno.

I could kill Ignis, send him back to Dunham and live free to protect the people of Atlanta for at least one more day.

Or I could abandon my chance at freedom and save Sabrina. Ignis would burn me to death, capturing me in Dunham's trap and enslaving me to the Fae Kissed's will.

No matter how much I might hope otherwise, there simply wasn't any time to do both.

Hedingham flashed into my thoughts. Scowling villagers marched torches toward oil-soaked wood at my feet.

I hurled myself at Sabrina's car, Karambits slicing away her door. Another flash of watery blades freed her from both airbag and seatbelts.

Ignis's voice held resignation. "You should've slain me."

I whipped around and hurled my wings at him. The combined water cost me strength, but bought enough time to snatch Sabrina from her car and race her onto the nearby lawn.

I hurried away in full retreat the moment I set her down, drawing Ignis with me.

"Your plan won't work."

Plan?

"That's a fire inspection station, a training location not a full fire house. There's nothing there to help you."

I wasn't sure what he was talking about.

"I don't even know why you of all people would think a training center would do you any good, Quayla."

I bolted for the building, using the last of my strength to sprint across the lawn and dive through a glass window into someone's office. I was on my feet and out the office door in a moment. I rushed through halls, cutting water fountains open and pulling fire alarms—anything to give me a drop's more water.

Even so, I knew it wasn't enough. Ignis would just light the building on fire and gain strength from the inferno. There was a certain irony in Ignis Round, Fire Inspector, burning down a fire inspection center, but the thought barely had a moment to roost.

Come on, there has to be something here.

The training center was a multistory office building. I hadn't seen any evidence of a live fire building. It was a place for book learning, new procedures and familiarizing firefighters with new techniques.

My breath caught in my lungs.

I threw open the next marked classroom and ransacked the cabinets.

Nothing.

I scavenged the next one, the trilling fire alarm dying in the increasingly humid air.

Nothing. Where would it be?

Ignis called from somewhere on the same floor. "Quayla? You can't hide forever."

I searched another classroom. Ripping the door off a tall, locked, metal locker delivered hope to my hands. I snatched two half-foot wide red balls and shoved them into my chest. I'd have been able to keep them handier if my current body had possessed breasts, but I had to keep them protected. Besides, Ignis might've noticed a sudden unexplained change in my bust size.

I hurried out the door, backtracking to a ladies' room I'd passed.

Ignis appeared in the hall, disappointment on his face. "I'd started to think you slipped away."

He charged.

I threw myself into the bathroom, transmogrifying into a winged, pure water human and slicing open sink feeds.

A blazing Ignis filled the doorway, flaming Katana in both hands.

"You're trapped."

I blew a raspberry at him, folded my wings, dove into a stall, and flushed the toilet.

Ignis's blade sliced away the first stall and then the second, the door closing behind him. "You won't make it down the drain in time."

I shrank my wings to putti size.

His blade barely missed me as he cut away the last barrier between us.

I raised my hands in surrender.

"I'm very disappointed in you," Ignis sighed.

I shrugged. "Right back at you."

The motion allowed my wings to lift the two red balls into easy reach. I snatched both, sucked in a breath and brought them slamming together into Ignis's burning form.

Pushed into contact with such high heat, the balls exploded instantly, filling the small bathroom with extinguisher chemicals.

My Karambit hilts scissored through his skull the moment the blinded Ignis fled chemical extinguishers into human form.

My voice broke as a quote from one of Dylan's favorite movies echoed off the bathroom tiles. "I fear you're underestimating the sneakiness."

Chapter Twenty-Three

In the Trap's Teeth

Vitae

My Mercedes came to a stop in the Sugarloaf Mills parking lot, a caravan of SUVs following me toward the Medieval Times side of the mall where Scurith reported the incursion was located.

I peered through squinting eyes at a seemingly-empty parking lot. Rolling down the window admitted taint to swirl through the car. The strength of the aroma left me choking and confirmed I was in the right place.

Enforcers poured out of the SUVs. I didn't have any of the winged fighters yet. From the big, beefy finger pointing toward an open loading dock door, they wouldn't have been much use anyway.

I rolled the window back up and left my Mercedes parked where it was—far away from mortals' cars that might scratch it. I affixed my fighting canes to one another, extruded crescent blades to complete the lajatang and led the others toward the yawning doors.

If the numbers Scurith relayed from the oracle were correct, I was about to deliver a decisive blow that in the end would teach Vusolaryn and Mariena not to trifle with me.

The loading bay gaped empty.

Horses stomped and blew out protests at the scent of both my enforcers and the Sidhe fighting in the mortal place of play war. Gestures hammered into my trollmen's decayed brains sent enforcers left and right to check for flankers.

My path followed taint to the entrance of a great arena. I stepped onto the sand only to have spotlights blind me.

Scurith's voice rang through the speakers around the arena. "Ladies and gentlemen, allow me to introduce Shieldheart Vitae, so-called overlord of Atlanta."

Applause broke out as the house lights came up, revealing two Sidhe armies. Immediately to my right, Knight Gherrian raised his head, curtaining hair falling aside as his tongue caressed his lip. He froze for three blinks then tightened up on his golden blade. His head rose. On the opposite benches in the red section, Knight Dolumii marched down the stairs toward me. He hesitated on the last step before wrapping his other hand around the growing Champion blade's hilt.

I spat the name. "Scurith, you traitor."

Scurith's voice filled with mock distress. "But, Mistress, isn't this what you wanted?"

"You'll find out once I finish with these insignificant worms."

Goblins, gnolls, and troglodyte lizard men swarmed down narrow aisles, shoving one another for a chance to die at my talons. Elves, orcs, and ogres raced across the sand from the far side of the arena, several, including one half-ogre, mounted on slavering beasts. Hergies, sprites and pixies swarmed out of the arena's rafters. My enforcers reached me before the Sidhe tide crashed against us, leaving the sauntering Champions—Gherrian and Dolumii—to face my virtually-immortal bodyguard.

"It will be my pleasure to reclaim my trophies from you, elves."

"The only way you're getting this sword back is in the back," Dolumii snarled and slashed.

"You cannot defeat my guard," I said.

"Perhaps that was true before," Gherrian hamstrung one of my enforcers. He reached into his vestment and shattered a glass vial on the fallen trollman. "Unfortunately for you, Vitae, Scurith has given us the knowledge necessary to defeat you."

I pushed through a sudden gap in my guard, trodding on lifeless enforcers somehow slain in a way that prevented their regeneration. I pressed my attack, whirling the lajatang back, forth and around.

Dolumii's blade met my own at every spin. His jaw set in a grim line and knuckles wrapped white beneath the tormented faces in his sword's guard.

Gherrian bounded over a melting trollman, lunging for my own hamstrings.

I leapt his attack, thrust the crescent blade at Dolumii before jerking it hard backward at Gherrian.

Dolumii lunged.

Gherrian sliced.

I flipped over Dolumii's blade, bringing my boot across his face. The impact delivered all of my momentum, forcing me to roll under the slice. Gherrian turned his slice downward, cutting into my side—though not as much as he'd intended. A glow enveloped his blade, making my rapidly-disappearing blood shimmer along the metal.

I swept his feet with the staff and then my own boot. He leapt the first only to be brought down by the second. I reversed the spin and swept Dolumii's feet out from under him before he could recover. I made my feet, chopping down at Dolumii.

Dolumii rolled to one side and thrust. The tip of his blade bit skin, sucking the warmth from my flesh.

Gherrian met my retreat with a hilt to the back of the head.

The world rang like the inside of Notre Dame.

I elbowed Gherrian in the face, splitting my staff into the two fighting canes and reshaping the essence blades into three-quarter axe heads. I brought one down at Gherrian's head and whipped the other at Dolumii, launching the essence blade into his gut.

Dolumii and Gherrian deflected their respective blows.

An elven arrow sliced through my right lung.

A serrated goblin sword sawed into the back of my knee.

A gnoll's teeth caught the wrist delivering a death blow to the goblin, fangs piercing my flesh and a jerk of its crushing jaws breaking my wrist.

Eyes wide, I realized my enforcers all slain.

I summoned all my essence and transmogrified, protectively cushioning two small vessels secreted on my person.

Armored and healed by changing into phoenix form, my talons lashed out.

"Now!" Gherrian and Dolumii shouted in unison.

A net of interwoven silver and iron chains hit me from above. Pain seared me in a hundred places. Sidhe hands deftly drew me down by the silver links, beating me with clubs.

I tried to transmogrify to a purely liquid form, but the iron bit harder from every angle in response to my magic.

I shifted back to flesh, protected from the iron by armor and cloth that did little against the downpour of clubs. I curled around my secrets and let them beat me.

Vitae

I awoke in a wide, cobbled hollow under a nighttime sky. Thunderheads shrouded the horizon. Torches burned a circle around the clearing. More lit the space beside two curved tables occupied with various Sidhe. A small table between the feet of the greater one seated the rotund goblin known as Thatch.

Flames illuminated twin knights guarding silk tents beneath tall pines. Knights and tents matched either icy blue and raspberry or daffodil and crimson. A knight on either hand held small, but familiar pixies on their shoulders.

Thatch refused to look at me.

There were no feast tables.

The Sidhe played no games.

Vusolaryn and Mariena entered from their tents dressed in battle attire. Dolumii and Gherrian followed them, restored to the glorious livery they'd worn before I'd...before they'd been slain in the sanctum.

My blood raced through my veins. My hands itched to strike them down, but my hands were bound and my neck collared.

"Shieldheart," Mariena scowled. "Enslaver of my servants."

"Our servants," Vusolaryn corrected.

Mariena inclined her head. "What have you to say for yourself?"

Laughter bubbled out of my throat. It rang through the quiet clearing and the unexpecting crowd.

"This is your answer?" Vusolaryn snarled.

I shook my head, unable to wipe my eyes with my hands still bound. "Apologies, the irony struck me funny."

Mariena frowned. "I do not see anything humorous."

"And your laughter will be short lived, I swear it," Vusolaryn said.

I laughed again. "Is that an oath, faerie? On your life and honor?"

"You're damned right," Vusolaryn said.

"Something isn't right here." Mariena peered into my face. A hint of fear edged into her eyes. "Laryn..."

"I have two sets of last words," I interrupted. "First. By the Undying Light, I command you to surrender or face summary judgement."

"You're more Sidhe than Light, *Vitae*," Vusolaryn said.

"Hmm," I offered them a thoughtful look, trying not to allow my triumph to reach my face. "You may be right, Sidhe, but I hope to exemplify the best—dare I say perfection—of both."

"Bow." Vusolaryn's voice hit me like a physical blow. I fought the command, but his will proved stronger than my own. I fell to my knees, still holding my expression.

"Laryn, stop. Look into his face," Mariena said. "Something is horribly out of balance here—a riddle that must be addressed."

Vusolaryn took Dolumii's sword, marching my way. "We can solve it once I've added this bird to my Champion blade. Maybe you'll even be reunited with the Aqua that saved your neck."

Anger backed Mariena's words. "Blight take it all, Laryn, stop and look at him."

Vusolaryn raised the blade over my head. "I've seen him before."

"No, really look."

"Not now, Mariena."

"Bide your strike but a moment, *Great Prince*," I almost kept the sarcasm from the title I used to stroke his ego. "I have yet my last words to utter."

Vusolaryn hesitated. "Well?"

"Silence him!" Mariena shouted. "Don't let the Shieldheart speak."

"I free you."

Vusolaryn scowled. "What?"

A smirk curled my lips. "I wasn't talking to you."

Magic surged through the clearing.

Two Arches opened, one between the tableau and the Seelie tent, the other opposite it. Twin armies of trollman enforcers poured into the hollow. Dozens of smaller, winged enforcers swooped through above their heads—readied just in time for this assault.

Perhaps I should reward my thrall...later.

I transmogrified my arms and leapt to my feet as the enforcers started killing. I caught Vusolaryn's downward stroke and drove sharpened wing tips into him like spears.

Sidhe forces fought the superior numbers of enforcers. On their home ground, the Sidhe proved far more powerful. Scurith having warned me of the possibility, I'd stacked the odds ten to one. Mariena shrieked, trying to throw off the trollman covering her mouth and breaking her arms.

I picked up the fallen sword. It writhed in my hand a moment, but I pushed my will into the blade, forcing it to submit.

An anguished voice sobbed my name. *<Oh, Vitae.>*

The sound of Mare's voice in my thoughts was like the light of heaven itself, but I had no time to bask in it. I could enjoy her presence once she was free.

I kneeled next to the bleeding and gasping Unseelie prince, holding the sword beneath his gaze. "Release Mare from this blade."

"Rot in hell," Vusolaryn snarled.

"Very well, if you will not bring her to us, I shall send you to face her."

"Shieldheart!" Thatch exclaimed. "No, stop!"

"For Mare." I slashed a claw across his throat, letting the faerie's blood spray out for seven heartbeats before I thrust the blade through his heart. I twisted the blade and willed it to drink his soul. Whether or not the Sidhe prince had a soul, the blade consumed him greedily, sucking him into the blade like it was a straw. I rose, pointing the blade at the Seelie royal. "Bring Mariena here."

"Vitae," Thatch begged. "You must stop."

My enforcers frog-marched the struggling princess my way.

My enforcers forced Mariena to her knees before me. "I'm sorry Laryn's champion slew your shield."

"Free Mare from this blade."

"I-I cannot, even were it my blade there is no way to free a consumed soul. They're gone."

"She's not gone," I snarled, slashing a bloody gash across the Sidhe royal. "I've heard her."

Mariena shook her head, terror sending tears from her cheeks. "Your shield is dead."

"She's alive!" Another slash turned the previous wound into a gaping, bloody wedge. "Release her."

"The sword is just tormenting you, Vitae, driving you mad for its own amusement."

"If that's so, I have no further need for you." I drew back the blade.

"Stop, Shieldheart," Thatch held up his hands from across the clearing. "If you do this, there will be a reckoning. Slaying them both will bring both queens down on all Creation in a war the likes of which you cannot imagine."

"Let them come," I snarled. "None are greater than what I've become. When I've finished punishing the Sidhe for what they did to Mare, none shall remain to threaten Creation."

"You sound like Lucifer," Mariena snarled. "You remember what happened to him."

I scoffed. "Except I'm on God's side—perfecting His plan. Once I've destroyed the Fallen and all their children, I'll have proven both my ability and my loyalty."

"Wearing the visage of our Fallen sister Viviane? I think not."

I tore out her throat, waited seven heartbeats, and thrust the blade into her. "Tell Mare Vitae sends his regards."

The Unseelie blade drank the Seelie princess, consuming her from the inside out.

A laugh escaped me. "Perhaps I'll be elevated beyond a simple Divine One. Is not the left hand of His throne empty?"

"This is madness." Thatch ran for his tent. "You've summoned hell into Creation—literally."

One of my winged enforcers scooped him off the ground and dropped him at my feet. "No, dear Thatch. You've overlooked one thing that prevents what you fear from coming to pass?"

"What is that?"

I thrust the blade into the goblin. "No one is going to survive this to tell the queens."

Once the blade left nothing of Thatch, I gestured to my enforcers. "Bring Gherrian and Dolumii here. Let's hope for your sakes, gentlemen, that you can release Mare."

Chapter Twenty-Four

Offers of Alliance

Quayla

I collected Ignis's ashes even though I wasn't sure how well they'd work mixed with the fire balls' chemicals.

Maybe I can run them through my essence like a filter.

Since I had no illusions about facing Ignis again, I returned to the locker for another couple extinguisher balls. I might not be able to sucker him into a small room again, but it was worth having them.

Paramedics were tending Sabrina when I exited. I inclined my head toward her and strode toward the edge of town where she could see me go. She'd follow or not at her choice.

If she's smart, she won't, but I hope she's as stupid as I am.

The walk back to Terrance's house took more out of me than I expected. Even transmoging, rebalancing and essentially recreating my human skin didn't manage to wash away the pain left by Ignis's strikes. Maybe it was phantom pain and maybe his essence just had the ability to harm me.

I didn't want to think about it, so I didn't.

Terrance's house was whole when I arrived. There was no

police tape, no burn damage to the nearby fences, not even scorch marks on the lawn.

I went around back to find the back wall repaired, but the garden still a ruin.

He said he was a putto.

I found the bronze statuette on the kitchen bar. Anima's voice nearly shouted from it the moment I came into line with its astonished expression.

"Creator, Quayla, you were amazing!"

I shook my head. "I nearly lost."

"But you didn't," Anima said.

"She's right, Quayla."

Panic flashed through me as I recognized the voice. I whirled around, blades at the ready.

Viviane lifted her hands in supplication. "I'm not here to fight."

"What do you want?" I rasped.

Her expression hardened. "Dunham has gone off the rails."

"Boo hoo for you."

"He-he killed Caelum—True Death," she said.

A hollow in my core ached for him. "I heard."

"I tried to stop him."

"If you say so," I said.

Viviane crossed the distance impossibly fast and slapped me so hard I hit the floor, then she kicked my hilts out of reach. "I didn't come all the way out here offering help just to be disrespected, little bird."

I struggled back to my feet.

She didn't try to stop me, but she didn't help this time either.

"Why did you come here then?" I asked.

"I need your help."

I laughed, but in a few seconds it transmog'd into crying. I was too tired, too heartsore for Sidhe games.

Maybe if I stab her in the head.

Viviane slapped me again. "Snap out of it. This is important."

A growl rumbled out of my throat. I pushed on my essence, sharpening my fingertips to talons.

"If you attack me, this deal is off."

"What deal?" I barked.

"I can get you the eggs. Ignis, Terrance and Vitae. I can even get you essence to fill replacement nests."

"Why would you do that?"

"Dunham's vengeance is interfering with my plans."

"What do you expect me to do about it? Kill him?"

She shook her head. "No, he's too dangerous. I know. I made him that way. You need to help me thwart the Seelie and Unseelie Courts. Do your job, just when and where I tell you. That's all."

"I don't think so."

Viviane darkened. "Right now, I've got my people covering up all the incursions and all of Dunham's attacks on the city. If you don't help me, I'll stop keeping things quiet."

I looked around Terrance's house.

Did she do this?

"I don't believe you. Why would you even want to cover up things? Sidhe live to create Fae Kissed."

"I don't want the other Courts to know I'm in play until I have the upper hand."

I frowned at her, unsure what she was talking about.

"Helping Dunham was the last straw. The other two queens ganged up on me to stop me from screwing with their games. They exiled me from the Dark Trinity and forbad my people a ruler. Mortality has suffered because of it."

I scoffed. "Yeah, I'm sure one less Court playing with mortal lives has really made things worse."

"Ever tried getting two people to keep a secret?"

"Yeah, but I don't see the correlation."

"Think about it. All three of us are trying to collect power. When three of us are in the game, it's damn near impossible to trade and treat for an unchallenged run at Creation. Reduce that balancing point to only bargaining with a single queen and humanity suffers far more often."

"Why would you give me the eggs?"

"So you can convince your Shield to help me by destroying our shared enemies."

"Shouldn't that include Dunham?"

"The boy's gone rogue, but he's not my enemy yet. Besides, empowered by your Divine One, you'll never beat him."

"Don't you think recruiting me will change that?"

"He'll never learn of this."

I considered her and her offer. Regaining the lost eggs would make a huge difference There'd be no way for Dunham to just kill my brethren outright. Anima could probably help remove the spells from the eggs or we could destroy and recreate them. Either way, so much would be better if I agreed to help her—a Sidhe queen who'd let Dunham murder Caelum.

"No."

"No?" Viviane's brow rose. "This is the only way you'll ever get those eggs back. The only way you'll save your friends."

God help me, but I can't make myself beholden to one of the Dark Trinity—not even to save my Shield.

"No."

"You're going to regret this decision."

I shrugged.

She was probably right. I'd probably regret turning her down, but enlisting under her command—even to destroy Sidhe like I was meant to do—felt so wrong.

Like selling my soul.

I'd managed—if barely—to defeat Ignis. Maybe I had a chance against Dunham.

Quayla

Sabrina turned up two hours later with the stone basins from Vitae's warehouse. I wasn't sure where she'd come up with another car, and I was just too tired to ask.

I stared at the ashes piled in the basin Sabrina retrieved. There weren't enough for a rebirth and after learning of Caelum's True Death I feared defeating Ignis had sent him back to a similar fate.

Three other nests rested in line with the first on the tiles of Terrance's foyer. The caches of essence Terrance had left around the city neared enough for a rebirth once collected. Until they were assembled, his was one of three empty nests. The fourth—Caelum's nest—wouldn't ever be filled just like I'd never again hear his horrible jokes.

Fortunately, I was too emotionally wrung out to cry no matter how much I felt like I should.

"What now?" Sabrina asked.

I shook my head.

I didn't have any answers.

"Will these be safe here?" she asked.

"Probably not."

Her hand slipped into my own. "Quayla?"

I looked down at her strong fingers gripping mine then up at the concern in her face.

"I don't know," I whispered.

"Didn't you say you contacted a supervisor? Could they help?"

I shook my head. "He's not answering. I'm on my own."

"You're not," Sabrina said. "I'll help you. If you woke them up like you did me, Mrs. Cox and Dylan would help you too."

"Dylan's dead. Vit—Vitae killed him."

Sabrina's expression hardened.

"Leave him to me," I said. "Take the nests and hide them at your place. At least there, no one will come looking for them."

"What are you going to do?"

The sound of the ocean rose in a slow crescendo as a fire

kindled from the ashes of my sorrow. "If Vilicangelus won't come to me, then I'll go to him."

"How? Where?"

"England."

Sabrina's brows rose. "There's no closer help?"

"It doesn't matter. He's responsible for this mess. It's high time he helped fix it."

Sabrina squeezed my hand. "Good luck."

THE STORY CONTINUES...

Keep reading for the excerpt from
***Blood Phoenix Chronicles 4:
Rise of the Exiled Lady***

Thank you for reading *Vengeful are the Drowned*.

Word of mouth recommendations and book reviews are insanely helpful, not just to other readers, but to an author's success. Moreover, we use these reviews to know what *you* want to read more of. Please consider leaving a short, honest review—nothing special required, just a sentence or two about how you felt about this book. I can't thank you enough.

If you loved this story and would like to stay up to date on the latest book releases, promotions, giveaways, and a free story, please be sure to become a member of the Delirious Scribbles Readers Group. [Your email address will never be shared, and you can opt out at any time.]

Begin your journey, just scan this image with your phone camera!

Keep reading for a sneak peek....

Sneak Peek:

Rise of the Exiled Lady

Vitae

Scurith rushed into the faerie glade, entering along the cobbled path through blood-soaked mud. He bowed his grey and tan furred canid form in a hasty bow. "Master, more Sidhe are coming. For your plan to succeed, we must depart before witnesses arrive."

I turned to the faithful thrall who'd sold me out at my request. "Quite right."

Rage and adrenaline eased slowly.

My trap had succeeded perfectly. It was in the Sidhe's nature to betray one another. They expected it. After Aquaylae's betrayal, I knew there was little chance of reclaiming my Champion blades from within Creation. The two elven knights pinned to their knees before me had died too many times, failed too many times to risk one-on-one combat in the mortal realms.

So, I played to their expectations. I'd fabricated a drama with myself as the fool, but it was I left laughing in the end.

My hands massage the grips of the Seelie and Unseelie Champion blades. Both swords responded to my touch, wriggling to fit the hands of my newest and most superior body yet.

"I very much wish to slay you. Nevertheless, I am willing to be merciful on one condition. As we are low on time, I should give you five seconds to oath your cooperation. Swear service unto me in releasing Mare from this blade and you shall not share the fate of Mariena and Vusolaryn."

"Master, we must hurry. They will not cooperate. Slay them and let us be away."

"Will either of you submit to reason?" I asked.

Dolumii spat in my face.

A growl escaped the trollman holding him.

Gherrian closed his eyes. "I am disinclined."

Scurith whined, ears pressed flat to his head. "Master, if too many arrive, we will not be able to slay them before they are able to report what you've done here."

Irritation flashed through me my fingers tightened around the swords. "Fine. We'll take Dolumii and Gherrian with us."

"Begging your pardon, Master, but I thought the plan was to slay all witnesses," Scurith said.

I let my cruel intentions play out along my raspberry painted lips. "I'd like to play with them before...well, let's not spoil the surprise."

The coyll bowed, gesturing to my enforcers. The hulking, black-washed mortal corpses my thrall had animated with troll DNA collected the glade's many bodies—living and dead—while the winged, reanimated children's corpses flew over watch.

As they did so, I transmogrified into pure life plasma. Stepping carefully through the battlefield, being mindful to control my essence lest it burn or stain the ground, I drew all of the spilled blood into my body. As I absorbed the powerful essence, I kept it separate from my own. Even so, A nova of magic exploded up my legs the moment I drew in Mariena's spilled blood.

My lips curled.

I'd spoken true. This newest body infused via rebirth with the essence of two powerful knights felt nigh unstoppable in a way none of my previous rebirth experiments had been. Being reborn with the essence of two Nephilim, first children of the fallen themselves, would make me the greatest shield in history—the Hand of God in Creation.

And with this kind of power, I will wrest Mare from the Champion blade.

I drew in Vusolaryn as I had his rival and stepped through the Arch opened to my palace, leaving behind an immaculate glade and a mystery served up to confound the Sidhe.

Just desserts on a silver platter.

Ignis

Ignis struggled to draw essence around his soul, focusing on dwarfism instead of his customary form. The valve in the stone basin's bottom restricted the flow, but he knew how it worked. He knew essence waited in the reservoir beneath.

Like a flame struggling to catch on an oil lamp's dry wick, his body flickered and faded only to grow to life in the end. His smile blossomed the moment lips formed to hold it.

Quayla beat me.

His center of gravity settled, and he knew by the feel his new body was female. Mahogany locks hung nearly enough to curtain proud bronze breasts. In his new compact body, his dark-walled cage left plenty of room to move. He shifted muscular hips to get a feel for his new flesh.

An angry face bent left and right trying to see Ignis appeared beyond the heat-stained square window. "What the hell happened? Why isn't Quayla here?"

Ignis's body flashed to pure flame without a thought, riding the surge of fury through a full body transmog. He raised himself to float where he could meet his enemy's eyes. "I know full well you are watching us, so you know exactly what happened Dunham. She beat me fair and square, so you can take your questions and shove them up your ass with a hot poker."

A massive weight pressed down on Ignis. Had he still been in a human body, bones would've splintered, but compressing flame only created stars. The pressure eased. Dunham's face disappeared. He returned ahead of a sudden wash of agony. Every atom of Ignis felt as it were being torn in half.

"I ordered you to feel pain when you even thought such comments," Dunham snarled.

He did at that.

"Why aren't you suffering for your insolence? Tell me the truth."

Despite not having lungs, Ignis's breath left him as Dunham's fingers throttled Ignis's stolen heart.

"I am."

The simple phrase was the literal truth, so no more agony worsened Ignis's ordeal.

"If you don't want to die—"

"Screw off, Dunham. You can't afford to kill any more of us. Besides, I obeyed you to the letter."

Dunham darkened.

Ignis's pain intensified.

The Anseelie Queen appeared over Dunham's shoulder. Her delicate fingers drew him away.

"Where the hell have you been?" Dunham demanded.

For the barest fraction of a split second, fury tightened her eyes. Her face relaxed into a smile. "Little angel's room."

Ignis's pain waned as Dunham's attention shifted away. "You're suppose—"

The anger returned to transform her face into something terrifying—angel to demon in a blink. "I am not actually your assistant, Dunham, quite the opposite in fact. I have a war to wage, one my general isn't tending properly. Since your attention isn't on what's important, that leaves me to take care of business, doesn't it?"

Dunham glanced over his shoulder at Ignis, his face that of a teen called out for rebelliousness. He raised the burning ruby of Ignis's former heart into view and squeezed.

Pain lanced through the fire phoenix again. He dropped to the floor of his cage, curled into a tight agonized ball.

You wait, Dunham. Just wait.

Dunham

Dunham turned his back on Vivian marching to the control console. Her fingers slapped down on the shoulder like a vice.

"What you think you're doing?" She asked. "I'm talking to you."

"I'm sending the Terra to take care of Quayla."

"No, you are not."

Dunham darkened, gesturing for the nearby Windows. "I know where she is. I know she's beat to hell. I'm sending the Terra to finish her off, didn't you say we needed her?"

"Vitae has slain Mariena and Vusolaryn. Local Seelie and Unseelie will be in chaos. Now is the time to slay as many of them as we can."

Red rage ignited along Dunham's skin. "No! I want Quayla!"

Vivian's hand slammed into his face turning rage molten. Magical energy rushed through him until eldritch magic coalesced into green power throbbed between his fingers.

She hit him again. "Don't challenge me, boy. Even with Summus's essence you are no match for me."

Dunham glowered at her. It had been at least a century since he'd last tried proving himself her equal. None of those attempts had ended well. Still, he had tried without the power of divine phoenix on those occasions.

Divine phoenixes replaced archangels like Michael. Shouldn't Summus's power more than match a Fallen angel's strength?

Except Vivian wasn't just any fallen angel. She had reigned as one of the Dark Trinity. She'd been a Principality of Hell, one of Lucifer's three chosen captains—the Lady of Water. She had eons of experience fighting and surviving creatures far more powerful than Dunham.

He eased the magic back into his core.

"Good." Vivian smiled. "Now dispatch Terra to Sugarloaf Mills mall. Have her clean up the Sidhe at Medieval Times."

Dunham matched her smile. "Of course, mother."

Vivian's eyes narrowed. Warning filled her voice. "Dunham this is too important. Whatever your thinking, don't do it."

"All I'm thinking about is sending the Terra to eliminate your enemies. That is what you want, isn't it?"

"If you're speaking specifically of my enemy Sidhe at the Sugarloaf Mills mall, yes."

"Whom else would I be speaking of?"

Her expression hardened. "No one else if you know what's good for you."

Dunham folded his hands behind his back. "Have you had any luck obtaining a new source of life, air or water essence?"

She remained suspicious but allowed the change of topic. "I may have a way to gain us another water phoenix. As for life, Vitae is playing right into my hands."

"If you can get us another water phoenix to help keep Summus contained, what are you waiting for?"

Vivian watched him for several moments in tense silence. She arrived at some conclusion without her eyes giving away its contents. "Some things must follow other things. There is no other way."

She marched across the room, descending the spiral stair toward her apartments. Dunham gave her fifteen minutes to change her mind or return. When she remained absent, he flicked the intercom open. "Terra, I have a mission for you. You will go to your home, slay Quayla, and proceed to the Sugarloaf Mills mall to exterminate a Sidhe enclave."

Appendix A: Cast of Characters

Phoenixes:

Aquaylae (Quayla Buckler): A water phoenix assigned to the Atlanta Shield. Recently released from house arrest. Employed running a florist shop in eastern Atlanta. Dating Dylan Snyder. Preferred weapon: karambit knife

Caelum (Caelum Kite): An air phoenix assigned to the Atlanta Shield. Employed as Head of Charitable Projects by Circlestone Corporation. Preferred weapon: handgun or battle fan.

Ignis (Ignis Round): A fire phoenix assigned to the Atlanta Shield. Employed as a firefighter and arson investigator for the City of Atlanta. Preferred weapon: duo hilt bow and katana.

Mare: A water phoenix formerly assigned to the Atlanta Shield. Lost in a battle with Unseelie forced.. Preferred weapon: short swords.

Summuseraphi: A divine phoenix assigned as new praefectus of the shields of the southeastern United States. Formerly Lympha, Summuseraphi was recently elevated to divine status and placed under Villicangelus for training. Preferred weapon: chain blade.

Terrance (Terrance Wall): An earth phoenix assigned to the

Atlanta Shield. Employed at the Department of Motor Vehicles. Preferred weapon: cestus battle gloves.

Villicangelus: A divine phoenix assigned as overseers of the shields functioning in Southern Britain. Formerly overseer of the southern United States. Training supervisor over Summuseraphi. Preferred weapon: unknown.

Vitae: A life phoenix assigned to the Atlanta Shield as Shieldheart. Responsible for overall operations. Concerned about mortal deaths in her former shield, Vitae placed Quayla on house arrest. Preferred weapon: lajatang—bladed staff and baton forms.

HUMANS:

Detective Sabrina Foxner: Atlanta detective currently assigned to the robbery division. The former homicide detective is investigating the Howell Mill break-in.

Doctor Bradley Sky: Intelligent and enthusiastic junior assistant coroner working in Atlanta's morgue. His memory has been rewritten multiple times to remove discovery of the Fey.

Dunham Heffernan: CEO of Circlestone Corporation

Dylan Snyder: Quayla's bisexual boyfriend. Dylan is aware of Quayla's true nature. He's employed as an IT professional

Emma: Fae Kissed human who made a deal to resurrect her cat. Employed at Howell Mill Humane Society

Judith: Pessimistic and disinterested Korean college student employed at Ponds de Leon Flowers.

Mara: Employee of Camp Woof doggie daycare

Miri: Atlanta PD tech ops.

Mrs. Hadley Sage Cox: Quayla's sweet but nosey landlady. Superstitious with detailed knowledge of Fey folklore.

Nicolas: Owner of a hole in the wall grocery store near the Atlanta Sheild's HQ and Caelum's supplier for honey candy and milk used as currency in the Goblin Market

Pete: Owner of Camp Woof doggie daycare

Tommy: Doctor at Grady Memorial Hospital Long time friend of Bradley Sky.

Valerie: News anchor. Subject of lingering crush by Bradleh's friend Tommy

Viviane: Dunham Heffernan's executive assistant

FEY:

Grynnberry: A Seelie nymph. An informant that provides Quayla with intelligence.

Knight Dolumii: Knight Champion of the Unseelie Court.

Knight Gherrian: Knight Champion of the Seelie Court.

Lady Esloah: Knight of the Seelie Court

Oshyn: Half sized elf merchant in the Goblin Market. Provides brownie cleaning services.

Princess Mariene: Unseelie sovereign and royal court adjunct between the Seelie queen and the phoenixes.

Prince Vusolaryn: Seelie sovereign and royal court adjunct between the Seelie queen and the phoenixes.

Thatch: WyldFae representative for the Sidhe's Georgia Shire near Atlanta

OTHERS:

Anima: Monitoring entity assigned to the Atlanta Shield

TWISTED GALAXIES
MYTHS REBORN
MULTI-LAYER
CHARACTER-DRIVEN

Acknowledgments

So, that's a wrap on the third Blood Phoenix novel. I hope you've enjoyed the story so far. We're a bit past half way through the series, and I'm glad to have you along for the journey. I can't speak for you, but I wrote BPC3, I got many shocks and surprises from all of my characters.

Vengeful are the Drowned showed off the talented Andrea Fodor once more—not to mention her patience with a certain author's pickiness about the cover. The rest of the crew have been put under the gun by this quick release schedule.

Rebecca and Sarah, Billy and Scott all contributed to the various stages of reading and editing, and Tina, poor Tina, once more carried a massive burden to help get these pages as error free as we all could manage.

I'd like to thank the personalities of the Blood Phoenix Chronicles—those that survived anyway.

The road from here gets rocky, but I'm sure the road again swings back to a happy ending. Thanks for joining me on this adventure. I'll see you in BPC4: *Rise of the Exiled Lady*....

About the Author

Photo credit: Jim Cawthorne

Michael J. Allen is a star-lord, goofball, and USA Today bestselling author of character-driven, multi-layer, full-spectrum science fiction and fantasy novels - pretty much whatever madness sprouts from his head... (Learn more at www.deliriousscrib-bles.com)

Let's Connect

I love chatting with my readers, and hope you'll join my reader groups. If you'd rather stay up to date without joining in on the fun, there are plenty of ways to follow along.

— Michael J Allen

Reader Groups:

Discord : https://discord.gg/WeM4bwq
Facebook: https://www.facebook.com/groups/dsreaders
MeWe: https://www.mewe.com/join/dsreaders

Follow the Scribbler:

www.deliriousscribbles.com

amazon.com/-/e/B0096GEILG
bookbub.com/authors/michael-j-allen
facebook.com/deliriousscribbler
goodreads.com/deliriousscribbler
instagram.com/thedscribbler
twitter.com/Thedscribbler